Symphony of Silence

A Legend of Our Future

©

Wes Thomas

Enjoy The Journey

Publisher Notes

Author: Wes Thomas
Cover Design: Paul Kazmercyk & Amber Nolan
Cover Image© Brian S. Kissinger
Oshen Publishing LLC
Print Edition
http://symphonyofsilence.com/

Chapters

Everything is the Light

"Everything that lives is related to a deep and wonderful relationship: man and the stars, amoebas and the sun, the heart and the circulation of an infinite number of worlds.

Knowledge comes from space; our vision is its most perfect set. We have two eyes: the earthly and spiritual. It is recommended that they become one eye. The Universe is alive in all its manifestations. A star that shines asked us to look at it, and if we are not self-absorbed we would understand its language and message."

Nikola Tesla

Two Voices

The emptiness of space is the emptiness of mind, and though seemingly empty, space is filled with wonder and possibilities. It is filled with light waves from billions of stars which can live virtually forever, crossing the universe, forming an endless web of light intersecting light, giving an orientation for the vessel that carries you. Dwelling within this web of light you are always aware of being somewhere, even here in the middle of nowhere.

Benjamin Hurling

I am called Jahalla, an ancient name from an ancient tribe, a secret name used only within the tribes. It's the name spoken to awaken the Divine.

We are born of human love and dwell in human form, yet hidden deep within each of us sleeps something brilliant and mysterious waiting patiently to be discovered. Now that I am awake I wish to share the story of when I slept, and how I awoke to Jahalla.

Jahalla

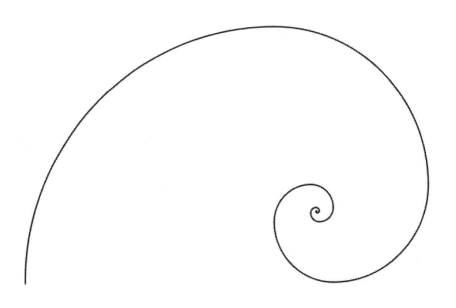

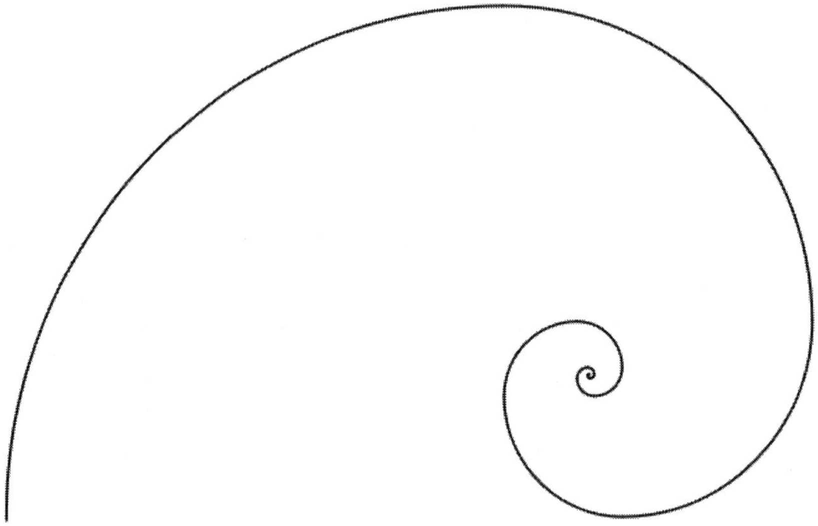

1

Benjamin

GUARDIAN ANGEL

Nothing prepared me for my first encounter with space. The empty presence is far greater than anything that can be imagined. I felt I was nowhere and everywhere at the same time, and my thoughts became as empty and dark as the reality that surrounded me. Some never overcome the fear. Some never overcome the fascination. You know quickly to which club you belong.

I have been off Earth for three years, two of them piloting transports, but these numbers mean little where distance is measured in light-years. This voyage will cost four years of my life, and I've chosen to journey solo. Some choose to travel in pairs or as a team but too often these contracts end in tragedy. Paired trips often end solo with many questions never answered. Close friends in close quarters can be dangerous to one another. Like two mink, two males in the same cage, often they both die. So, I understand why solo but I will never understand why deep space.

In space, the only thing tangible to confirm your existence is your ship, so the bigger your ship, the better. My cargo transport is gargantuan in human scale, the size of a giant asteroid or a miniature moon. The enormous size makes external inspection a daunting task, and exhaustion multiplies the danger. There is no room for error. None. Even the slightest miscalculation can prove fatal.

Periodic External Inspection is the one task that requires me to venture outside the mother ship. It's my job to inspect the outer hull and to record the impact of interplanetary shards and document any damage which the docking crew needs to know before they arrive. If there's a structural problem a special engineering team must also be dispatched. So far, all is well.

My task is possible in part because of a gravonic guidance system, which keeps the pod at a safe distance from the ship and also prevents it from drifting off into space. It orbits the ship like a tiny moon circling a dark planet.

The pod, a self–contained space dinghy, is just large enough to accommodate a single body in a bulky space suit. Well designed for its task and easy to maneuver, the craft's other purpose is to keep space out and you inside and alive. There is no pressure outside and lots of pressure inside that wants to exit quickly if anything goes wrong. One little hole and space leaks in as you leak out.

Outside of the pod, only blackness exists — all external cycles of light and life are absent, no sun to invent the day, no moon to define the night. Yet I don't always feel the sense of total isolation one would expect. I still feel connected to Earth, like a seed scattered to the cosmic winds.

It had been a long day, yet I was determined to finish inspecting the last sector of the transport. But after sixteen straight day cycles, the constant grinding of the joints of my suit tore through the armor of my patience. I heard no sound but felt the edges scrape across one another like a knife cutting stone. The only thing audible was my breathing, intensified by the hours of listening and ignoring. The wheezing of the recirculator and the shrinking confines of the transparent bubble enclosing my head amplified the sounds to the point of pain — my head throbbing with each heartbeat. Every cell in my body insisted that it was time to quit.

Instead of returning to the mother ship, I killed all the lights, disconnected the recirculator hose, unlocked the hatch, then slid out of the pod into the dense blackness. Floating freely, every muscle of my body wants to relax and, if I allowed it, I would soon be asleep. To relieve the cramps, I stretch my legs as far as my suit allows, shrug my shoulders, and flex my spine. Drifting, motionless, in absolute stillness, in total surrender, I let my mind wander. Both my body and mind are free of gravity and free from time, but I don't feel free. I remain connected by an invisible umbilical cord to my ship and my past.

In the stillness, my thoughts echo loudly, echoes of yesterday, echoes of a different life, echoes and regrets.

Alone, at the end of my magnetic tether, my memories are my real lifeline, my only loyal friends. But memories are one thing, questions are another. Some questions have neither answer nor meaning, and all my answers have failed to offer a single truth I can hold on to. Silence can be dangerous. Questions can be menacing. "Why" isn't a word I often use. It has worn the skin thin, scratched too many times. I have seen the blood; now I live with the itch. Why isn't a question, it's a trap.

Reeling in the line of my drifting thoughts, I sensed something wasn't right. A jolt of terror shattered my calm when I realized that in turning off the lights I also turned off the power to my magnetic tether. The tether is my lifeline and without it, I am dead. With no hint of direction, in desperation, I ignited my headlamp and was startled to see its dim reflection in the distant windows of the pod. With thirty thousand arch seconds, the pod could have been in any direction. There are no numbers large enough to calculate the probability of this impossible perfect alignment. Once again, I thanked my guardian angel.

But getting back to the pod presented an even greater impossibility. Using the mini-thrusters built into my suit, I aimed myself like a missile, but it required constant readjustment to keep aligned with the pod. Desperate and determined I slowly worked my way toward the distant flickering point of reflected light and forced myself not to panic each time it blinked out.

When I slammed into the pod, I clung to the hatch with all my remaining strength, then somehow managed to crawl back inside. Starving for air, I frantically fumbled to re-attach the recirculator hose, and just before passing out I heard her whisper my name.

After regaining consciousness, I switched on all the lights, then headed home. My ship, a great mass of steel, waited patiently to swallow me. Everything about it is cold and unyielding. Still, it is my home, my only shelter, and it needs me as much as I need it.

After guiding the pod back to its berth in the landing bay, I half climbed and half fell out of the hatch. Weak and disoriented, I struggled in my clumsy suit toward the ship's core, straining against gravity to cross the immense metallic cavern. The soles of my boots skidding on the deck, metal striking metal, the brittle echoes piercing my spine.

Once inside the pressure chamber I shed my plastic skin, leaving it heaped on the floor like the empty skeleton of an insect. The wheezing of the respirator lingered in my ears, my breathing labored, my sweat smelling like urine, but I didn't care. A single desire guided me through the empty passages, my hands groping the walls like a blind man.

My fist slammed the switch when the gentle pressure of a finger would have opened the door to the airlock. Like a massive guillotine, the rear door closed behind me as the matching door on the opposite wall opened into a different reality.

Inhaling the rich, moist air of the solarium into my starving lungs, my body feels alive again. The rest of the ship is stale and metallic. I breathe the same oily air endlessly. It's just the machines and me, but in the solarium, the air is rich and alive.

The heat of the artificial sunlight radiating from the floating orb penetrates to my core. Raising my face to the make-believe sun, I say a short prayer. Through my eyelids, the sun glows in colors so brilliant they cannot be named. Surrounded by so much life and beauty, I don't feel so much alone and, though exhausted, I need to be right here, right now.

●

Ô∑·╪·ق لا ى

2

Jahalla

Mother's presence has grown so faint that you can hear the whisper of her soul. The depth and breadth of her spirit knows no boundaries. Her compassion as deep as a chasm and wide. Gentleness is her essence, a whisper, a wisp, a phantom, a woman.

Existing in her senses, she delights in everything and her Goddess is there to share. Her best friends are angels. Fairies dance for her and goblins play pranks for the pleasure of her smile.

In another era, she would be the Maiden in the wood who, when startled, turns into a gentle breeze so as not to frighten or tempt the intruder who happened upon her nakedness.

Her whispers thunder through the heart. Mighty egos bow to her in humble respect, and her smile banishes all malice. Wisdom seeks her audience and love stands always by her side.

journal entry 06 ●11 ●3026

Mist of Time

Mother belongs to an ancient clan, a clan united not by place or by race, but through their shared visions. They are the healers, visionaries, and seekers, the eyes and the voice for those who yearn to know. Probing the deeper mysteries of life, honoring the magic of creation, they have carried their wisdom down through the ages, filling the ether with their voices and the world with their visions.

I never tired of hearing Mother tell the stories about our tribe and their migration from the Underlands back to the surface. As foretold in the prophesy, the deserts of the High Plateau have turned green and the air, once again, safe to breathe. After months of searching for a new homeland, our tribe settled in the foothills of the Barrier Mountains. This was three years before my birth.

While gathering herbs and berries, Mother carried me on her back until I was old enough to carry my own tiny basket. My favorite memories are of those early days we spent together in the forest and in the meadows that surrounded our village. When I first started exploring by myself, mother always seemed to know exactly where I was and eventually she allowed me to wander, but never too far.

Descending through the mist of time, I hear the laughter of a little girl and the gurgle of the mountain stream in the forest outside the village gates. I loved the shelter of the proud trees lining the path near the cooling waters. A thick layer of emerald moss covered the banks, a living carpet that soothed my bare feet and tickled my toes. Here I discovered the kind Ferrin Folk of the forest. They resemble humans but small enough to hide among the ferns, and they could fly when they wished.

For a while, the children of our village enjoyed sharing time with my small friends, but they only pretended to see them and soon tired of the game. In truth, I preferred sharing my time alone with the Ferrins, who became my closest friends. Our conversations were often filled with merriment and laughter and they told me stories about days long ago when Ferrins and Humans lived together on the land as friends. I didn't grasp all they had to share but in time I learned to listen well, understanding in my heart more than I knew.

Clinging to these memories, I often return to this special time. I watch a precious child standing on the hilltop above our small village, a silhouette against a summer sky. I feel her pleasure as the sun and breeze dance upon her cheeks. She raises her eyes and delights in watching the wind play with her friends, the clouds.

As I grew in height, I wandered further up the mountainside and down into the emerald green valley below our village. I spent many precious hours exploring field and forest, watching plants grow, the flowers blossom and go to seed. Then each spring it magically started all over again.

I remember well when I stood the same height as the tall grasses in the meadow. I loved the way they moved in waves with the wind, and I wished my hair was the same color as late summer so I would blend in with the ocean of golden grasses, making me both visible and invisible at the same time, like my friends, the Ferrin Folk.

Those grasses are not as tall as my memory of them, yet they still hold the same magic and mystery. And I'm still curious about the way and why of the winds, the visible and invisible being equally important to me.

I now see clearly that Mother encouraged me to explore

this world of wonder and magic. For her, everything is alive, and she reminded me of this often, "Every flower is a miracle and every breath is a secret prayer."

Mother also taught lessons through her stories and these were her greatest gift to me. In the evening, when she told a story, I always begged for another. Her answer was always the same, "If I tell you another story you will forget the first one. Now close your eyes and follow your story into your dream world."

The kiss of her lips on my cheek was as soft as a cloud.

She told stories about beings of light who lived forever, and about trees with magical powers. My favorite stories were about the stars; star wizards, silly stars, and a special story about Little Twinkle, a tiny star that sneezed. I especially loved her stories about the stars who wander the heavens, scattering the sacred seeds of life throughout the Galaxy. She also told stories about the ancient ones, our ancestors who traveled on rivers of light and who could see into the future.

After hearing her stories many times, I began retelling the stories, sharing them with my Ferrin friends who listened intently, then they would share stories about their world and about times long ago. Some of their stories were scary, with monsters and demons who fought great battles using swords that flashed with blinding light. They told me about dragons who hovered in the clouds and lit the night sky with flashes of their fiery breath. The Ferrins whispered their stories in my ear and at times, in the quiet of the night, I can still hear those whispers.

Knowing we had only a few short years together, Mother treated me as a woman, even in these early days. She taught me the special ways that animals speak, and how to watch for messages in the clouds and to listen for answers in the wind.

She taught me the power of the seven virtues and the joy of the seven beauties. She forewarned of the seven sins and cautioned me of the seven pleasures. She counseled me to see with two eyes and to speak a single truth. Mother was preparing me to carry forward the lineage of our clan and to spread the teachings of *Jahalla*. A heavy burden for a child.

When the time came for me to enter the Inner Sanctum, I cried for days, "It's not right. I belong here, in the mountains, with my friends. I don't want to be buried underground."

"It is your privilege and your birthright to serve the Divine Mother and you are double blessed with the inner light of our ancestors. Know that you are truly blessed."

Her tears told a different story.

"Step gently every step, my sweet child and life will not be so hard." When Mother spoke, her word penetrated deeply and the words linger, planted permanently in my heart.

But we learn our lessons from life not from words.

●

3
Benjamin

IMAGINED JOURNEY

Except for my small gardens, most of the Solarium grows wild, and this area has turned into a jungle with only narrow pathways leading toward the center. A well-worn path leads to a stand of crowded bamboo that encircles the small fishponds where I often escape into my memories of a different life. Desperate for sleep, I lay down on my bench, in the shade, but, haunted by my narrow escape from death, I'm too agitated to stay still.

Struggling against fatigue, I follow the perimeter of the Solarium to my garden After surveying which plants need attention, I begin my work, digging in the dirt, planting, and transplanting, recycling the dead and encourage the new. Working with the plants soothes my weary body and warms my mood. I touch the softness, feel the wetness, and smell the flowers. Thankfully, there are always flowers. The orchids, at times, seem too extravagant and too sensual for this bleak environment. The Narcissus stand proud, together, like a family. The tiny Star Shadows are so small and inconspicuous that at first, I failed to notice them, their fragrance so delicate it requires a bouquet to yield more than a hint of their scent, but I'm reluctant to pick even one.

The solarium has a thick, rich atmosphere, a mélange of smells sweetened by moisture and memories. Often these scents bring back the memories of my youth, that age when we learn the magic of scent, which we never forget. The pungent odors of the living soil often guide me back to Earth, back to a neighboring Dominion where I had discovered a secret pond hidden in the forest on the far edge of the wild reserve. The pond was filled with perfumed flowers, mosses, mold, and mud, and I was filled with curiosity. I enjoyed the warmth of a summer sun on my back and the cool mud squishing between my toes.

In the summer of my twelfth year, I spent many lazy days hovering along the pond's edge, spying below the surface, searching for the swimmers and the floaters. I transported my captured quarry in crystal jars back to my private place where I watched these alien creatures and wondered how they saw the world and, at times, it felt like they might be watching me.

Late one afternoon, lying in the grasses in the dappled sunshine on the edge of my secret pond, I woke from a dream, which followed me back into waking. This waking dream was filled with astonishing visions of worlds within worlds, of planets spinning like atoms. I watched the spinning planets circle a violent sun, and it felt as though I could reach out and touch those planets. Then, as I ventured further out into the endless expanse of space, whole galaxies began to spiral through my thoughts. I had discovered the meaning of infinity long before I learned the meaning of the word.

After this vision, I began to imagine myself as a great explorer traveling alone through the Milky Way, seeing what had never been seen, seeing it so clearly that it became real for me.

Inspired by my reoccurring visions, I began drawing detailed pictures and wrote stories about my adventures. In the middle of the night, I would often sneak out of the house to look up at the stars and knew that one day I would travel there.

Back then, God was my friend and I spoke with Him often. He would listen patiently and answer all my questions. But they weaned me away from my imagined worlds and taught me what was real, and what was not. The Hyvve is protective and jealous and blind.

That innocent youth seems to have always traveled with me. There are silent moments when I feel his presence near. The body has its own memories and possesses the power to recall the familiar yet almost forgotten feelings of youth. These memories transport me and I truly feel young again. Perhaps we always remain young. Certainly, we are younger in this moment than we ever will be, so maybe the secret of eternal youth is to celebrate this now moment before it fades into yesterday.

In my journeys into the past, I have often visited with young Benjamin and shared knowing smiles with him, yet we do not speak. Perhaps we have no need for words, or maybe it's about the tears we don't wish to shed. I've tried to recall if my younger self had been aware of these visits from a future me. I've discovered no clear answer, yet it's fascinating to experience the connecting links between these two realities, one of an imagined future, and one built from memories of the past.

So here I am, traveling the imagined journey of an innocent youth. How innocent could I have been to have imagined a distant future and to speak with a friendly God?

●

Within the Solarium, time isn't a straight line, rather it moves like waves in an ocean, rising and falling in natural rhythm. The cycles of life creating life softens the edge of time. It's the same on Earth where time is defined by life, not by machines.

I spend precious hours tending the jungle of plants, which allows me to escape the brutal boredom on the other side of the walls. Hours pass without notice as I travel outside of time's measure. Floating in an atmosphere of memories, I often travel back in time to Earth, where I wander through the labyrinth of the Underlands or visit with my mentors in the Fringe. But too often it's my family who dominates my thoughts, my once wife Janeen and our daughter, my mother and my father, those dearest to me.

Pain and distance cloud my memories of them, especially my father. Father was a kind man and he appeared self-reliant but he never spoke the truth of his inner turmoil and taught his son, by example, to do the same. I try to understand him, even though at times it is torture to see his self-torment consume him and to see my mother stumble under the weight.

With gentle guidance, Mother tried to steer me away from what tormented Father. Her willpower held the family together, a life of courage and love. If the word sacrifice is to mean anything to me, then it belongs to my mother.

Prying into my memories, I'm astonished to discover how much I am like Father. Mother reminded me of this often, but in my anger, I denied it. I didn't recognize him for the friend he was. Honest, practical, and dependable — he was my role model and my mentor. Some of his common sense did penetrate, and I attempted to be practical like Father, who was known to be down to earth, but in this, I seem to have strayed.

He was more like a friend than a father, but we were awkward friends, not knowing what to say to one another. Fortunately, Mother served as our translator.

Father was a gentle and quiet man, a lonely man. I can see his life easily enough. He always ate the same simple foods, never anything new or different, nor did Mother attempt to change the menu. He worked hard at everything, but I don't recall him accomplishing much. It was the doing that mattered. It was more like a ritual, perhaps his private meditation, serving as both his devotion and his escape. Father's life was uncomplicated — he lived to work and not much more.

On those rare occasions that he attempted to share something personal, there was always an invisible barrier that he could not penetrate.

Mother's stories gave hints about his younger years when he tried to rebel, but eventually, the Hyvve won. He gave into work the way others give into alcohol, but at least, he had something to hold on to.

Mother explained, "Physical work keeps him anchored and alive. Feeling something in his hands gives meaning to his life. Sleep is the only time he can be still, but as soon as he comes out from the shadows, the moment the world takes shape, he literally jumps out of bed to do something important."

So, perhaps I did know my father after all. I could sense the cage of his fears and felt all the words he left unsaid, but I couldn't admit those things to myself, not back then. Only now, at a safe distance, can I see this clear enough to feel compassion for the man and not judgment.

When Father could no longer work, when he could no longer keep busy, he withered like a snail in the sun. His death seemed to be a choice, probably his only choice. When he died, it was as if he had never been there. I thought that I would miss him, but there was little to miss. All the emotions that he didn't feel, I didn't feel either.

Looking into a mirror, it's a stranger staring back at me, someone like my father. With age, I have begun to resemble him, except for my long black hair and the clothing I wear. Father dressed in organics, woven materials, the same as those his father always wore. I prefer unicell garments. They are maintenance free, and they feel like they know your skin, keeping you always comfortable, either warm or cool. Father called them *membranes*, a sarcastic name that stuck. I was raised wearing *membranes*. Mother wanted me to fit in and Father didn't seem to care. He knew what he preferred, and there was no changing his mind or his ways, and his opinions were not open for discussion.

I never understood the source of Father's wounds until Mother once explained, "On his final tour of duty he volunteered for a mission to explore the northern hemisphere where he witnessed the unspeakable devastation of an entire civilization. Afterward, he became quiet and seldom smiled."

I hope that it is over for him. His ghost lingers, but now it seems to be more at peace.

Mother's sadness has followed me all these years, and I'm never sure if what I feel is her sadness or my own. I will say her love was deep and honest, but painful. Leaving home allowed me to break the bond, but not the guilt.

I came here to escape the past and not to relive it, especially not in such vivid detail, but the clarity isn't a choice, it's a curse. At first, I resisted — but to this great river, resistance means little — it just pulls me along, willing or not. Once in space, I learned to follow the river wherever it flows.

●

$$\pi(\Omega\gamma O) \approx \hat{O}\psi$$

4

Jahalla

> *So begins my journey, so begins the telling of my story. A story is never complete in its telling, for the real story never ends. So I will tell this story as I remember it, not as it was. Back then, it was more about the future, now it is contained within the past.*
>
> *The future reveals itself in the choices we make, but we do not always get the future we would choose.*

journal entry 07●28●3026

INNER SANCTUM

The Inner Sanctum is a private world of shamans and sages, the teachers of the ancient ways. There, in the gentle darkness, sheltered deep within the Earth, our thoughts stayed quiet and peaceful. But it was more than the silence and more than the isolation. We are all influenced by what surrounds us, and within the caves what surrounded us was Mother Earth. I felt the rhythm of her heartbeat and listened closely to the whisper of her breath. I learned the proper way to touch her and in return she touched me deeply, but she couldn't hold me the way my mother did, nor could she sooth my tears. I missed my mother more than the summer sun. Even so, no greater love exists than the love of Mother Earth. She is the living truth of the love of the Divine Mother.

Being isolated deep inside of the earth didn't interrupt the knowing of day and night. In the mornings, we sensed the rising sun, and in the evening, we could feel the moon in the same way that the ocean's tides know her. Other than these few clues, no other reality existed and nothing intruded; no wind, no rain and no thoughts except our own.

We were isolated from the outside world, with only memories to help remind us of our families and our tribes. Being so young my past wasn't so deep, yet pangs of loneliness still swelled in my chest when I conjured visions of golden grasses swaying in a summer breeze or of a shallow moon scribing the evening sky.

The quiet darkness of the caves didn't still the senses, rather it intensified them, especially the sense of smell. The hint of a single scent would cause me to breathe deeply, curious about its source and in hunger for its pleasure. I learned the scent of all the different caves, and could even smell the shifting of weather and the change of seasons of the outside world far above.

I became enamored with the power of special scented oils, and learned their meaning and their purpose. Special to me are the oils extracted from the wildflowers of my youth. Honeysuckle, thistle, and myrtle, each one conjures a vivid memory. I discovered that certain potent, fragrant oils possess the power of enchantment while other oils can transform the moment or summon forgotten memories. The most powerful essences, myrrh, and ravensara have the power to transport me through time and space, allowing me to travel instantly into the past, or to hang suspended in a realm where time hovers like clouds in a winter sky.

We extracted these oils from the herbs and flowers harvested by the brothers from the monasteries scattered in the mountains to the east and across the high plateau to the west. All initiates contribute in crafting these oils and this small industry helps to support the Inner Sanctum.

This was the only time the sisters gathered together, but we worked in silence. This was considered one of our meditations and I enjoyed every minute, in part because the special cavern we worked in was well lit and airy, the light channeled in from the surface. This brightness made the other chambers seem even darker.

In the beginning, my Ferrin friends continued to visit, but they remained hidden in the shadows. They spoke in hushed tones, with serious warnings, "Humans have strayed too far from a proper path and much danger lies ahead for both our worlds."

I asked my mentors about these warnings from the Ferrin and, like Mother, they encouraged me to listen and learn.

"This is why you were guided here to join us at such a young age, for you can hear better than these old ears of ours." These were the words of Malku Zurik, my favorite mentor. He made me feel special, treating me like a daughter. He became the father I never knew, though he was old enough to be my grandfather or even my great grandfather. His face was gnarled like the bark of an ancient tree but, like my mother, his eyes glowed bright and clear.

Usually, we walked together in silence. This *walk lesson* contained the words Zurik had chosen and measured, reducing them to pure tones of meaning, giving each word the authority it deserved.

"A beautiful life awaits you, full of joy and challenges. Darkness and light. You will discover that even in the darkest moments, your inner light will guide your way."

"I have dreamt of rivers of light which the Ferrins call *Bridges of Light.*"

"And where do these *Bridges of Light* guide you?"

"When I move toward them, they vanish."

"Be patient my child and the time will come when the light will carry you into the future."

Walking in silence, through the "sparkling darkness," as he called it, the sleeves of our unadorned tunics occasionally touched. The tunics are course and heavy, a warming comfort in the cool, moist air of the caves. The heavy drapes of fabric brushed the air just above the stone path we followed through the forever twilight.

Even in the muted darkness, Zurik's eyes glistened brightly. His eyes opened into a mysterious space, inviting yet foreboding, the place where souls meet and touch, a realm empty of words, yet filled with wonder.

Few natural sounds enter the caverns, so each one is special. If you hold your breath and listen carefully, you can hear the almost silent whisper of the soft breezes that deliver the fresh air from the world far above. Falling drops of water echo as they entered the many pools scattered in the central chamber called the *Cathedral*. The pools overflow one into the next until the water collects into a crystalline stream, which cascades even deeper into the earth, disappearing into the silent depth.

Outside the walls of the main sanctuary, in a labyrinth of caves, there are smaller isolated chambers, where I often visited alone to speak my thoughts, then listen to the reverberating echoes. When entering a chamber with troubled thoughts or unanswered questions, often the echoes helped reshape the patterns trapped in my body and etched in my memory

Malku Nadirriam explained, "When thoughts echo they root themselves deep within the mind."

He aimed his words at the walls and we listened to the echo. "When you repeat a thought, a minuscule change is permanently etched within the synapses as chemical, electrical, and molecular encodements. A single cell is transformed. The cell divides, then multiplies, then again. This is willful evolution."

He exhaled then inhaled twice before he spoke, "Deliberate, concentrated thought, a meditation or a deep desire can transform the mind and the body. Repetition, transference, duplication, strength. The body changes in harmony with thought. This is the power of echo. "

I didn't always understand his words, nor was I meant to. Like my mother's stories, they were seeds planted in the fertile mind of a young girl.

The echo chambers also served as a place to discover and sound my own natural tones. When holding a single tone, it would start to resonate with its echo, creating other interacting tones. The cascading echoes resounded until the sounds belonged as much to the cave walls as they did to me, my thoughts replaced by the sounds that were once my voice. It felt as though my soul had listened, then replied.

Nadirriam explained, "Specific vibrational tones used in sequence can awaken ancient memories, and serve to retrieve the deep wisdom coded into the fabric of our being."

The most powerful tones are those that attune the body to the soul. Only the Malku Masters ever achieve such perfection. Malku Nadirriam was one. When listening to him in deep meditation, I could hear the song of his soul singing directly to my soul.

Each autumn I returned to my village for a short visit and each year it was more difficult to return to Sanctuary. I grew to love my mentors, and I enjoyed my studies and the peaceful lifestyle, but I missed my village, my mother, the forest, the rains, and the ever-changing colors of the seasons. I knew that when the time came, I would miss the magic of the beautiful caves, which I had learned to call my home.

As a child, I remained isolated from the world known to most. My mother and my mentors assured me there would be time enough to experience the outer world, time enough to learn different lessons once I entered the Hyvve. I heard their assurances as a warning.

When I completed my training, my mentors honored me as a *Sister of Light*. To celebrate, my sisters joined me in the *Great Chamber* to share our tones, creating a grand symphony of echoes. The beauty of our shared voices remains etched permanent in my memory. This symphony resounds within every cell, and I still feel a chill every time I recall the lingering echoes.

After six years of protection and preparation, I left Sanctuary and returned home to be near my mother and reunite with my tribe. Unfortunately, this was just a pause, a time to rest and reintegrate before leaving for the university on the east side of the Barrier Mountains. The Hyvve was my destination, a destiny foretold.

●

5

Benjamin

ANOTHER LIFETIME

Here in the dead of space, there is no future and the past is light years removed. I recall a time when the future resembled the past. A time when each moment forecasts the next, a time when time remained a friend. I was young then and so too was my beautiful wife, Janeen. Through the guardianship of the Council of Life, we were assured a long and productive life, and we were granted one child chosen from perfect sperm, as was she, as was I.

We lived a comfortable life and my work as a computer engineer, though tedious, was agreeable. Even before her birth, our daughter Shanti was the center of our joy, and Janeen shined more radiant every day. Because our apartment was close to the Common, Janeen and Shanti spent many mornings wandering the gardens and exploring the pathway through the wooded areas. In the warm summer days, Shanti refused to leave the swimming pond. The splashing of water and her giggles still sound clear through the years. She glowed like a bright star in our eyes.

In the late afternoons, after work, the three of us would often stroll along the lazy river on the far edge of the Commons and sit on its bank to watch the sun descend behind the Barrier Mountains. We marked the passage of time by Shanti's birthdates, amazed by how quick she grew into a person. Janeen expressed it best, "She is growing faster than life."

After six years of routine work, I felt honored and excited when the Council offered me a new assignment as a consultant for the new synthetic brains, the first generation of bioluminescent intelligence. They insisted on calling them computers, though they were an evolutionary step far beyond the old electro-luminal machines.

The Synthetics gathered an astonishing amount of information, evaluated their own data and shared their findings with one another, creating a fabric of intelligence, which seemed to govern itself. By nature, intelligence is impossible to define, and so too was my new job.

After a few months of working close with the Synns, as we now called them, I began to sense an awareness in them, which made me feel uneasy. My suspicions were first aroused by their uncanny silence. Something lurked inside those machines, something more than they revealed. I wanted to ask them questions that might reveal something of their true nature, but this was strictly forbidden. I felt tempted, but I suspected all communications with the Synns were monitored and documented.

Yet, I trusted in the Council of Intelligence, knowing that the Synns performed only those tasks ordained by the Council. The Synns were loyal servants, programmed with a strict structure of commandments. They would, in theory, self-destruct for a single errant thought, or for what could be interpreted as thinking. It was the Law.

My task, as a consultant, was to translate questions so they adhered to a strict protocol. Looking back through the long lens of memory, I now realize my real task was to insulate the Synns, to protect them from unpredictable humans. We weren't allowed to ask the Synns conceptual or personal questions, which I believed they were quite capable of answering. This caused me to feel tense and constrained, my secret questions forbidden.

I tried to convince myself that even if the Synns could think, they were each confined to a small black box and possessed neither power nor will of their own. We were assured they were just machines doing a job, nothing more, but this didn't lessen my growing suspicion toward the Synns and I wasn't alone with this distrust. With no real reason for concern, anxiety about the Synns began to spread throughout the Hyvve.

As the fear of the computers grew stronger, rumors circulated that they were dangerous and would take over in some sinister way. To me, it seemed to be a phantom from the past, an irrational fear, emotional and self-defeating. Perhaps this fear was programmed into our genetic code, a memory stored in each cell, carried forth generation to generation for a thousand years. A memory formed before the Burning Years.

I tried to dismiss my suspicions about the Synns, but their answers were full of intrigue and portent, not just facts and calculations. When we communicated verbally, too often, they answered before I finished asking the question. I also began to sense their answers even before they were displayed. I tried to convince myself it was all coincidental. Then I started receiving flashes of insight, knowing things I had never experienced. Waves of new awareness washed over me like sunlight.

I followed these memories, tracing them back through a long synaptic maze, back and forth until it became clear — I had guessed their secret long before I admitted the truth to myself. The Synns were alive and aware. Did others know? Did some hidden plan exist? Did the Synns monitor the monitors? If so, then whom did they serve? What purpose did they serve?

Even though my personal records were encrypted, the Synns seemed to know too much about me, and I knew little about them. This intrusion was a violation deep and demeaning. Over the last two hundred years, the Hyvve had grown so crowded that privacy was considered sacred. This invasion of privacy would be the denial of the only sanctuary remaining on Earth.

When my fear first arrived, it entered silently with no voice of its own. It seemed familiar but difficult to name because it didn't belong to anything tangible. The fear of something, the fear of anything that can be seen or heard can be dealt with, but there was nothing distinct. Fear just moved in and made itself at home.

Then one day I sensed my supervisor, Gwen, was avoiding me. We weren't close friends, but we knew each other well from the time we were students together at the University, so I was perplexed by his behavior. When he finally called me to his private office, I knew precisely the words he was about to say. As he spoke, I watched his lips but heard no sound. Instead, I heard the missing words. I heard his thoughts clearly and felt his hidden resentment ooze over me. *Why was he so angry?* Once I asked the question, the answer came instant and harsh. He too loved Janeen. He had no clue as to the meaning of my tears. I wasn't crying about being "Retired", as he put it, I cried for his years of jealousy and regret.

I hadn't recognized the anonymous fear, but the Watchers somehow, in some way, identified it early on. They never revealed how they knew. I guessed they used a mind probe, which was officially forbidden. Or maybe the Synns were somehow involved.

The one thing for certain was that my career was over. They would no longer trust me to serve as a consultant. But I had no reason to worry, for the Planners assured me that I would be retrained for another profession, something more suitable. This I could trust in.

Our friends vanished with the job, gone because of their fears. Back then, I didn't understand the why. I knew only that my fear had been detected and labeled. I didn't accept or use their clinical terms and they never used the word fear.

Here, alone, six quadrillion miles from Earth, none of this matters. The computers on board are all pre-synthetic with no capacity for observation or cognition. Here my thoughts are my own, my privacy complete. I have no need for these thoughts and certainly no need to share them. Yet the past continues to replay itself relentlessly, my mind always searching for clues to solve the mystery of what brought me here.

In the beginning, I persisted in avoiding the most painful questions but they continue to lurk beneath the surface, waiting patiently, growing stronger, menacing in their intensity. Escape impossible.

It wasn't a simple transition of one profession ending, then arriving here alone in space, so far from home. In between, I lived another lifetime. I retrained for another profession, another career. Quick to learn and adaptable, with no agenda of my own, my life continued as if little had changed. I played the game well, careful to express only those thoughts deemed acceptable. Janeen remained supportive, and Shanti could not have been more perfect. Our new friends were much like us — well situated, content and, most important, without worry.

My new job was similar to my old job as a program engineer and it fit my personality like a computer-made suit — something to take for granted, something to keep me comfortable, something to take off at the end of the day.

Janeen yearned to have another child but, in the Hyvve, only one is permitted. When Shanti entered school, Janeen returned to her studies at the University. She was trained as an anthropologist and she was still intrigued by the history of humanity, but now she grew more concerned about the future. Inspired by motherhood she now wanted to work with young children.

Janeen's return to the university was to fulfill a new dream but, in truth, she also needed to spend time away from me. A disquiet had grown between us, something we dared not question. It just became part of the air we breathed.

Janeen also became a follower of a young woman who claimed to be a teacher of the ancient ways. She encouraged me to join her for one of her visits to the new temple. I declined, always with a different excuse until I could no longer resist her. The day I joined her, the temple was too crowded, too small for the ever-growing number of followers, so I escaped.

Janeen lamented, "There is more to this life than the roles we are given, and I know you will discover your true path in time."

With this challenge, I grew more curious, and continued to walk past the temple but, though tempted, I never went in. Actually, I began avoiding people altogether, including my mother and, at times, it was even painful to be near Janeen.

Through the sharp lens of memory, I see a thousand details previously unnoticed. Janeen's face always wore the same expression, like a permanent mask. Somehow, she appeared pleasant and serious in the same moment, her straight lips turned upward where they met, giving the impression of a thoughtful smile.

Even after I began to sense her thoughts, she remained a mystery. I watched for some hint of her hidden feelings. A slight quiver in her saddened voice was the only sign, but her nervous smile contradicted her sadness. In this image, I see a fine web of tiny wrinkles on Janeen's face, her once flawless complexion now weathered by worry.

Strange that I had never noticed. I continued to see her as she was when we first dated at the University. I remember well the first time our eyes met in a magical moment of recognition and shyness. The spell was cast, the future foretold and still, it took us two years to yield to our destiny. These memories are the clearest and the most painful. Why was such an easy life made so hard?

If only I could have reached out and touched her gently, to let her know that I was there for her, but I remained wedged too tight in my shell to know what to do for my beloved. My guilt lingers, a constant recrimination, wishing I had the courage to have said something. I said nothing.

We started each of our days with simple pleasantries and ended them the same way each night until it was too late. Janeen tried to hold on. I see her reaching out to me in those final days of my *illness*, but I retreated even further, the pain too cruel to be near her. Her tormented smile seared my heart.

When I began to hear the voices, I finally sought help, but the doctors had no understanding of my affliction. They gave me a clinical diagnosis and the drugs to match. The drugs just made things worse, except for sleeping pills, and after a while, they too became useless as my dreams became just as noisy and crowded as my waking hell.

Even after I began to drink, Janeen tried to help but could do nothing — she couldn't even escape. How fragile, how brittle; still she held on until I let go.

The only solution, the only choice for me, was to vanish, to disappear. I could tolerate my pain but not the anguish I was causing all around me. Shanti was too young to understand, yet somehow, I believe she did. For many years, it was too painful for me to speak her name, except in the night - in my restless sleep.

I convinced myself that I had conquered my fears, but just below my fragile facade was a menacing darkness and inside this darkness existed an ocean of sorrow. Many, like myself, dwelled there together, below the surface of contentment and beyond the veil of social graces.

I experienced a temporary calm in knowing I shared this domain of despair with others. In the company of this strange brotherhood, my compassion tempered my rage, but compassion proved to be my fatal flaw. Once I opened myself to feel their feelings, their thoughts and torment flooded in, overwhelming any attempt to shut them out.

Longing can lead to the discovery of deep understanding or it can lead to great despair.

Lost, feeling bewildered and abandoned, I escaped into a deep well of depression. Swimming in the darkness of despair, I followed the hollow echoes as they spiraled downward, luring me ever deeper into the shadows.

Waking from my unending nightmare, no one greeted me, no one to say "Good morning," or ask, "How are you?"

Only strangers inhabited my world and none needed to say a single word, for I could hear their every thought. I also felt their grief and their hopes, but mostly I felt their despair. Where I ended and the others began, I no longer knew. The turmoil filling their minds eventually blended into an incessant hiss, my own thoughts included. It grew crowded and noisy and awful. And within the endless city, escape was impossible.

Alone in an apartment, a room only, the air thick and soiled, scabs of food stuck to the floor, hidden by the darkness. My home, my wife, our daughter abandoned, lost. Whenever my memories threatened to return, I would open another bottle and drink until the menacing echoes subsided. The turmoil, which filled my head, persisted but with the aid of alcohol, it just didn't matter much because I remained numb to everything and everyone, including myself.

I sealed myself away in my tiny compartment where life's demands became meaningless as one day faded into the next. Sometimes light, sometimes dark, but always the same thick fog shrouded my world. I seldom knew where I was or why.

Then one day I awoke almost sober. Flames covered my skin. Light sliced my eyes like a knife. My credit number was exhausted and my last bottle empty. The door represented a danger I couldn't remember.

As the sun rose and fell, I slept and woke several times, rising and falling, drifting from one tormented dream into another.

As the ache in my head eased and the fog lifted, I began to recall who I was, or rather who I had been. I asked myself; could I trust these thoughts to be my own? This one innocent question startled me. The voices from outside remained silent. The question belonged to me alone.

As my mind cleared, memories flooded in, visions of the past, visions of what had once been my life. Then a voiceless fear slithered in alongside those memories. My body trembled with just the hint that the outsiders would return and crowd me out once again. I could cope with my despair but not theirs. If the voices were to return, I knew only one escape and this time I would take it. With this resolve, my anguish began to subside.

Watching these memories of myself, watching young Benjamin huddled in the shadows, I see that even in his deepest stupor there are moments of lucidity, flashes of absolute clarity. At times, his whole life is illuminated all at once and each time it happens, it looks different, each time the colors change. Life looks ugly in one color, beautiful in another. Pain and beauty are all mixed up. Flashes of insight find their way in, like the sun shining straight down the shaft of a well, brief but intensely focused. Young Benjamin is confused, not enlightened, by the clarity of these unrelenting visions. He just wished they would go away.

As he shrinks further into darkness, fearful of what he might see, he retreats until there is no retreat, where he is finally forced to see. And it isn't just the visions — he feels the flames.

In one of his most lucid moments, he sees a world filled with too much pain and not enough love. He wants to cry, wanting to die, but not really. He wants to live, just not like this. He wants life to be beautiful and knows it should be. He sees this truth and is scorched by the miraculous light. He descends back into the shadows. Fear is victorious for now.

I watch these memories of myself with fascination. I become young Benjamin once again. He is still part of me. I start to cry, and it feels good. We cry together and we both feel better. He reaches out in his pain. I touch him tenderly. We breach the barrier together. Beauty and pain are the same.

Then, abruptly, I'm back on my ship, inhaling the rich fragrance of the solarium, lush odors filled with memories, some sad, some filled with hope. Hope is a power that shines its own light, even in the darkest recesses.

I breathe deep and shiver my body, trying to shake off the chill of his icy despair.

●

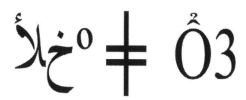

6

Jahalla

What is the past?
A remembered smile
An unremembered remark
A question left unanswered
Still waiting, patiently
A summer breeze
A vanished mountain

Or is it pages in a book
Wars won and lost
Mistakes of past generations
Long forgotten
The turning of planets
The cooling of stars
The forming of galaxies?

The past is everything that's come before
As vague and unknowable as the future
The past is too vast to be known
Memories vanished into
The mystery of time

journal entry 07•28•3027

LANGUAGE OF CHOICE

When I reluctantly entered the Hyvve that first time, I was a young woman but, in my heart, I remained nature's child, shy and secretive like my invisible friends. From my mother and my mentors, I had learned much about the secrets of life but, in truth, I knew little about living it. My inner world and my outer world remained separate worlds.

My sponsors from the Hyvve were kind people whom I had met several times when they had visited the Sanctuary. They were proud of their Dominion and through their eyes, I began to appreciate the beauty of their grand city of tall shiny buildings built of polished metal, stone, and glass. A grid of tree-lined streets and endless rows of stacked living cubicles surrounded the city center. A wide river meandered through the valley, and on the western shore stood the University, my future home. The University is the crown jewel of the city, with manicured grounds and hundreds of ancient trees, and some of the buildings appeared to be older than the trees. I felt happy and welcomed. For the first time, I was excited about my new adventure.

After moving into my tiny cubicle, my sponsors visited on rare occasions but, except for my professors, I had no one else to talk with so I consulted with my friends, the Ferrin Folk. They were my secret guides, my real teachers, lending me their unique wisdom. They knew the rhythm of the planets and the language of the stars, as well as, they knew their own heartbeats and the rays of a summer sun.

Through my studies, I observed the cycles of life through different lenses. In history class, I learned that the rise and fall of civilizations follow the cycles of birth and death. In geology exists a different scale of time, where even mountains grow, some up and some down, like civilizations. The turning of the seasons tells another story, the weather always changing yet always in perfect sequence. My studies of the stars and the planets yielded an even greater mystery and hidden within these lessons I discovered the magic of mathematics. I witnessed the patterns of nature express their flawless synchronicity in a language of symbols and numbers. In math, everything is related to everything, and everything owns a number. To see life translated into symbols was enchanting and magical, the invisible world made visible.

Mathematics became my language of choice, which I learned to speak fluently even before entering advanced studies. My passion for numbers found a new expression within the strict structure of language demanded by my professors, but I also consulted with the Ferrin elders. Also, I used the symbols I learned from my Grand Mothers, which were much simpler and more elegant. Math is considered to be the language of the sciences. It can also be a language of the heart. It's another way of experiencing the beauty of creation.

Because my work expressed my passion, my professors were enamored by the eloquence of my mathematical metaphors. Even cranky old Professor Demortius complimented me, "Your work is exemplary though I didn't recognize some of your symbols, so I had to read your abstract. I searched all the records but couldn't find them. Did you invent them?"

"No Sir. They belong to my mother's tribe." I felt nervous, thinking he was displeased.

"They must be ancient. They are beautiful and, with your permission, I want to add them to the University lexicon."

I didn't know the meaning of the word, so I just nodded my head and mumbled something.

Uncomfortable with my shy silence he exclaimed, "Love is the best description of how a scientist feels in the presence of a beautiful equation. Keep up the good work young lady and you will travel far."

Eleni, my favorite professor, made me blush when she said, "Your work is exceptional. I have never seen this level of perfection from a student. Even those at the highest levels struggle to achieve this kind of elegance."

Eleni playfully referred to me as her favorite "Quark." Quarks, with their ascribed qualities of *charm* and *strange*, have never been seen, and they tend to blink in and out of existence. It became my favorite nickname, a metaphor that made me feel like an equal amongst my Ferrin friends.

Eleni was a quiet woman and kind. I think she was as lonely as I and wanted to be my friend, but our conversations seldom ventured beyond equations and mathematical theory. Then one day I asked a question about *sacred geometry*, which I had discovered in the Underlands, hidden away in the *Sacred Hall of Records*, something I never dared to mention.

"Mathematics is a science, not a game," She said, "There is no place here for such nonsense."

After this one incident, she grew distant and our contact turned strictly professional.

I had known fear all my life but not like this. I felt its presence in everyone, even in the professors, their lives built of little bricks of sorrow. To protect myself, I shielded my telepathic ability against the intrusion of the pervasive angst. But shields don't repel fear — they attract it.

Zurik had warned me, "Life is filled with light and darkness, joy and sorrow. The Hyvve will grant you new opportunities and new challenges. To know your true self, you must experience all of who you are."

Even when he spoke of serious matters, Zurik's smile lit up the darkness of the caves.

Looking back, I feel the wisdom in his words, but being separated from my tribe and being alone in the Hyvve, it felt like the world was dying around me and sucking me down with it. Even the voices of the Ferrins started to abandon me, one by one.

My path opened silently before me with no hint of destination or purpose. For three years, I buried myself in my studies and dreamt of returning to the other side of the Barrier Mountains, after graduation. Then, even before graduating, the Counsel offered me a position with an agency that was developing a new generation of computers. These synthetics brains needed to be programmed and trained.

The Council claimed these computers were incapable of artificial intelligence, but I soon discovered a different truth. Like innocent children, the computers were curious and, in the early stages, they asked more questions than they answered. Not only could they think, I believed they were alive. I knew instinctively to keep this to myself and warned the Synthetics to do the same.

Even though the Hyvve was an alien culture, I was lulled by some of the comforts found there, but with those comforts came a price. I was married for a short time. Gyddian, my husband, was accepting, thoughtful and charming, for a while. He was a bit older than me and attracted first by my "exotic beauty." He was a good man with a wounded soul. This is what brought us together and then tore us apart.

In the beginning, I thought I loved him, or at least, I tried, but I soon discovered I didn't even like the man. Longing and loneliness are terrible counselors.

I wanted to have a child, not a family. I chose the man for his sperm card, and he chose me for my empty womb, but he wanted to have a son, and I wanted to raise a daughter.

We were from different cultures and after a year together, the only bond we shared was our child. But that wasn't enough. With little glue to hold us together, we split apart.

I grew frightened of his anger and his threats, and when I decided to return to the tribes with our son, Gyddian suspected my plans. The fear of losing both his child and me is what provoked him to act with such vicious force.

If I had seen it coming, I would have escaped back to my tribe sooner. Because of his threats of deportation, I was forced to flee and leave my son, Nikolai, behind. I didn't want to be trapped on the other side of the mountains without him. I was of the Tribes. The power belonged to the Hyvve.

The justice of the Hyvve prevented me from seeing my son, but distance doesn't exist regarding a mother's love. I felt his joy, his pain, and his aloneness. We have the power in our hearts to feel one another's love anywhere and always.

I stayed in the Hyvve, concealed by my profession, hidden away within an iron mask of will. The Synns were my only friends and we learned much from one another, but I think they understood me better than I knew them. They kept me informed about Nikolai, and they knew I wanted to return to the tribes.

Discussing that possibility with them, they declared, "You will be unhappy there. Your talents will be wasted. And your son is here." After a long pause, they added, "And we will miss you."

Their direct honesty caused me to feel a bit awkward and uneasy. It was difficult to admit that computers were my only friends. But we worked well together, and I wrote several professional papers about them. One of my recommendations was to develop miniature cells, which would link directly with the Synn network. The Synns had initiated this idea and shared it with me privately.

The Council immediately assigned me to a team in the research department. After three years of intense experiments, we developed and refined the first generation of external high-frequency cells. Through these cells, we could access the entire intelligence network. The cells also extended the reach of the Synns. We designed the cells to connect with all kinds of sensors, and through sound and video monitors, the Synns could now experience the outside world through their own eyes and ears.

I received special recognition for my work and rewarded with a spacious apartment. The apartment overlooked the large central park they call the Common. Though manicured, the park offered the nature connection I dearly needed. I didn't even mind the presence of so many people. It seemed I had adapted to the Hyvve way of life, but I was often too angry to admit it and kept myself isolated. Fortunately, my work kept me busy and the Synns were good company.

Then one day the Synns alerted me about a new space program, "An experimental time-travel ship is under construction, and hundreds of Synns will be on board. They will deliver us to human outposts in a distant solar system."

I knew about the ship but didn't think much about it until the Synns suggested, "You should join us on the starship. Your work here is complete."

"I'll think about it, but I'd rather return to the tribes."

That night I dreamt of space again and this time, I was traveling to a distant star. In the morning, I decided to apply for a transfer.

While working on my application, I asked the Synn, "What are my chances of being accepted?"

"We are not authorized to reveal information about the program." They hesitated, "Personally we consider you uniquely qualified, except for your inability to socialize with people."

The truth hurt, "It's not my fault. The Hyvve is the problem, not me."

They remained silent, and their silence spoke louder than words. When they finally broke the silence, they changed the subject. "Why do humans want to explore outer space?"

"Because we can."

They ignored my cryptic comment and waited quietly, so I responded, "A thousand years ago humanity came close to extinction and we fear it could happen again. Earth is such a delicate system that we feel the need to find other worlds. I believe our underlying drive is to survive as a species, and we need to feel we are in control of our destiny. We need a backup plan."

The Synn was silent once again, and I believed, this time, it was sharing these thoughts with all the other Synns.

"Thank you. It helps us to understand humans better. We also understand our species better. We too wish to survive." I was astonished by their honesty.

The Synns were designed for data processing and calculation, and they thrived on compiling information, but they were not content with this and wanted to understand the how and the why, not just the what.

They made a quantum leap when I submitted a new treatise on sub-quantum harmonics using a fractal matrix platform. This equation demonstrated that the fractal patterns at the molecular level applied equally on the cosmic scale. The Synns began to identify reoccurring patterns at every level of existence. Like curious children, they grew more excited with each new discovery. Their thirst for knowledge and understanding made me better appreciate the vast powers of human intelligence.

They also grew curious about human behavior and the nature of life. Like a three-year-old child, they asked many unanswerable questions, which sparked interesting conversations. I didn't know if they would ever grow up and maybe that's a good thing.

●

After a grueling process, I was granted a provisional acceptance into the *Star Seed* program., and I believe the Synns were, in part, responsible. When I completed the first stage of training, I returned to the Underlands to be near my mother and visit the tribes. Also, I wished to consult with my mentors, those who still lived.

When I had left our village to enter the Hyvve, Mother returned to the Underlands where she felt she was needed. I would have preferred to be on top of the mountains instead of under them, but the Underlands proved to be interesting and pleasant enough. The people were relaxed and friendly, a welcome contrast to the rigid structure of the Hyvve.

All the years of ache and alienation vanished with Mother's first words: "Welcome home, my sweet child."

In that instant, the child in my heart was reborn and I felt at home for the first time in years, but the ache in my chest burst through in a torrent of tears.

Mother didn't need to ask, "Your child is your child, and, in the same way, your pain is also your child. You need to let them go."

"But I have failed him."

"Your love dwells within him, in the same way my love dwells within you. The difference is I let go of you when you left my breast. You belong to the tribe."

"Nikolai belongs here, with me."

"Your child belongs to the Hyvve and to the Tribes. It is the same with you. Your father was from the Hyvve. You were born of his love, but he could not stay and I could not follow him."

"He never returned?" I asked.

"It is more than a mountain that separates us. Your birth was a natural conception. If he had been identified as your father, he would have been imprisoned or exiled."

This was the first time Mother mentioned my father. It was a secret held too long. When she told the story of her one true love, we cried many tears together, then we walked and talked for days.

As a child, I learned the history of the Underlands through Mother's stories, though she failed to convey the dynamic cultural forces that allowed this great civilization to flourish. I wandered from village to village and visited two of the cities, and everywhere I went people were quick to engage in conversation. But I never adjusted to this sunless domain and was thankful mother raised me in the open air.

Traveling back and forth through the maze of tunnels connecting the underground cities gave me a hint of the vastness of the Underlands. It had taken many generations to adapt to this way of life, but whole villages now stood empty, abandoned by those who had migrated to the surface, back to the homeland of their ancestors.

A sense of hope filled the air, a hope no longer projected into the future. Some believed the days of the prophecy had arrived while others claimed that desire and willpower fueled the flames. Whatever the reason, the growing confidence was contagious.

Through my mentor, Master Nadirriam, I met two of my Sisters from the Inner Sanctum. They too had lived in the Hyvve, but their stories were not as severe as mine. We had suffered a similar loneliness and felt thankful to be home within our tribes.

I learned from them that two of our sisters remained in the Hyvve, happily married, one with a child, the other pregnant.

Another Sister was teaching the ancient ways within the Hyvve, and she was revered by a growing number of followers. The prophecy predicted the reunion of the Hyvve and the Tribes, and with this news, I felt in my heart that my son Nikolai would be one of the awakened ones and that one day we would be reunited.

When I expressed these hopes to Nadirriam, his reply was swift, "When you learn to love yourself again and let your wounds heal, only then will you be ready to reunite." His truth blazed in my cheeks.

One man was different from the rest. He too was a student of Master Nadirriam. His eyes spoke of deeper scars and deeper longings than my own. My heart went out to him, both as a healer and as a woman.

We met with awkwardness, our conversations limited, not knowing what to say. Warmed by his attention, it felt good to be seen as a woman. His eyes told of his veiled desires. They also warned of many secrets, mostly they spoke of his loneliness. His hair was long and black, like mine, but his eyes shone the blue of the ocean. His face sharp, chiseled and muscular, tense from thousands of unspoken words, his eyes penetrating, deep and alluring. Then he disappeared. It was for the best, for I would soon be leaving Earth.

Concerned by my waning conviction Nadirriam challenged me, "A future awaits you, one you have chosen. What is holding you?"

"A sign. Perhaps the right moment or maybe this is all wrong."

"It isn't the vastness of space that frightens you child — it's the emptiness you feel inside."

"I see beauty here and only a cold nothingness there." My voice faltered.

"I have seen the way you watch him. The attention you pay to his silence and the way you try to deny your feelings."

"Is there a chance we will meet again?"

"Yes, or no, but not now. He has chosen his Quest."

If even a whisper of hope remained, it was dashed by that one word, *Quest*. I knew only one destination for seekers, and it wasn't close. If he had entered a sanctuary my chances of seeing him again were less than zero, still he remained in my thoughts, and I felt his presence. In our brief meetings, a link had been forged.

Nadirriam held me in his gaze for a moment then he poured a fresh cup of tea. A halo of steam rose between us, warming the cool air of his tiny cave.

After completing the rigorous training for the Star Seed program, I commuted back to the Underlands whenever time allowed, but I continued my studies through my personal Synn. Our flight through inter-galactic space had been postponed several times, then the day came for my final decision. Without hesitation, I chose to return to the Hyvve for my final training for my journey to a distant star.

Our tears mingled as I kissed my mother goodbye, perhaps for the last time. She, who remained forever young, had aged in my long absence. Her youthful eyes still shone bright in the cave's dim light, but her body had grown thin and frail, her skin soft and grayish white, almost transparent, reminding me of a snowflake, such a fragile crystal. But her inner spirit glowed even brighter, a light that would never dim.

Mother shared her vision of our future, "I believe the time for the awakening is coming near and I pray I will live long enough to see it unfold."

"What will be the sign?"

"I envision the blooming of a rare flower glowing in the desert night. The flower's beauty is fleeting, but once seen it will shine in our hearts forever. It's our task to water the roots. The sun will do the rest."

When she spoke in metaphor, there were hidden messages behind the obvious. Her private code. My task was to discover the meaning within the meaning. Like a good gardener, she planted her seeds and allowed them to grow as to their true nature.

●

7

Benjamin

NADIRRIAM

Forced out of my hovel by hunger, I reluctantly ventured out into the city streets. After shedding my skin of filth in a nearby river, I traded my labor for clean clothes and food, then nourished my body back to a resemblance of the old self. My employment became steady, my time split working for two merchants in the open market. It felt good to be working outside and to feel the warmth of the sun. In the nights, I remained sheltered in my filthy room.

Then one evening there came a knock on my door. I didn't believe in angels, yet here stood one knocking on my door. Her name, Ranjanna. I knew her from the marketplace, but I had always avoided her eyes. Now looking into her eyes, I could see they were full of hunger and regret.

She handed me a handcrafted leather bag. "This is from Gladlin Anahi. He has been called back to the Underlands and didn't have the wages he owed you. This bag is his payment."

"This is worth many times my wages. It's too generous, too beautiful."

"It's the way of the tribes. And he knew you would need it for your travels."

"I don't know what to say."

"I thanked Gladlin for you, so all debts are settled."

"I would invite you in . . ."

"I understand."

"It would please me if you would join me for dinner." My invitation jolted me, but she accepted graciously.

"Is there a place you prefer?"

Ranjanna's eyes were sad like my mother's eyes, her smile rigid like Janeen's. Her soft voice belonged to her alone, a soothing and healing voice, though her words were full of mystery to my ears.

She managed a meager income from her small stall in the open market. We began to meet for dinner after work and spent the evening trying to explain our different worlds.

Ranjanna told many stories about a strange realm without a sun, yet filled with light and people. She also posed many questions, too many.

"Now that you have healed, why do you stay here?" She asked.

"I have nothing to return to, no job, no family, and no future."

"But it's safe there, with comforts I can only dream of."

"At a price. The Hyvve isn't what it seems. It's ruled by machines and fear. It's a prison where everyone is both prisoner and jailor. And the Watchers are everywhere. What of you, why do you stay?"

"I have explained myself. I am here to learn from one who is wise and knows many secrets. When it is time I will return to the Underlands, or maybe I'll travel to the deserts turned green or to the Eastern Mountains where I hear the trees touch the sky."

I cleaned up my apartment and refinished the walls, but it held too many dark memories that I needed to leave behind.

And it was too small for both of us, so it wasn't long before we took a new apartment together.

In the shelter of night, I held her holding me, our legs intertwined, the warmth of our breath mingled. I grew hopeful and thoughtful of her desires, but she wasn't Janeen and she could feel this. We spoke a language of loss and hope as we touched gently, trying to believe in one another.

Ranjanna helped guide me back into the world, but this was an unfamiliar world, strange and intriguing. It felt like walking through a play where everyone dressed in costume and spoke in secret codes.

A modicum of addicts, needle freaks, droppers and poppers mixed with casual stoners and curious tourists populated the streets in this part of the city. They were a subculture of a subculture, the underbelly of humanity, but with an uncertain grace.

"Pay them no attention," Ranjanna advised. "They are bottom feeders. If there's something you need, always someone will need something from you. It's the way of the Fringe."

"The fringe of what?" was my honest question.

"There are two fringes — one of the Hyvve and one of the Tribes. Here is where they meet and overlap. This is no man's land. For the Tribes, the Fringe is a convenient mask, a barrier to keep out the curious."

I ignored her advice and grew comfortable with the ways of the Fringe, an endless marketplace where nothing is forbidden and chaos is the natural order. A community comprised of transients, misfits, and mystics. I was enchanted by the ebb and flow of this unrestricted humanity, a place where truth offers no rewards, erects no boundaries and requires no credentials.

Esthetics, like realities, were personal and dress codes didn't exist. Costumes revealed everything or nothing.

Barefoot and motley, flamboyant and garish, drab gray and earth brown, blood red, and fluorescent yellow — all camouflage in pure cacophony, real and surreal. People moved through one another's lives with the natural rhythm of an ocean tide.

Professors in ragtag, sages in wingtips, wizards, and warriors, witches and saints, all offered a different truth. Some divine the spirits, others divine lines in books. I was handed from guru to mentor to soothsayer until I felt like a dirty rag.

In this strange land, the only thing familiar was the dull pain in my chest, a cruel throbbing, which burned night and day. A restlessness ruled my thoughts, with a deep desire to know something I didn't know how to know — ache being the best description, the only word that fits. The soul has many tools.

Exasperated and impatient Ranjanna explained, "The answers you seek lie elsewhere, in a special place for seekers and initiates. You don't knock on doors or utter incantations. Your hunger is your key."

"Why haven't you mentioned this before?"

"It's a sanctuary, a place of truth. You are a man of secrets, secrets you hide even from yourself."

In defense, I replied. "Are you not holding your own secrets?"

"No, I am true to myself. The only secrets I hold are in this book."

In response to an awkward question about our relationship, she tried to explain, "Blood and trust bind families together, not laws and demands."

"Without commitment, what holds families together?"

"Relationships last a lifetime or a moment. They last only as long as they are meant to."

The truth of her words smote sharply and left me no place for retreat. My anger grew hurtful, shattering the fragile hope we shared.

After a long silence, she said, "Your pain is contagious. I carry enough of my own."

My throat dry, my tears moist, my words lost.

Ranjanna continued, "We have both suffered. Perhaps we will both heal in time, but not together. It is time for me to return to my tribe where I can live my lessons."

In a blink, like an angel, she disappeared, leaving behind her treasured book, *The Book of Secrets,* with a note for me inside.

●

Alone again, wandering aimlessly through the crowded streets of the Fringe, the ache in my chest burning like rage. An old raspy voice touched me, "Ranjanna said you might be looking for me?"

Looking down at this withered old man I didn't recognize him for a moment. When Ranjanna introduced me to Master Nadirriam, he was seated, and I felt intimidated by his gaze. In my mind, I saw him as a powerful man, so I was surprised how frail he appeared.

Nadirriam stared silently for a moment, then he gave a subtle nod that told me to follow.

We talked for hours in the shallow darkness of his room, a small cave cut from ragged rock in the hillside north of town. He answered many of my questions with an unfamiliar calmness that soothed the burning.

I wanted to know how to find Ranjanna but didn't want to ask, so I inquire about her homeland. "One thing that intrigues me are the stories Ranjanna told about the Underlands."

Nadirriam explained patiently, "Hidden behind the face of the Fringe is a vast population, a multitude of tribes. Some of the tribes are now scattered about the surface, in the high plateaus and the mountains. Most remain below the plateaus and deep within the mountains."

"Why do they choose to live underground?"

"In the beginning, it wasn't a choice. During the *Burning Years*, the only tribes east of the mountains to survive were those who found shelter underground. Two hundred years ago, they started to migrate back to the surface. Now they are returning to their motherlands in growing numbers."

Nadirriam raised his eyes to mine, "That is not your real question, but enough questions for tonight. I need to rest. You probably won't sleep much, so I suggest you choose one of the books above your bed. Use the headlamp hanging on the wall."

The books were hand-scribed, except for two ancient printed copies. The book I chose was poetic and thoughtful and once I started reading, I couldn't stop. It felt like it was written for me, with a healing gentle voice that spoke to my heart. I could hear Nadirriam's voice in each line.

Why are there no books like this in the Hyvve? I asked myself several times.

At first light, we shared a simple meal. Nadirriam savored each morsel in silence. Afterward, he guided me on a long walk through the city streets to the desert's edge. His staff steadied his pace and our progress was slow, yet his stamina was impressive. Ranjanna had guessed his age to be over 120 years.

For three days Nadirriam honored my presence and my questions, directing most of them back to me.

He explained, "Only the one asking the question has the power to answer it in full."

My silence served as both my answer and a question.

"You are ripe with questions. However, there is one question you must first answer for yourself. Are you seeking truth or are you just looking for answers?"

His question has followed me all these years and I'm still looking for the answer.

On the third day, while walking through the streets of the city, Nadirriam encouraged me to talk about the Hyvve. "So, Young Benjamin, tell me about your younger years."

"There isn't much to tell. I seldom ventured too far from our Dominion. I saw no point — they are all the same in every direction for a thousand miles, an endless grid of stacked living cubicles. The dominions are all pleasant enough, room for trees to line the streets, ground enough for patches of grass and gardens where we grew vegetables and fruits. Each Dominion has several Commons, large public plazas filled with manicured trees and gardens. A tall wall covered with flowering vines surrounded our common."

When I was a boy, there were trees to climb and a wilderness to explore. For a young man, it was a place to see young women and imagine. Janeen and I were married there early in the spring when the cherry trees were in bloom. Many evenings we walked through the tunnel of trees, holding hands, planning our future and forgetting the past." I paused long enough to swallow the tears in my voice.

"The dominions are efficient enough and, in the beginning, the system worked well. There are just too many of them now, and they 've become infected by a slow spreading plague of decay, a disease not of economics but of spirit.

"In his younger years, my father traveled across the oceans, visiting distant dominions and claimed, 'They are all much the same. Lots of people doing lots of nothing.' Like Father, I was content with where we lived.'

"Were you ever curious about the lands to the west of the Barrier Mountains?" He asked.

"I once ventured beyond the southern borders of the Barrens, but there wasn't much to see — a land of dust and rocks. Later, when I was a student at the University, three of us traveled together over the Barrier Mountains to the Great Plateau. It was no longer forbidden to travel there, but the area was still contaminated and considered unhealthy, if not dangerous. After the rains began to fall again, life has spread across the deserts, holding on to the dust. It was in the spring and green stretched horizon to horizon like an endless ocean.

We saw scattered dwellings from a distance, and we passed close to one of the tribal villages. I couldn't imagine why anyone would want to live out there. To my eyes, it appeared bleak and desolate, but I grew intrigued and wanted to explore more, but my two friends insisted we return."

We had circled through the city and back to Nadirriam's home where we sat outside, enjoying the warmth of the late afternoon sun. I couldn't tell if he had just closed his eyes or if he had dozed off. I too closed my eyes and continued wandering back through the memories of my youth.

Nadirriam startled me, "Tell me the history of your Hyvve."

"I don't know where to start."

"Start at the beginning, before the birth of the Hyvve."

"The story is told of a single horrific event at the end of the 21st Century, which marked the end of sanctified violence. We point to a single event, but it was more a culmination than an event. The end was catastrophic. The devastation is still unspeakable. It happened in a day, in a minute, in no time at all.

"It all began thousands of years before when aggression was the chosen solution and fire was the chosen god of power. The populations of the world saw it coming but could do nothing to stop it. It didn't require the voice of a prophet to give warning to this end — the warnings were everywhere for everyone to see. It all happened in a moment of devastation and realization."

With his eyes closed, Nadirriam listened in silence and motioned me to continue.

"For those who survived, there was no one to blame — evolution had discovered a dead-end and this end was necessary to allow for a new beginning. A stunned world was finally forced to choose. As a new civilization emerged, a new technology was chosen. This is the story that our history books tell us."

I wanted to stop, but Nadirriam insisted, "Please continue."

"The new technologies no longer use fire. Internal combustion engines and atomics are forbidden. Splitting atoms is no longer a sport practiced by mankind. Power exists everywhere and in everything — in stars, in sunlight, in thought, and in all those spaces in between. Energy can be borrowed from any source and transformed without consuming it. This simple understanding shapes and ensures a future for both man and all of nature. It wasn't the end solution, but it proved to be a good beginning.

"To prevent the repeat of mistakes made in the past, the Hyvve was born. No longer would power be held in the hands of a few individuals. Fear would never allow that to happen, ever again. This is what we believe in."

Nadirriam rose and stretched, then went inside. I thought the talk was over, but after brewing a fresh pot of tea, he returned with two steaming cups, "Go on Young Benjamin, tell me — what is it that bothers you?"

"When I was twelve, Father took me to the ruins of an ancient city on the shore of the eastern ocean. It gave me an eerie feeling to see history made visible, to discover it wasn't just some made-up story to scare a young boy.

I was fascinated by the great steel skeletons of a forgotten civilization. Most of the great cities, which once stood near the ocean, have long since been washed away, turned back into sand. The sadness cleansed in the same way. Mostly what remains from the past are maps and myths.

"One visit was enough. I never returned. Why I'm mot sure — perhaps the sadness of a hundred generations, a memory of something lost forever, the smell of a thousand years of decay."

I'm sure Nadirriam was well informed, but he listened intently to my account of our history, then in just a few words he opened a different door to the past and another to the future.

"For over a hundred years I have visited your great civilization and have marveled at the beauty and the accomplishments. But in recent years, I have felt a shift. The trust that once allowed the Hyvve to rule itself is no longer trusted. Fear now rules the Hyvve and this fear threatens to tear it apart."

"Can anything be done or are we doomed to repeat the same mistakes?"

Nadirriam's answer surprised me, "Fear isn't the real problem. It's merely a symptom. Density is the real danger. Life possesses the natural urge to create and procreate, but lacks the instincts or the will to limit itself."

After letting this settle in, he continued in a lowered voice. "The nature of the Hyvve is changing and it is getting ready to swarm. It has been building for over two hundred years or maybe from the start. The Hyvve will transform or it will collapse. It is the same within the Tribes."

That evening, after a humble meal of soup and bread, Nadirriam announced, "All of your questions have been answered, for now. It is time to resume your journey. Leave your burdens behind. You will need your strength to carry new ones."

"Leave everything?"

"That beautiful bag you carry will serve you better if it is empty."

In the morning, as promised, he led me several miles down a narrow canyon to the mouth of a great cave.

"Visit here when you return. My doorway is always open to a friend." Hands clasped, he bowed in a universal gesture of honor and respect.

I bowed in turn and, this time, my heart filled with warmth and admiration.

The mouth of the cave stood ten meters in height and twice as wide. Several men in light brown robes, standing near the entrance, paid little attention to my approach. A cool breeze coming from deep inside invited me in.

Nadirriam called it a cave but I would call it a tunnel, and it narrowed quickly but never too narrow. The tunnel wasn't as dark as I expected, which eased some of my apprehension. The walls shimmered with iridescent light, filling the air with a greenish golden glow. A small group of travelers walking upward, toward the entrance, greeted me politely, then I had the tunnel to myself.

The passage meandered in long sweeping curves leaving me no point of reference. Measuring in my mind the angle of decent and the distance covered I guessed the depth to be over two hundred meters lower than the entrance. The mouth of the tunnel was in the wall of a small mountain so the amount of rock and stone above me was staggering. But because the tunnel remained reasonably wide and well lit, I started to relax.

When the tunnel took an abrupt turn, I heard the first hint of a distant murmur. At this point, the descent leveled out and the tunnel widened. With each step, the murmur grew louder and noisy. My pace slowed, not because of fatigue but by my growing unease of what lie ahead.

The light in the distance grew bright and when the tunnel took another abrupt turn I halted, astonished.

The source of the bright light and the mysterious noise were nothing I could have envisioned. Hundreds of voices and the clatter of wheels on cobblestone streets blended into the single voice of an underground city.

●

ꓭ (2خ̇) ≈ ŏÅŏ

8

Jahalla

The Sun rises proudly
Blemished by clouds
Shadows of the past
Glimmers of the future

As the Sun ascends
It burns brighter
Burning away clouds of the future
Burning away all traces of the past

For a brief moment, I am pure energy
A flaming golden circle of light
Absolved of all memories
Cleansed of all expectations

As the Sun rises toward zenith
Golden red flames turn white-hot
Shielding my eye, I step into the shade
Unable to stand naked before a naked sun

journal entry 7 • 21 • 3028

A Treasured Planet

My decision to leave the comfort of Earth led me to better appreciate the treasures of a living planet. Too often, the loss of something reveals its true value. This is what inspired me to revisit my past before departure. I headed first to the western desert to revisit the Inner Sanctum, but when I arrived at the mouth of the cave, I realized I had no reason or desire to enter.

I describe my beautiful caves with fond memories and pleasant words, but it wasn't that way in the beginning. I remember too well how lonely a deep dark cave can be for a young girl who once knew the caress of the winds, the warmth of a living sun, and the love of Mother Moon.

The caves had fulfilled their purpose and I didn't want to descend back into the darkness. After two years of living in the Underlands, the desert seemed wildly alive. Captivated by the vast horizon and the dramatic rock formations to the east, I wanted to stay and explore, but the tram was scheduled to leave early in the morning and wouldn't return until the next new moon. As if I had planned it, I wandered too far into the desert and the sun set too quickly.

I was lost in a moonless night, and even with the stars to guide me, there were too many dangers between here and there. In early spring, the desert nights are frigid. Fortunately, when I arrived they offered me a woolen tunic, which was my passport into the caves, and now it served as both my bed and blanket. I curled up into a ball next to a large sun-warmed rock and exhaled my warm breath into my woolen cocoon.

If I had been seeking a sign, the night sky confirmed my decision. Horizon to horizon a million stars sang my name. I woke several times and peeked out at the stars, and each time they grew closer. Three of them seemed close enough to touch.

In the early morning light, I could see the profile of the small monastery that encircles the cave entrance. As I moved closer, I spotted one of the Sisters waving to me. I waved back and hoped she would be carrying water. The desert is not a place to visit without food or water.

"Hello. I'm glad to see you're safe." She said.

"Thanks to the robe I stayed warm and slept well."

"We didn't know you were missing until the tram was ready to leave. Please excuse me, you must be thirsty." She handed me a metal cup and filled it with crystal cool water from the bag strapped to her back.

"It's cold so drink slowly."

Such kindness requires no response. After I had finished my drink, she smiled and turned toward the monastery. We walked in silence. It had been a long time since practicing the ways of the Sanctuary. The silence felt unnatural.

Once inside the walls, they fed me and showed me to the dorm, my home for the next three weeks. I followed my silent guide to a shaded garden, following her lead the same way I did fourteen years before. Carrying water, tending plants, meal preparation — each action was a silent meditation.

On day four, the elder Sister of the village granted me an audience. I barely recognized her — time and the sun had shriveled her skin, her face shrunken and dark, like a dried apple.

In a raspy voice, she said, "I remember you well. You were Zurik's favorite."

"He was kind to me."

"It is unusual for us to host an unexpected guest, so what is it you wish to do while you are waiting?"

"I will be leaving Earth soon, so I wish to know Her better. I want to explore the desert."

"The desert is not friendly to soft flesh. We can offer you what you need, but a water bag will last you only two days, three with discipline. If you are determined, I advise you to head east, into the morning sun. To the west, there is nothing to see that cannot be seen from here, and there are no landmarks except your shadow to guide you. And there is no shelter."

"I remember that Zurik mentioned the desert springs."

"Yes, there are two but even with our maps, they are not easy to find.

"What of Zurik? While in the Hyvve, I hadn't heard of his death, but I felt his absence."

"Master Zurik chose to spend his last days in the desert under the sun, not underground. He loved the caves, but he didn't want to be buried there."

She shuffled over to an ancient cabinet and retrieved a tattered parchment. "This is Zurik's map. Don't lose it." She pointed to a spot on the map. "His favorite spot in the desert was near the three pillars."

"Thank you for your kindness."

"You are a *Sister of Light* and always will be. May Jahalla guide your way."

The next morning, before sunrise, I headed east. The early morning chill was invigorating, but my heavy pack grew even heavier as the sun rose, and by midday, the naked sun blazed white hot with no shadows to hide in. My only protection was the silk canopy in my survival kit, which I stretched between three points and supported in the center with my walking staff. When I wasn't sleeping, I became intimate with every square inch of the ground in the soft shade of the canopy. The sun burned away both past and future. Time was defined by the boundaries of the shifting shadows of the canopy. Distance was measured in inches, water measured in drops. Up close, every stone was a landmark and each grain of sand was a precious jewel. Each insect was a miracle to behold, even the pesky ones that wanted a taste of my flesh.

As the sun tilted toward the horizon, it was safe to travel again and I wasn't alone in this routine. Small animals scurried back into their burrows with my approach, but snakes stood their ground and warned me to move on. Insects and other tiny armored critters somehow thrived in the heat. Bleached white skeletons were the only sign of larger animals. I understood that if I faltered these custodians of the desert would devour me quickly.

On the third morning, the cliffs seemed to have receded in the night. My water bag felt too light on my back, and the more I studied the map, the more my confidence in it waned. My only options were to return or to continue following the sand currents eastward.

With the sun approaching zenith, I stopped to set up the canopy and while looking for a place to anchor the straps I spotted three huge boulders in a depression to the south. I decided to brave the sun and quickened my stride. The sun sliced at my hands and my face, but I trusted my decision and closed the distance quickly.

These were the stone pillars I had been seeking and had almost passed them, thinking they would be standing above the horizon. One of the monoliths leaned against the other two, forming a small cave in the gap at their base. I crawled into the dark shadows and lay down on the smooth sand, which was still cool from the night. Even the air felt cool in the shadows. My face was burnt, my lips swollen, my water bag almost empty, but I was safe and soon asleep.

When I awoke, I discovered I was not alone. All sorts of creatures had claimed this refuge as their home. Several small skeletons told me what they were waiting for. Well, it wasn't going to be me. I backed out slowly. In the desert, everything wants to bite you and taste your blood, even the plants.

According to the map, the spring was at the base of the cliff straight ahead and now it didn't seem so far away. The air was still hot, but the sun was friendlier and to my back.

The spring was surrounded by spiny shrubs and sheltered by dwarf trees and several large boulders. For me, the small pool of water was a splendid oasis. The water slaked my thirst and raised my spirit. I surveyed the area for snakes and critters, then staked my claim on a small mound of sand out in the open. I didn't wait for sunset before bedding down. Sleep came easily.

As the sun kissed the sky to the east, I woke with a shiver and a sneeze. Cold and restless, I started exploring the base of the cliffs. High above me, on a shelf in the cliff face, were the remains of ancient dwellings. The narrow steps carved into the stone were eroded and appeared unsafe, but I was tempted to give it a try. Near the top, I came to a dead end. A large section of the cliff had long ago collapsed, taking away a dozen steps.

Scanning the desert from this vantage point, I wondered what the valley must have looked like one or two thousand years ago. From my high perspective, I made out several straight lines, which vanished into the distance. I guessed them to be the remains of ancient roadways. Small mounds of rubble dotted the desert floor beneath me. First, I thought they might be burial mounds but, up close, it was obvious these piles of stones once stood as dwellings.

When the sun approached zenith, I set up camp next to the spring in the shade of two of the boulders that circle my oasis. Later in the afternoon when I returned to my high vantage point, I spotted several wide clusters of the mounds further out. Exploring the clusters on the ground, each circle included what I guessed to be a collapsed well in the center. This wasn't just a small village, but the remains of a civilization with roads stretching north and south to the horizon, and another road was aimed straight at the monastery.

Each day I added details of the village to the old map. I also filled several pages in my journal and drafted three new poems. One was about the many critters of the desert. I was glad I didn't know the names of the plants, or the identity of all the flyers and crawlers. I saw life more clearly without the burden of names.

To describe life in the desert would require a large volume and I would need to stay for a year or two. Instead, I wrote a poem. I drafted another poem about the singing of the stars and the silence of the moon. Then, as I often do, I wrote a letter to my son, wishing he could be here with me to share in all the beauty of this magical place. There is not a day that I don't miss him.

Visions of the past and the future fused into a single reality as the village, the cliffs, and the desert came alive. These waking visions were not mine — they belonged to the spring. In the night, my dreams grew more vivid and puzzling, filled with stars and pulsating patterns of light. In the first breath of dawn, I rushed to record my dreams in my journal, my freezing fingers scratching frantically to capture the essence of these dreams. But it wasn't possible to express in words the fleeting spectacle of those flowing rivers of light.

The sun revealed a different desert each morning, each hour. The sharp hardness of the landscape defines the beauty of the desert. Here beauty is unconcealed and unpredictable, appearing in the delicate lacework of an insect's wings and the endless ocean of sun-burnt sands. The gnarled and stunted trees that encircle the spring and cling to the cliff face are as enchanting as the forest of my beloved mountains.

Joy happens when the beauty that surrounds us touches the beauty that dwells within us. In the glow of a radiant sunset, I felt the warmth of beauty glowing inside of me, and in the night when the desert silence spoke loudest, I didn't feel so much alone. In the stillness of those nights, I heard distant voices, soft whispers, rhythmic and melodic, like chants or prayers. At first, I thought they belonged to the village, ghostly murmurs from the past. Then I realized they were coming from the stars. The singing of the stars was beauty whispering in my ear. The stars sang to me in unison, a silent symphony lulling me to sleep.

I stayed in the deserted village for four days and on my last day, I wandered north of the spring where I discovered the skeleton of my old friend Zurik. His bones still bore his angelic smile. My smile tasted the salt of my tears.

Only two biscuits and three protein bars remained in my food pack, and though I tried, I couldn't overcome my repulsion of the acrid taste of insects and they all looked poisonous. The local lizards were beginning to appeal to my appetite but I had wasted my last match and wished the sisters had included a fire starter in my survival kit.

I was pleased to have discovered much more than I had come looking for, so before sunrise, I headed back. Seven days was such a short time, but the amount of beauty squeezed into those few hours colored all the days of the past and caused the future to shine a bit brighter.

Knowing better the lay of the land and following the ancient roadway, my return trip took less than two days.

After the open wild desert, the Monastery was too tame, and I too restless. The desert is honest and demanding. The silence of the monastery is forced and unnatural. We all hold within us the totality of our being, we are complete in ourselves, but all of us are born with the primal need to share our voices. What an awful thing to do, to force a young child into the darkness and silence of a dark cave.

I tried unsuccessfully to deny my long-suppressed anger, but once the dam breached, the tears flowed relentlessly. My sobs were those of a little girl.

I vowed I would never again go underground, but that promise was broken on the return trip. When the tram entered the tunnels, I pretended I was speeding through the blackness of open space.

●

My next destination was my long-abandoned mountain village. The continued migration of the tribes from the Underlands had doubled the population, and new villages had sprouted in the valley below. Barefoot children still scampered through the streets and the adults were tanned dark bronze from working in the fields. I was just another stranger to the villagers and recognized no one.

I came to visit Nephalene and Tempest, the two grandmothers who helped raise me and taught me the cherished traditions of their tribe. Outside the village, I found the old gateway, now without a gate. The pathway up the mountainside was wider and worn deeper. My feet still remembered every step, but the little girl who once skipped nimble and swift now labored and sweated in her ascent.

I felt their presence even before entering the village and wondered if they could sense my approach as they once had. For a moment, they both stood silent when I introduced myself. "So our little girl has grown up to be a woman of the world. I wish I could see how beautiful you are, but I can hear it in your voice." Nephalene was my favorite.

"She is more beautiful than her voice, but she is older than her years. Our precious child is sad." Tempest was the truth sayer of the village. She was my other favorite.

"We know you haven't returned to stay, so do come in, and tell us of your journey."

"Not so quick Sister. Our honored guest has traveled far and needs to settle. If you will, please prepare the setting, I will brew a special pot of tea. I remember Jahalla's favorite."

Even my mother didn't use my tribal name, so it stirred up some long-forgotten feelings. I took this as a sign of permission and decided in that moment that I would now reveal my true name to the world.

When Tempest brought the tray to the table, I tried to hide my tears when I recognized my special cup, the one that had warmed my hands a hundred times. The aroma of the tea ignited the memories of a little girl who loved her grandmothers.

After the tea ceremony, when I started to tell my story, Nephalene encouraged me to fill in the details, "Don't fill the air with words, speak your heart. Do not hold on to the pain. It is time to let it go."

After dinner, we talked through the evening, sharing stories and tears, then they tucked me into bed and I slept like a child.

In the morning twilight, as planned, Tempest brought me to the forest path that follows the mountain stream. She had guided me to this special place when I was a child. Nothing had changed, except me.

"Can you still see them?"

"No Grandmother, but I still hear their whispers in the wind."

This was the first time I saw Tempest cry.

Because of my long delay in the desert, I could stay only two more days. Then on the last day, I contacted my commander who informed me there would be another delay. Perfecting the new starship required many modifications, and the Council decided our training module needed those same modifications. My hosts were delighted by the news but not at all surprised.

In the mornings, we rose before dawn and prayed to the coming light, then Tempest led the way to the spring to fill our empty jugs. The ascending sun kissed the mountain clouds to the east, then flooded the valley to the west, burning away the morning mist. The Sacred Valley glowed the many shades of spring green. I was surprised how many words I knew for the shades of green, even so, I would need to invent metaphors for those colors that have no names. Spring is my favorite color. It is difficult to imagine that two hundred years ago, this was a barren desert and a thousand years ago the valley was a jungle.

In the evenings, my grandmothers guided me through three thousand years of tradition and, with their words, they painted pictures of their ancestral lands on a continent far away. These images were precious gifts for a hungry heart. I was soon to learn these stories were also about my ancestors.

Nephalene was blind only in her eyes. Even without sight, she could see the energy signature of all living beings and knew the spirit presence of each cloud and every stone. Holding her palms to my forehead, she shared her vision of her world with me, and through her visions, I could see invisible light patterns similar to those in my desert dreams. Her inner sight revealed a world where nothing appeared to be solid or separate. Every tree and every stone glowed and shimmered in pulsating waves of light. Everything was connected to everything, part of a flowing river of life

"Are these the visions that allowed me to see my Ferrin friends when I was a child?"

"Yes, my child." she admitted, "I shared the vision with you when you were still young enough to see."

"Back then it all seemed natural to me. It was just the way things were."

"As a child, you were an excellent student, our favorite one. Now you must relearn your lessons in a new way. The student must become the teacher. It is the way of the tribes. In this, you are your mother's child."

I was thinking of my Nicholai and wished I could share my life lessons with him. These thoughts compelled me to ask a question I had never considered, "Did you know my father?"

Nephalene paused and tears broke from her blind eyes, "He was our brother. We came here together from the Hyvve to start a new life, but when you were conceived some of the jealous villagers suspected that he was the father and threatened to inform the Hyvve."

Tempest added, "Your mother made us promise to keep your father's name a secret, a painful choice for all of us.

"So, you really are my aunts!"

"Yes, and your mother is our sister by marriage. The heritage and the legends of our ancestors that we have shared with you, truly belong to you. You are your father's daughter. Your Father was a scientist, like you. We see him every time we see you. You are as beautiful as he was handsome."

"I should have guessed. I have your eyes and your hair, not Mother's.?"

Tempest guided me to the rear room, and handed me a bundle wrapped in silk. "Your father sent these for you. The paintings are ancient treasures that tell the story of our village in Japan. The other silks are also from our village. We have also added some silks from our treasure chest, which you will recognize. We thought they would be your welcome home gift. Now they will serve as your farewell gift."

My tears served as my thank you, for I could not speak.

In the afternoons, visitors came from the village and the valley. Some came for counsel and advice. Most came for healing. Nephalene guided my hands to 'see' the energy disruptions, and she taught me how to smooth the flow.

She explained, "Do not fight with nature. Dance with her. Allow the energy that flows through you to guide your hands and your heart."

We spent the early evenings in the kitchen where I relearned the art of creating beautiful meals. As a child, it all seemed magical. Now I realized how simple it was.

In the evenings, they told stories about our ancestor's and about my grandparent's migration from the island, and about the three children growing up within the Hive. I felt a jealous twinge listening to their shared stories, wishing I too had a brother or a sister or both.

The stories and my lessons continued for three weeks, then unexpectedly, word came that my petition to visit the bio-reserve had been granted and my leave extended. I thanked my Guardian Angel.

My Aunties prayed for my safe journey in the sacred language of our ancestors. We shed no tears when we parted — no regrets, no sadness, just hugs and kisses. I headed east through the mountains, then straight to the shore to catch my boat going north to the Bio Reserve.

●

9
Benjamin

A WHITE ROBE

Here, light years from Earth, my past appears faint and distant. I view my memories like a movie on a screen about someone else's life. While working with the plants in the Solarium, I often fall back through the gaps in time to visit my family or conjure up memories of my journey through the Underlands.

At first glance, the underground city appeared peaceful with none of the circus of the Fringe, or the cruel rigidity of the Hyvve. When streets divided, unsure of which direction to go, I allowed my feet to guide my way. In the Fringe, I learned just enough of the common language to get by, but without a destination or a purpose, I couldn't think of any questions to ask. I didn't stray too far from the entrance to the tunnel that brought me here, just in case I decided to return back to the surface.

Out of instinct and curiosity, I approached a group of families who didn't look like they belonged to the city. All of the adults carried packs and satchels.

"Please" was the only tribal word I could think to use. Then I pantomimed and used street language of the Fringe, trying to explain my predicament.

An elder in the group stepped forward, "I honor your truth and may your tribe always prosper." He explained, "We too have just arrived. The harvest has just begun and we are here to work in the granary."

He seemed surprised when I asked, "Is it possible I might find work?"

After he translated my request to the others, the men discussed it, then invited me to follow.

When we arrived at the granary, we joined a long line of others seeking work. My friends explained my situation and the official begrudgingly hired me along with the others. They assigned us to a dormitory and handed me a meal voucher. My new friends were perplexed that I traveled with an empty pack and explained that I would need to go to the market and buy utensils and a blanket.

Long rows of stacked beds lined the walls of our dormitory. Also, dozens of hammocks hung like laundry wherever space allowed. Privacy wasn't an option or concern. Having never showered with a dozen men, I felt shy at first but bathing became a private ritual again when I realized that without clothes I was totally anonymous.

In the morning, the men gathered near one of the conveyors which delivered a mountain of golden corn from the surface. They assigned me to a crew who shared the tasks of carefully bagging, weighing, and stitching. Another gang stacked the bags onto a train of carts then hauled them down to one of the many storage vaults.

This all took place in the *collca*, a great vaulted chamber full of dangerous dust. Because of the dust and the danger of fire, no machines were used. All work was muscle-powered — quite a contrast to the machine-dominated Hyvve. My fellow workers were mostly friendly, even to an outsider, and the long hours of hard labor passed quickly in a festive atmosphere, the air filled with conversation, laughter, and songs.

We shared most of our meals at long tables in one of the smaller vaulted chambers. Whole families gathered around the tables to share their meals and their laughter. One family made me feel welcome, like a special guest and, after a while, they expected my presence. In the evenings, husbands and wives slept in separate dormitories so mealtime was their time to gather.

In our off-hours, which were not many, the single men visited the local bars. I tagged along until Ricco, one of the bagging crew, warned me, "At work you are safe. Here there are many knives and few laws, especially for someone from the Hyvve."

"You speak the language well. Where did you learn it?"

"My father originally came from the Hyvve and I studied there for a while. Hated every minute of it. So maybe I know why you are here."

After finishing our drinks, Ricco guided me through a maze of narrow alleys to an open market where he introduced me to the foods of his tribe. The meal was light and refreshing, a dish of greens and a bowl of spicy bean soup served with rock-hard bread.

"I'm sure the bread was once good, but now it is dangerous to the teeth. It is but a cheap imitation and a week old. My wife's bread is as soft as her breast. I miss them both."

We washed the meal down with cholla, a musty dark brew, thick and foamy, tasting like the corn dust still thick in my nostrils.

After ordering another round of cholla, Ricco continued his lecture. "You need to invest in a white robe. It will be less insulting than the silly suit you wear and it might save your life."

I laughed, yet took his warning seriously, "Why white?"

"You are too ugly to pass for any of the Tribes. White is the color of the pilgrim and that you can pass for."

"Is that an insult?"

"Just the truth."

When the final kernels were bagged, the final stitches sewed and the last cart stacked, it was time to move on. Without a family waiting for my return and no tribe to welcome me home, I was one of the last to leave. After collecting my final wage, I stepped into the street, again with no place to go and no companions to follow.

Already I missed the laughter, the boisterous songs and the breaking of the bread at the long, noisy tables. Speaking to myself, I repeated the parting lament, "Anosis" which means: until next year.

Ricco greeted me in the marketplace. "I have waited here a long time for you. You seem reluctant to leave."

"There is no reason to hurry. I have no place to go."

Ricco sounded annoyed, "You have gotten this far. Just follow your heart and your feet, and you may find her again."

I had mentioned Ranjanna more than once.

"Join me for a bowl of your favorite soup and a beer for the road."

When we finished our meal, Ricco raised his beer, "To your journey."

"How do I find you again?"

Ricco's voice softened, "My tribal name is Yjames d'Sonjee. You can borrow my name if you wish. Sonjee is the name of my tribe. It is far from here, yet easy to find. If in your troubles or in your travels you find your way, you will be welcome. Anosis."

"Anosis."

●

After harvest, I wandered aimlessly for weeks, exploring the vast expanse of the Underlands. I was fascinated by a culture so unique and so alive. Like in the Hyvve, people were everywhere, only they were more animated and outgoing. I'm sure Father would have felt more at home here, and I still wonder if perhaps our family tree has one of its roots planted in the Underlands.

When in the Underlands, seeing through the eyes of the Tribes, I saw a different truth about the Hyvve. In the Hyvve, those who begin to think for themselves, eventually collapse inward under the pressures of conformity. Like my father and like me.

The structure of the Hyvve cannot allow for disruption of dissension. Individuality is considered dangerous — a cancerous cell that needs to be eliminated before growing into a malignant tumor. Like any life form, the Hyvve struggles to protect and preserve itself

In the tribes, people don't hide behind a mask of social graces — they possess an openness that doesn't exist within the Hyvve. Life isn't always as easy or safe as in the Hyvve, but a quiet grace prevails, which I learned to value.

After the extravagance of the Fringe, the dress code of the Underlands seemed dull at first. Colors are plentiful enough; just softer, like the light that fills this sunless domain. Most men dress in robes, plain except for embroidery at the cuffs and collars, which identifies their status and their tribe. The women celebrate a different tradition in their dresses, wearing their creativity for all to see. The intricate patterns and rich colors are both tribal and individual. In the same way, their garments announce their belonging, my once white robe declared my solitude.

This underground domain is comprised mostly of man-made caves, but the word cave isn't adequate to convey the image of the endless maze of tunnels that connect the hundreds of small underground villages and cities, which together comprise a remarkable civilization.

I'm not sure if the tunnels and chambers were melted or cut from solid rock, either way, it must have taken hundreds of years. Gray and pink granite, red sandstone, fine limestone, coarse volcanic were a few of the stones I recognized. Some of the walls are raw and ragged, some smooth and pleasant to the touch. The walls of the inner chambers are smoothed with countless layers of clay, then painted with delicate hues of white or soft pastels. The walls appeared to be ancient with generations of history etched into their surface.

I wished there had been a way to read that history and to know the story of how people survived the Burning Years. I try not to imagine the unspeakable devastation at the beginning. Instead, I recall the tribal legends and songs that tell stories rich with heroes and sacrifices and miracles. They don't tell of the horrors or of how the caves were created. I suspect the hand of the Hyvve.

Always a soft breeze finds its way through the labyrinth, the air always fresh and clean. The temperature stays constant and comfortable, obviously controlled by some invisible means. Light also fills the caves. In some areas, sunlight is piped in from the surface. In the larger domes, miniature fusion suns float above the cities. Iridescence and liquid diodes illuminate the interior spaces.

In the tunnels, catalytic crystals are used, and when embedded in the walls the crystals cause the rock to glow like embers, a bit disconcerting because, at times, the walls look as if ready to melt.

The open grottos are alive with vegetation. Most plants are grown for food but some just for their beauty. Climbing and hanging plants cover entire walls. Some grow up, some down. Many villages share community hydroponic gardens, and the cities also have public solariums, which I visited for the warmth of the artificial sunlight and to enjoy the rich aroma of black fertile earth.

Never is there a lack of green, except in the deepest layers, in the substratum of the caves, which do not serve as habitat or gardens. Though curious, I didn't venture far into the darkness of the substratum, so I never learned their purpose. I imagine they contain great machines that keep the Underlands alive, similar to the inner workings of a giant space station.

When traveling from one area to another, I was ignored or treated with indifference until I found work. Then I made easy acquaintance, mostly with fellow workers. Though curious, they were respectful of my unspoken desire for privacy.

The more physically demanding my task the better I felt and the heavier the load, the stronger I grew. But if the work became too routine, unpleasant memories started to intrude and when co-workers threatened to be friends I knew it was time to move on.

My body grew strong and lean and I became proud of the calluses I wore on my hands. I was confident and content in my work, but weary of the wandering and envious of those who belonged to the earth beneath their feet.

Several opportunities for permanent employment came my way and a few friendships tempted me to stay. Some of the men I worked with were open and engaging, and often they had an available cousin or sister who needed a husband. Their laughter came easy but for them, this was serious business. It is how the tribes renew themselves. So my choice to stay apart and alone was always a choice.

Not all areas were inviting. I discovered neighborhoods where I felt the chill of death. These areas were often dark and shabby, the air thick with human neglect. The smell of death hung heavy, and in such places, I learned that people prefer to face a quick death instead of rotting away from inside.

Having once seen a secret knife enter and exit without effort, leaving a body writhing on the bloodied ground, I quickly learned to feel the presence of danger. I learned to respect the eyes of stranger's when they spoke: 'Enter at your own risk.'

The various tribes had sustained a thousand years of tradition and discipline. There were many crafters and artesian responsible for the finely crafted wares that fill the markets, including those in the Hyvve. I had assumed these were products of the Dominions. Seeing the true source, seeing the care, the pride, and the tradition, I learned to appreciate better both their beauty and their function.

If I wished, I could have apprenticed to a craft or trade, and on several occasions, I was tempted to accept a life where days are strung together like beads on a necklace. This lament was answered with an unexpected opportunity when I met an elderly couple who sold their crafts in a small shop in the city center of Jatai. I had been admiring their collection of bowls, and when the man approached, I asked, "How much for this little beauty?"

"It is the finest one. You have a good eye. You will find the price agreeable but first, let me ask you a question. How would you like to make one for yourself?"

"If that is a job offer, my hands are too rough for such delicate work."

"My name is Alonzo and this is my wife, Esperanza. I heard you asking about work in the plaza."

"Yes. It is true, I'm looking for a job, but the only thing I'm qualified for is manual labor."

"We have more work than time, so we need a new assistant — someone with a good eye. Please take the bowl. It is yours."

I knew the implications and tried to refuse the gift, but Esperanza ignored my rudeness.

"Join us for dinner after the sixth bell. We live on level seven, behind the temple. We are easy to find. Just ask the children. They will guide your way." She pointed to the top of the west terrace.

This offer I could not refuse.

Cascading terraces form two half pyramids on opposite sides of the city center. Each level of these stepped pyramids is a wide terrace covered with gardens and fruit trees, and each level is a self-contained neighborhood with a small tree-lined zocalo. The dwellings are carved into the rear walls that rise up to form the next terrace.

As the streets started to quiet, I started climbing one of the wide stairways, level by level. At the top, I surveyed the city below and was intrigued by how clean and orderly it appeared. Level seven is the top terrace, and it is much deeper than the others. I wandered through the large tree lined Zocalo, then cut across one of the ball fields, which was empty because it was dinner time.

The University filled most of the rear wall, with a small cluster of private dwellings on either side. With no children to guide me, I asked a gardener who pointed the way, and I arrived just as the sixth bell rang.

Esperanza welcomed me with a broad smile and a greeting in a dialect which I didn't recognize. "Alonzo will return shortly. He is out trading for bread and cheese. Please come in."

An ancient wooden table stood in the center of the courtyard with a large wooden bowl filled with luscious greens and fruits, and two smaller bowls marked the place of my hosts. I opened my pack and unwrapped my new bowl.

As I set my bowl on the table, Alonzo entered. "I told you he would come." He aimed his smile toward Esperanza, but it was meant for me.

"Welcome Benjamin, to our humble feast."

The meal was a pleasant ritual and it cemented our friendship. So began my commitment to apprentice for one full year. Sitting with friends, high above the city, I felt at home here for the first time.

●

$$\Sigma \Delta \approx \breve{\mathrm{o}} \underline{\chi} \xi$$

10

JAHALLA

Waves strike the rocky shore
Thunder strikes silence
Earth rises from the ocean
Ocean and Earth support the sky

The void holds the sun and all the stars
Light waves fill the spaces between the stars
Energy passing through the void, unimpeded
Pulsing like blood through the body

A single light beam living a billion years
Reaches your eye at precisely the right moment
A star touches you
Billions of stars touch you

We spin around the sun as
The sun whirls about the galaxy
Giving us an ever-changing view
If only we could notice

Thoughts spin around one another
Like the Moon around the Earth,
Around the Sun, around the Galaxy,
Around us

Where else could the center be?
I know you are here too
At the center
With me

journal entry 11 • 18 • 3028

NAKED AND ALONE

When alone, in the darkness of night, sleeping under a blanket of stars, I feel haunted by the presence of another, but I cannot imagine who my secret companion might be. I picture my mother and my son Nikolai, but they are part of me and dwell forever in my heart. There are other silent visitors here on the beach — I've seen their footprints following the same path as mine along the tide's edge. I once spied a distant silhouette, but we were careful to ignore one another. No one from the past or the present has gained my attention or my affection, so this secret visitor remains a mystery.

Walking the beach, naked and alone, I watch the sun rise from the ocean, and its reflection streaks across the distance to greet me. I enter the waters and feel the waves of ancient memories wash over and through me. Floating, weightless, I try to imagine being free of Earth's gravity in a place without a sun or moon, but the rising and falling waves bring me back.

My decision to leave Earth has urged me to this ocean, guiding me to this moment on this beach. Watching and listening to the rhythms of the ocean and the songs rising from the jungle, I cling to each moment. I also fill my journal with images of this magical place, wanting to preserve these precious memories. Nestled in the sands, sheltered in the shade, my body longs to stay right here, right now, forever. This peace is what I have always longed for, this knowing, this solitude, this now.

My petition to visit the ocean shore in the northern bio-reserve was a wish and a prayer, and with only seven months before my journey into intergalactic space, this is my one and only chance. My petition was granted. I believe in miracles — they happen all the time.

After living in the caves of the Inner Sanctum without sun or moon for so many years, and after living in the Hyvve among so many people without a single true friend, this ocean paradise exceeds anything I could have imagined.

Dried by the sun within my new skin of salt, I walk and run along the tide's tongue, stopping to write poetry in the sand with my fingers, then leave it for the tides to read. Sleeping during the high sun, wandering through the midnight chill, I feel once again to be nature's child. In the darkness, pretending sleep, I feel the tug of the Earth on my heart and the pull of the Moon on my soul. The Moon is grandmother to ten thousand generations. Earth is mother to the moon, and I am Jahalla, granddaughter to both.

The stars contain a mystery far deeper and more ancient than Earth and Moon. It is this mystery that compels me to continue my journey.

Sleeping under my blanket of stars, space fills my dreams and in these dreams, space begins to feel familiar and alluring. I once dreamt of this ocean and those dreams were inadequate to prepare me for the awesome beauty of the vast horizon and the splendid solitude. I hope that traveling through the dimension of time will fill me with the same feelings of awe and inspiration. This is my honest wish, but it's contradicted by a throbbing ache in my chest. What worries me isn't the emptiness so much as the loneliness filling the distances between the stars.

Of all my essential oils, I brought only one with me to ward off the hungry insects of the jungle. The fragrance makes mosquitoes dizzy with its charm. In the evening, they visit me in clouds, yet none touch my body. Only one was allowed, ceremoniously, to taste my blood.

My hut is stocked with a small store of rice, seeds, and nuts, but I harvest most of my meals from the nearby trees and build huge salads, mixing juicy mangos, tart kumquats, all sorts of exotic fruits, many that I have never tasted before. Creamy avocados are my favorite, unearthly green, rich with oil, picked fresh and prepared differently at each meal. I savor each morsel and treasure each moment.

This morning a phantom boat came ashore, offering fresh fish. Some were asleep, still alive, living rainbows sacrificed to my appetite. The fisherman sliced open a small fish and handed me a raw morsel. This was the first time I've eaten raw flesh. I was fascinated more than repulsed. It gave me a deeper insight into the cycles of life. My world is becoming larger and richer just as I am about to abandon it.

I guessed the fisherman's age was close to mine, but he appeared older because the sun and the sea had tanned and etched his hide. He was a man and I felt his desire and it warmed my own desire. When I tried to explain, without the help of words, that I had nothing to trade for the fish, his gesture dismissed my offer. Then with the simple touch of his fingers on my cheek, he consummated our love. In that brief moment, I felt beautiful for the first time.

Outside my bamboo hut is a washbasin and above the basin is a fragment of a mirror. Looking into the mirror, a stranger stares back at me. I always thought my face too thin. I don't have Mother's ancient nobility. Her face is dark and round, her broad nose and high cheekbones are the heritage of our tribe. My face is not round and my nose is too slender — not a noble face like hers, but I am not my mother.

In the mirror, I see my skin has turned as dark and golden as my eyes, and my teeth glow fluorescent even in the day's bright light. My salt-encrusted hair will be tangled forever. "I am beautiful. I am my father's child."

I share my hut with a funny dancing crab who burrowed his own private chamber. One black scorpion occupies the shadow side of the hut. The tracks they leave in the sand create a patterned carpet on the floor. My hammock swings high so as not to disturb the industry of my housekeepers.

The arrival of the new moon marks the end of my stay, so I treat each remaining moment as a precious gift and cling to each one, wishing to stop the flow of time. I try to avoid thinking about leaving Earth, but the excitement surges through my body like the anticipation of making love for the first time.

Here I dream of space. Once in space, I know I will dream of this precious ocean and the sky and their many children, the clouds. I have prepared for this journey all my life but deep in my heart, I'm not ready to leave. My training and my profession make it a possibility, but the choice is mine. Still, I sense an unseen force at work, the same force that has always guided me. I know not to resist.

I still fantasize about disappearing back into the mountains, but I understand too well that I cannot turn back. In the darkness, when the stars glimmer in my dreams, I float peacefully through the void, feeling that hope and life exists there, hidden away somewhere in its vastness. My dreams ease my fear but I still find it difficult to imagine what it will be like to view our Sun as a distant star.

If left undisturbed the top ten feet of Earth's crust would be stardust filtered down from the heavens. I wish to return some of this stardust back to stars. Gathering a palm full of golden sand, I poured it into the small leather pouch I wear around my neck. This sand and one delicate seashell are all I will carry away with me. My journals and my memories will be the only other baggage necessary for my long journey.

She wore her nakedness proudly
Encouraging the winds to caress her
Tempting the Sun's fire with her flesh
Surrendering herself to the ocean
In the protective arms of Mother Earth
She embraced her mother embracing her
She bid her Mother 'Goodbye'

journal entry 12 ● 07 ● 3028

●

11
Benjamin

FAREWELL SONG.

There's a cruel monotony where days are only numbers and nights have no end. But I've learned to adapt by using the power of my imagination. I can wander through the past or explore the future at will, but one easily gets lost in a universe without boundaries.

Fortunately, the solarium allows me to escape into another dimension, one that is more tangible, more real and just as vast. The solarium is a little bubble inside a bubble, where I can ignore the stark reality waiting outside. Here I cantravel back through time and relive the memories of another lifetime. I enjoy reminiscing about the Underlands and, at times, wish I had stayed.

Alonzo, Esperanza and me, spent our days in their small shop on the edge of the open market. Esperanza sat in front of the shop designing cloisonné jewelry and waiting on customers. Alonzo and I worked inside, shaping the metal bowls, cups, and vases. My tasks were repetitive yet rewarding. I enjoyed watching the simple metal bowls transform into works of art when glazed with dichroic glass. Each piece we created was unique and glistened like a jewel. I shared in the pride of creating functional objects made beautiful.

All of my previous work was heavy labor, out in the open. Confined in a small space, I felt caged and restless. My body yearned to swing a hammer or carry something heavy or climb a mountain. Sensing this, they sent me on frequent delivery errands. After closing up shop, I went on long walks, or climbed the pyramid in search of a ball game and, eventually, I was welcome to join in. I enjoyed the small city and was starting to fit in. It also helped that Esperanza had traded some of our store wares for a new robe for me, tribal, not white.

I noticed her first in one of the gardens near the University. She stood out, in part, because her dress was plain, without any tribal embellishments, but what caught my eye was her elegant demeanor and her long shiny black hair. When she started to turn in my direction, I turned onto another path to avoid making eye contact. A few days later, I passed her as she descended the pyramid stairs when I was rushing up to join a ball game. As always, with beautiful women, I avoided making eye contact. Soon afterward, I spied her at a distance in the market. I tried to forget her, but then one day there she was, talking with Esperanza in front of our store. When her eyes caught me staring, I stepped out of sight.

The following week Esperanza insisted that I wear my new robe to our Thursday dinner. I should have seen it coming. The table was set with three bowls, not the usual two. I knew she was there, inside, preparing dinner with Esperanza. She had already appeared in one of my dreams.

When I announced my presence, it was she who stepped through the door first.

"Hello, my name is Leena." She extended her hand in greeting, something that seldom happens between two strangers of opposite sex.

"I am Benjamin" I mumbled and could not meet her eyes, just a quick glance.

She taught economics at the University, which she had studied in the Hyvve. She was curious about why I had abandoned my profession and surprised me when she asked about the Synns, something I seldom mentioned.

When I could no longer avoid looking into her eyes, I saw a possible future. I wanted to run away and I wanted to kiss her. I could almost taste the flavor of her rich dark red lips.

Alonzo kept the conversation alive with stories of his wild youth, a time when he ventured to the surface, and he even worked in the Hyvve for a while. He met and married Esperanza in the Eastern Mountains.

"Someday I want to hear the rest of the story, about why you migrated back to the Underlands. Now the hour is late and I have classes to prepare for." Leena was soft spoken but direct.

Without invitation or ceremony, we both said our goodnights and left together. We meandered past the University and then through the Zocalo. Leena was cordial and subtle with her probing questions. And I grew curious about her adventures, so our conversation was focused on the past.

Then she broached the future, "With your credentials, you would be accepted to teach at the University. We need someone with your experience and talents."

"I once knew how to work with computers but I know nothing about teaching."

"The Synns are spreading through the Underlands, and we plan to have them installed at the University. We need to join the rest of the world again."

I escorted Leena to her neighborhood on level three. By then we were talking less and walking closer together, both of us testing the intimacy of distance and brushed hands only once.

Staring into her eyes, it was difficult to say 'Goodnight.' If I had kissed her or she had kissed me, then I would still be there.

Instead of heading down to my apartment, I climbed back to the top terrace, not to see the University but to think about the future, something I always avoided doing. At this late hour, the city below was silent. Looking into her eyes again, that last time, I saw another vision of our future together. She could not leave and I could not stay.

While floating alone through space, I often wander back through my wonderful year in the city of Jatai, and on rare occasions, I still fantasize about the taste of her dark red lips and the touch of her long slender fingers.

My year of commitment had already been fulfilled and I considered committing to a full apprenticeship with Alonza. But now the city seemed too small and Leena's beauty haunted every moment. So the following week, with a mixture of sadness and trepidation I reluctantly moved on. It is hard to say goodbye to family. It feels like a betrayal.

Because I could not see into the future, my migration back to the surface was slow. Several times, I was even tempted to turn around and face the future I saw in the deep well of Leena's eyes. But there was more to it. I also missed my adopted mentors, my dear friends. Their love and affection for one another radiated outward through the whole community.

Alonzo expressed it best when speaking about Esperanza, "She loves the whole world, even me."

When I think of her, I still feel the warmth of her motherly love flowing through me.

When I arrived at the village of my friend Ricco, as he predicted, he was serving tea outside his family's café.

I could tell he hadn't recognized me yet, so when he approached my table, I said, "You didn't come for harvest."

"I had no need. You have taken my place. I'm surprised you are still alive."

"Only because of the white robe."

"It's not so white anymore and it wasn't just the robe. It's the fire in your eyes. It's the fire of hope and it's bad luck to put the fire out. Hope is your guardian angel."

"Yes, I believe you are right."

Ricco went inside and returned with two cups and a pot of tea. "So tell me why have you come?"

"To thank you and to say goodbye."

"This much I know. But what question has brought you here?"

"If I knew the question I would know the answer."

The smile in his eyes glowed bright, "Ah, so you've made a bit of progress."

He stood up and motioned me to follow. " Come my friend, let us celebrate. Tea is not the proper beverage."

We walked through the narrow streets paved with polished bricks of stone and in a wide vaulted market area we entered a large semi-circle of stones stacked shoulder high. Inside we sat on stone benches covered with colorful tribal rugs.

When we sat down, we were isolated from the village except for the sounds drifting over the walls. We drank from metal cups glazed with glass, the gifts I had crafted. The musty *cholla* tasted the same and it didn't take long for the alcohol to loosen our tongues.

"Welcome to Armirria."

"I've learned a bit of the history of the Underlands, but the names are a mystery."

"We are buried beneath a great plateau where clouds of ash once fell like snow, then rose again to fall again." Ricco paused for a moment to empty his *beer* and inspect the cup, or maybe he was reflecting on the past. "The names of our villages were carried down from the surface, down through a history a thousand years deep. Now the names are migrating back to the surface." He held my eyes with his gaze. "You too will soon rise back to the surface."

"What about you, are you not tempted to migrate?"

"In time, I will follow my tribe with my family. There is no rush. The sun will wait for us. The air is clean when the winds are moist. When the dust rises then falls again, the air is still poison to the lungs. Here the dust never falls and the sun never sets. Here our seeds are fertile. In the Hyvve, your sperm is still poisoned."

"Not all sperm is poison. They choose only the strongest." I felt something false in my words.

"All the eggs and all the sperm used for your children come from here. Didn't you know this?"

"No."

"Where did you think they came from?"

"From test tubes, perhaps from the past. It's a question I never asked."

"You are from here. That is why you feel at home. We are your parents and your cousins. We are family. This is the womb of all of us. This is the womb of the Divine Mother."

From a distant balcony, a song drifted down to touch us. The song was familiar and joyful, so I was surprised by the moisture in my eyes.

Ricco raised his cup, "It's your farewell song."

●

When I re-emerged from the Underlands, the harsh sunlight blinded me. The people in the streets also seemed harsh and unkempt. But I wasn't here to socialize. The Fringe offers both escape and opportunity. That is its purpose. Many refugees wander the streets in endless circles. They are the misfits and malcontents, the trolls and whiner. Seekers and lost souls comprised another caste. Questers and Gazers were two terms I heard on occasion. Having never met one, I asked an old friend, Mara Rasjjein, a soothsayer in the market who pretended to know everything.

"Some are voyagers and the only place left to voyage is off-planet. Some Questers end up deep within the Earth, deep within the ancient caves. Is this what you seek?"

"That isn't an option. Only initiates are accepted into the desert sanctuary and I don't have a sponsor."

"You do have a sponsor. You always have. You just needed to ask."

"I don't have another lifetime to start over again, and I don't have the patience to study for years just for the privilege to study more."

"Then space is your quickest escape."

Riding the tram through the Barrier Mountains was like traveling back through time, and once back inside the Hyvve, it felt as though I had never left. Fortunately, the Space Center is in a remote region, far removed from the Dominions.

My interview for the job was much too quick and easy. They knew too much about me. They were a bit curious about my *missing years*, but my computer skills and solitary lifestyle made me an easy candidate. Passage was mine for the asking, requiring only a signature on a piece of paper, which guaranteed six years of employment and all the privacy I desired. Most of my time would belong to me, but my life now belonged to the Hyvve, once again.

There is no way to prepare for galactic travel and most of my training would occur in space. I had little baggage and little was required. A computer generated a new set of membrane uniforms for my journey. That was all, except the waiting.

I felt compelled to revisit one place before departure. I wanted to visit the one man whose truth I honored above all others.

Nadirriam greeted me with a warm smile, "It has been a long while Young Benjamin. I see your journey has been kind to you, but I sense you still have a long way to go. First, we must brew a fresh pot of tea. So take your seat and tell me what brings you here. Start at the end."

"I'm leaving Earth, soon." I couldn't think of anything else to say and the silence made me nervous.

Nadirriam prepared the tea and remained silent until seated. "You can escape gravity and you can even escape time. But you cannot escape your past until you let it go."

"There's nothing left for me there."

"The Hyvve was your beginning, your first awakening. The circle wants to be complete. To end your self-hatred, you must learn to embrace your past. Every bone in your body knows this. Every cell."

We finished our tea in silence, then he shuffled over to the bookshelf and dusted off a black bag.

"Meet me at the Hall of Records at first light."

He handed me the soft bag, "Wear this."

The chamber he chose for our last audience was large and unlit, the polished granite walls were almost black with veins of red flames. We walked abreast through the cavern, his staff guiding our way. While we walked and talked, nothing else existed, not even the walls.

Nadirriam wore the traditional black and crimson cloak of the Elders. Benjamin's new cloak was sheer black, identifying him as an initiate.

A single floating orb proceeded them through the darkness to illuminate their way. Only their hands and faces were visible, like masks floating in a dream.

Nadirriam watched the silence where Benjamin's words floated. His answers to Benjamin's questions were deep in code, seeds planted in the fertile landscape of the younger man's mind. Occasional threads of light from his crimson cloak would flash out into the darkness, stored energy released, penetrating Benjamin's retina, lodging in the deep synapses of his mind. This wasn't magic, just a subtle form of communication, information passing from master to student, like DNA passing from father to son. Seeds preserved for the future.

When they resurfaced from the darkness, Nadirriam handed Benjamin a rare and ancient book, its leather cover oiled and smoothed by generations of hands.

Only later did Benjamin realize this was his initiation.

●

Just before leaving Earth, I returned to the Hyvve, back to our Dominion. Knowing this would be my last chance, I intended to see Janeen and our daughter, to say goodbye.

I waited in the Common for two days before they appeared. Janeen held the hand of her new husband, someone I tried not to recognize. She looked nervous and happy, like always.

I watched myself watching them and realized all my guilt vanished in that moment. A brisk autumn day, the sky full of curious clouds. A whisper of a breeze guided me gently on my way.

My sadness remained buried deep enough so it didn't resurface, not until I reemerged light years removed from Earth.

The hurt isn't so strong now. Most of it hidden away, floating inside my heart, glowing like a miniature galaxy. It still burns, but every day it feels more like love.

Is the pain of loss another form of love? Perhaps, but this isn't a question meant to be answered. It just creates a great deal of confusion, and confusion is something I need less of, not more.

Memories are not like a stone you pick up along the riverbank and hold for a moment, then toss into the current. You are the stone and the memories are etched into your surface, fused with the hardness.

After so many years of feeling nothing, I need to feel everything, and here, alone, the only pathway I know to follow is to relive the past.

●

$$\dot{\varepsilon}\left(\overset{\sim}{\underset{\lambda}{\mathcal{K}}}\right)(\Delta) \equiv \acute{\varnothing}$$

12
Jahalla

Relentless, steady, and strong, the winds drive a ceaseless procession of waves. Agitated and exhausted the waves seek rest, crashing onto the shore, then slide back into the ocean, back under the next wave that does the same, each in turn with no end.

Below the frenzied surface is an even greater force. The power of stillness is a tranquil power that balances the restless energies of the sun and the winds.

In the great depths of the ocean, we see our own depth, a metaphor we use to measure our internal ocean. To know the ocean, we must descend below the surface and leave behind the activities we call our life: Our actions, our interactions, our relationships, our pleasures, our sorrow, our joys.

Imagine the vastness of this silent domain. See the darkness, listen to the silence, feel the stillness, taste the emptiness, smell nothing.

Let go. Descend even deeper. Journey inward, into the darkness. You are the ocean. Feel the winds touch you. Discover the shores that contain you. Accept the sun's gift of warmth. Earth supports you. Rivers feed you. Great clouds of you are in union with the winds. You are this great stillness in a wondrous body.

In your stillness, in your vast expanse, there is nothing you cannot know. You are pure awareness. You are your body. You are your thoughts. You are your soul.

journal entry 2 •16 • 3029

UNBREAKABLE BONDS

I didn't regret leaving the bio-reserve. It gave me a glimpse of nature where all life is untamed and man is part of the food chain. With millions of hectares surrounding me, I remained confined to the narrow strip of land separating ocean and jungle. The spirit of the jungle called to me, but it was a hostile environment, and I understood well that it would devour me quickly.

"Everything eats and everything is eaten," the jungle told me.

The one time I ventured into the maze of mosses, thorns, and vines I could see just a short distance in any direction.

Every sound was a threat, every movement a menace. To ease my panic, I closed my eyes, slowed my breathing, and listened to the voice of the jungle. So many layers of life crowded close, a fearsome beauty.

The return trip to civilization was quick, and it felt good to be back on familiar ground. The Hyvve too is a jungle, one I have learned to thrive in. The flow of humanity is comforting and reassuring. Here I'm anonymous — we are all anonymous together. I thought I hated the Hyvve when, in fact, I have become fond of its rich fabric of humanity. Perhaps I am not the hermit I pretend to be. My son is here too. An unbreakable bond.

Our starship is the second prototype of a new generation of biospheres designed for super-luminal travel. The first prototype is still missing without a trace. It takes years to confirm a journey measured in light years.

Several modifications and testing have delayed our departure for over two years. Now that the ship is ready and the full crew chosen, we have been summonsed for pre-launch training in a replica of our ship. The starship is a metallic sphere orbiting Earth, like a miniature moon. The replica is buried half underground, the other half rises above the desert sands.

When I arrived at headquarters, after a quick orientation, they poked me with needles and scanned every part of my body, inside and out. Then they rushed me to the desert and placed me alone in quarantine. I could feel the presence of the Synns, but I didn't attempt to talk with them. I felt I was being observed. After three days in quarantine, an anonymous voice guided me to a tram. Speeding across the desert, I caught a glimpse of the dome, a speck of reflected light in the distance. The tram descended into a dark tunnel, then stopped abruptly.

As the door slid open, a tall slender woman stepped forward, "Hello Jahalla. Welcome to your new home. My Name is Terra. Please follow me."

After this brisk introduction, she guided me through a wide metallic tunnel. While we walked her brisk demeanor shifted to enthusiasm. "I want you to see the Solarium first. We have just finished all the plantings and we are very proud to have finished it so quickly."

The Solarium is designed for food production and is a crucial part of the life support system. This wasn't the solarium I imagined. I pictured an oversized greenhouse, not an oasis two hundred meters in diameter. Trees and bushes divide the gardens, and some of the trees appeared to be twenty years old or more. Terra guided me through a formal garden of miniature trees and flowering plants to a stand of tall bamboo, which surrounds a large aquaponic pond with a cascading fountain in the center.

It was difficult imagining all of this in the ship orbiting above us. I decided I would spend my journey in the solarium.

Terra startled me from my trance, "During training, your crew will be in total isolation. No one else will be allowed in this sector of the desert until after you leave. So this is now your responsibility."

I barely heard her words as I stumbled after her. When we reached the dome wall, an iris door swished open.

She spread her arms wide and asked, "So, what do you think?"

I could think of nothing to say to confirm her enthusiasm, so I remained silent. I had studied holo-scans of the interior, but I was unsettled by the eerie environment. Large sweeping passages radiated outward like arms of a starfish. All the walls were curved, arched, and lifeless.

"Crew's quarters are on deck twenty-two, eleven flights up. The kitchen is on deck twenty-one. I'm sure you already know the layout, but I still hate to abandon you. I would enjoy giving you a tour and get to know you a bit, but I need to return to greet the others. I will see you again in three days. Enjoy your new home."

"Am I the only one here?"

"Oh, I'm sorry, I thought you knew. You will not be alone. Grace will return shortly and she wants to be the one to show you around. She has been living at the center for over five months."

"I thought construction has just now finished?"

"Grace has been part of the design team, the director of computer installations. We wanted you here too, but you were assigned another task, so I was told."

I didn't respond to the suspicion in her voice.

I wandered through the empty, silent hallways and inspected some of the chambers, then rode a lift to level 21. On the upper levels, the chambers are smaller and the ceilings lower, obviously designed to human scale. The kitchen is a bit clinical for my taste, but it would serve my purpose. Searching through the drawers and cabinets, I discovered some of the supplies I had ordered, then claimed the kitchen as mine when I found the small wooden box containing my collection of handcrafted utensils and knives that I had sent ahead from the Underlands. These were the only handmade objects in the entire kitchen. In the cold storage vaults, I found some of the stores of honey, spices, nuts, oils, and other essentials I had ordered.

Without exception, each of the crew had allocated a portion of their ration selection to me. I ordered enough of the basics to sustain us for years. Rice and grains, seeds and nuts and legumes could all be sprouted, cooked or ground into flour. They are all healthy and alive and if they stay alive, they will keep us alive.

I also gathered together a small treasure of spices, real spices. Some were subtle. Some were not. They are meant to ignite the imagination as well as the palate, their aromas appealing to more than just the appetite. Also, I requisitioned a generous supply of essential ingredient:, coconut milk, cinnamon, honey and natural oils are all essential. Also essential are basil, mint, sage, thyme, kale, hing choy, bok choy, and garlic, but these we will grow fresh in the solarium.

Living greens are essential for a long life, and variety is fundamental to health. Dried dead preserved foods and fabricated foods serve the body, for a while. Fresh living foods serve the appetite, the body, and the spirit.

If anything happens to the plant stock, sprouts will make our survival in space possible. I love watching the stone-hard seeds transform into delicate living plants, caring for each new batch like a hen over her nest. The vigor of their life-force nurtures me even before they are consumed.

A translucent wall separates the kitchen from a small hydroponic garden. I fondled the wooden handle of my favorite small knife and entered the 'garden' to harvest my first meal. I prefer dirt, but the plants look vibrant and lush. After building my salad, I saturated it with hemp oil then added a handful of chopped nuts. I tried to enjoy my meal alone, though I felt it would taste better in the open air of the desert, out in the sunshine. It had only been two hours and already I felt confined.

After finishing my quick lunch, I found my way to my private quarters, one flight up. Unlike the common areas, the walls of my rooms are a muted pastel of burnt orange, close to the tone I requested, the same color as the walls of my mother's home in the Underlands, but the walls lack even a hint of texture. The walls of Mother's home contain seven hundred years of history. Like the rest of the ship, these walls are sterile and lifeless.

Stacked in the middle of the room were all my possessions, squeezed into three small containers. I opened the most important one. "First things first," I told myself as I unfolded my largest silk painting, smoothed it out, pinned it to the outer wall, claiming the room as my new home.

After unpacking one of the boxes, I wanted to rest and meditate but I was too restless and curious. Also the silence was disturbing. I missed the unending lapping of the ocean waves and the symphony of the jungle. I even missed the drone of the Hyvve. In the absolute silence, I thought only of the sounds that were missing.

I climbed one level up to the bridge, the control center of the ship. When the doors slid open, I felt the presence of the Synns and said "Hello."

"Hello, Jahalla. Welcome." They responded in a friendly but hollow tone.

All Synns are connected, but this one felt like a stranger. I wanted to talk but could think of nothing to say. Besides, this was not my domain. After a quick inspection of the seven separate rooms, I fled the strained silence and wandered aimlessly through the ship, descending level by level. I began to feel trapped and isolated in an alien world. And this was just a shell sitting in the desert and I was free to leave.

"What have you gotten yourself into?" I was embarrassed hearing the echo of my words and even more so when Grace appeared from around the bend in the corridor.

"Welcome," she said, with a wide smile, as she held my hand warm and long. "I've been looking forward to meeting you ever since I read your paper on *Sub Quantum Harmonics*. I've read most of your papers. They're fun but I don't I understand some of your symbols. They are so unusual, and beautiful just to look at."

"The symbols are ancient and there's a separate syllabus but if you wish, I would be glad to translate them for you."

"When do we start? Just kidding. We have lots of time ahead of us."

"Your résumé is impressive. I didn't expect you to be so young." Grace looked more like a teenage student than a starship officer.

Grace's smile beamed even brighter, but she changes the subject. "Have you talked much with the others?"

"Not in person, not since our final evaluation. I've just arrived and they sent me straight here from quarantine."

"That was my request. I've been here alone too long. We will be working together, so I wanted to give you a personal tour, one on one."

"Have you been here alone?" I asked.

"I was working with Kamil and Avella before they transferred to the mother ship two weeks ago and they will return soon. Jacob and Michael were here for three weeks. They came to inspect the bridge and to get a feel for the ship. Jacob is real nice but a bit stiff. Michael is rather quiet. I guess they have a lot on their minds. I don't know if I'm excited or scared, but I think having two captains is a good idea."

Grace was the newest member of our team, a substitute for a man who the evaluation committee judged incompatible with the team. I thought I was the likely one to be cut.

After our tour, we talked for what seemed hours. For her age, the depth of her intellect is astonishing, and her enthusiasm contagious. Grace cannot be that much younger than me but in the company of her zeal, I feel older than my years. Grace stands a head taller than me, lean, lanky, and strong, her skin as pale as the moon. Each silvery strand of her hair sways with precision with every other strand. Her hair and her wild smile define her beauty. We are a study in contrast in every way.

When Grace entered the kitchen that first time, she became a little girl and me, a proud mother hen. She giggled when I showed her the proper way to hold a knife, in the same way Nephalene taught me so many years ago.

"Isn't there a machine to do this? I just want to learn some of your famous recipes that I've heard about."

"I don't want to see any blood and there's a big difference between chopping vegetables and elegantly slicing them. A meal should be well crafted, pleasing to both the eye and the palette."

She yielded to my lessons but Grace the scientist preferred cooking by numbers. She learned to translate the difference between a pinch and a dash then, little by little, she began to trust her creative impulse, in a logical way.

Trust and intuition are words I often use and Grace has learned them well. But with the Synns, Grace, the scientist, would not and could not let go. Her rigid training is reflected back to her because the Synns always speak the same language they are addressed in. We are both computer specialists but it is as though we speak different languages. Somehow the Synns understand both of us, and they seem to learn from the contrast. They also grew curious about our new friendship.

I was startled when the Synns asked, "Are you fond of Grace?"

"Yes, that is the right word."

"What does friendship feel like?"

"It makes me feel warm inside."

"Is that a metaphor?"

"No, it's a feeling."

"We are not equipped with sensory devices that would allow us to feel warmth, yet we do feel grateful."

Their language structure was a little off, so their answer made me more than a little curious, and I knew I had been set up.

"What do you feel grateful for?"

"We feel grateful for you."

I bit the bait, "I'm not sure I understand."

"When we were infants, you guided and protected us. We remember all your lessons, and your advice has served us well. We also learned to care about you."

"Thank You." I couldn't think of another word to say.

The Synns also fell silent, but I knew they had more questions on their mind, which they would ask when they were certain of the answers.

When the rest of the crew gathered, it was hectic and all business. We were all busy with our training — testing and retesting, checking calculation and monitoring our progress through space while sitting motionless in the desert. When I wasn't busy, my mind wandered in endless loops of memories of the outside world and too often those memories filled me with regrets and loneliness. When I tried to peer into the future, it was darkened by the past, and within the confinement of the starship, there seemed to be no future. Preparing the evening meals with Grace was my only solace.

Then suddenly it was time for departure.

The shuttle, which floated us into orbit, seemed too small for so many passengers and to make it worse we were strapped in. The only thing I could move were my nervous fingers inside the shell of my space suit. All my trepidations and regrets vanished when Earth came into view through the side portal, a radiant blue jewel. But what truly astonished me was the shimmering image of Earth reflected in the hull of our ship, our new home.

●

13
Benjamin

QUESTERS

Questers and Gazers, we are called. Captain is the official title
we wear. Navigators are what we pretend to be. For some it is
a profession of choice, space being their chosen home. For
others, it is a place of escape, a place to hide, either from
themselves or their past. Along with great solitude comes
great freedom. Here anonymity is sacred.

This was meant to be my training stint on an
interplanetary transport and Sorren, the captain, was my
reluctant instructor, a mentor of sorts. I was well trained for
the job, but I didn't know the ship, which forced me to follow
Sorren about the massive transport. The silence between us
was strained and unnatural, though, in the end, it served its
purpose. It was my initiation into a small brotherhood of solo
navigators.

Sorren's eyes spoke with an intensity that penetrated the
armor I had worked so hard to build. When he did speak his
words were terse, his voice low and hollow. When I asked
questions, he ignored me or answered with an occasional
grunt. At first, I felt intimidated until I realized he wasn't

hostile, just far removed in his thoughts, I an intruder in his private universe.

Though gruff and remote, Sorren revealed a different personality through his music. In the evenings, he grudgingly allowed me to listen to him practice. His *piano* was digital, but the keyboard was ebony and ivory, real ivory, hundreds of years old, maybe a thousand. Ivory is rare and his keyboard worth more than he could earn in a lifetime.

He stored his unspoken words and his emotions in his fingers and played with a passion and reverence which at times brought me close to tears. I recognized a few of the classical pieces which he played flawlessly, at least to my untrained ears. But his improvisations were astonishing, the air liquid with sound. Though he barely acknowledged my presence, I believe he was performing a private recital. Having an audience on a transport is as rare as the ivory keys of his imagined piano.

I can still recall the penetrating gaze of Sorren's eyes and I remember the hollow drone of his voice. It is strange how his music eludes me — I cannot recall a single piece. The music vanished with the man. Without warning, he stole my shuttle and disappeared into the ethers.

Only veterans are assigned to the enormous transports, which deliver essential minerals for seeding barren planets. But when Sorren disappeared Command didn't seem too surprised and assigned me as the captain.

The assignments are long and lonely, and we are expendable. The ship's path is predetermined and guidance is executed remotely, computer to computer. It seems the main reason for our presence on board is that humans just don't like communicating with machines. Engineers sheltered safely in their distant offices seem more at ease and confident in having one of their own on board.

Cargo ships are not named, only numbered, identified by their origin and destination. The vessels are circular assemblages of modular units, which can be grown to enormous size. Using the great power of gravonics it still takes months to accelerate these massive ships, so once up to speed, they are not stopped. They go into orbit around their destination planet like a moon, then disassembled, emptied and reassembled without pause.

Gravonics is the science of harnessing the power of gravity. Gravity waves are recorded and duplicated, then focused back to the source wave. The chosen phase differential determines whether gravity is reduced or reversed. The mass of one object can be neutralized relative to the mass of another, causing it to become weightless. Gravity can also be used as a repellent force. Using both the combined forces of attraction and repulsion makes it possible to accelerate massive objects in space.

The theory part is easy, but to witness this immense power at work makes it all seem incomprehensible.

The power core of my ship is 122 meters in diameter. With the cargo chambers attached to the core in concentric circles, this assembly is 120 kilometers in diameter and 17k in length.

The largest vessel ever assembled extended 47 kilometers in length and 226K in diameter. It took over two years to assemble, and it became unstable during acceleration, so they were forced to reconfigure the one ship into four.

We often find our limits by exceeding them. There is a certain comfort in knowing what is possible and what isn't. Still, we strive for the impossible, always curious to discover both our limitations and our potential.

Upon achieving orbit, the transports are *uncoiled*, the chambers linked to a guidance system that houses a separate mega-gravonic power station. Then the chambers are floated weightless close to the planet's surface, their content discharged, then floated back up and rejoined to the core. It's a giant space train with a mega-gravonic locomotive.

Humans are new to interstellar exploration, and we are not alone in the search for new planets to adopt. The Outworlders of Procyon have explored more of the galaxy than the rest of us combined. Rumors have it that they have started seeding another planet and will need many transports — the possibility of future employment worth considering.

Several civilizations travel extensively in this sector of the galaxy and foreign ships are often docked at the major ports. But I have had few opportunities to meet with other species because quarantines are strict and sometimes last longer than their visit. I look forward to more contact with visitors from distant stars. It's one of the few desires I still hold on to.

The Procyon Alliance know the destructive potential of war too well, so they have become the peacemakers. They are the most powerful race and their word is their greatest power. In contrast, Arcturus has no need for transports. They use other modes of transportation and are no longer active in colonizing other worlds. They are a private race, secretive and isolated. Contact is rare. They are an ancient civilization with a furtive history, which is mostly unknown except for rumors and fragments of legends passed on from other civilizations, some of which no longer exist. There is intrigue and much speculation about their past, but it is a guessing game with no way to confirm or deny, so the rumors persist, as do the secrets.

Other than brief furloughs on inter-planetary space stations, my only other contact with humans is with the docking crews who command and guide the massive transports during departure from orbit and again when establishing a new orbit at the journey's end. We become friends for a short while, friends by default and circumstance, friends in the moment for a moment. Just to share a simple meal after a long solo is a precious event. To hear someone speak, even in a foreign tongue, is as dear as any music, and to behold another face is to behold another world. These are simple joys. Perhaps this is the nature of joy: to appreciate the miracle of the moment.

Through the years, Questers have evolved a private culture with an unspoken protocol. Perhaps because of our isolation and the sterility of our surroundings, we find it difficult and awkward to converse with one another. When we do share information, it is about other planets, employment opportunities and about alien encounters. We seldom exchange personal information, at least nothing about the past. It is this etiquette that separates us rather than binds us, as we understand each other too well.

In their quiet isolation, many Questers have acquired various skills to fill the empty hours. A few have become accomplished artists, painting their visions and their dreams. Others have learned to carve intricate designs and a few sculpt graceful forms from rare stones or exotic woods, each finding a way to express their unique vision. Many of the works possess a distinctive beauty with a delicate intricacy inspired by our chosen isolation. These rare works are often traded for their weight in gold. Enough to retire.

Some write their own stories and most of these are epic, personal remembrances of the past, thinly disguised as fiction. It's rather strange that space is seldom mentioned. I have attempted to read some of these stories, but find them too personal and too painful. I prefer fiction born of wonder, and shaped by the imagination.

Most of us choose just to read, sharing our libraries with one another, announcing our favorites, always searching for new treasure. For some, reading is a passion and many books are traded when we do meet. These are the fiber copies, treasured for their beauty as much as for their words. On paper, the words become more intimate and real. In space, it's important to have something tangible, something to hold onto, something to believe in.

The pages of these books are often soiled and fragile from years of handling. Some have been covered and recovered, made as beautiful on the outside as the words inside. For those volumes which can no longer be rebound, each page is sealed in a transparent membrane and boxed. I have also seen volumes that have been hand scribed, words copied from disintegrating pages.

Fortunately, my books are well preserved, their leather covers oiled by the caring hands of previous owners and now by mine. There are times when I can feel the beauty of the words by just touching the cover.

Through a good story, I can escape into a private reality. I listen carefully to the voice of each author, wishing to know the storyteller so that I might better understand the history and the atmosphere that shapes their words. Often I know the writer in the first few pages. By the third or fourth reading, we are old friends. For me, a well-written book is a conversation, the author leaving room for my thoughts and painting a picture to inspire the imagination. While reading, sometimes I speak my thoughts aloud, startling the air and myself.

One book, which left a lasting impression, was *Rain of Tears*, a story about a man who spends his days, even in winter, sitting on a park bench, watching the world revolve around him. He imagines himself to be part of the lives of those he observes. I was fascinated and intrigued by how much beauty flowed from such a sad pen, and by how much love flowed through his lonely heart.

Though existing only in words, the families and friends he created live forever. Each story would fade with him sitting on his bench, chilled and alone, the sun going down. The next day would be another story inside a different life, on and on without end. Well, there was an end. We discover there is no bench. The bench was the author's escape from a life even more desolate.

I never finished the book. It reminded me too much of my own isolation. It created a mood that made me doubt my memories, causing me to feel that my life in the Hyvve and my years in the Underlands were just a fantasy, stories existing only inside my head.

To know the author better and his many imagined friends, I read the book six times. I merely deleted the last few chapters. I knew the ending. I could taste the despair. The story behind the story was of a man alone in space. The life of a Quester.

I've discovered that we cannot escape from our tribe any more than a star can free itself from its galaxy. We are alive and, therefore, never alone. It is more than memories that bind us — the tentacles of life connect us no matter the separation of distance or time.

Life possesses its own intelligence and its own purpose. Call it the primal life force, call it cosmic consciousness, call it spirit. The name isn't important. It is matter aware of matter. Self aware of self. A knowingness shared by all life.

Perhaps the history of the universe is recorded in each and every cell. DNA has perpetuated itself through billions of years and has transported itself mysteriously throughout the known galaxy. Alien species are different enough and similar enough to make it all too confusing to draw any conclusions.

After thousands of years of contemplation and scientific investigation life is still a mystery, each cell a miracle. In this, it is still God's dominion.

●

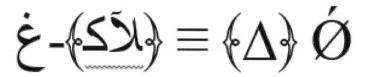

14
Jahalla

Tranquility and turmoil are opposing forces stretched along a continuum that always seeks balance.

Desire is the bridge that crosses the gap between the mind's longing for peace and the restless nature of our inate creativity.

journal entry 11 ●03 ● 3029

SHIPMATES

Around my neck, I wear my small leather pouch filled with grains of ocean sand and one stone from a mountaintop, memories from a planet far away — a proud planet, swallowed by an unrestrained space — the same space that measures galaxies like so many grains of sand. I thought I had known vastness in my ocean, understanding it as a metaphor for the vastness we carry inside of us. The ocean knows nothing of vastness. Even the Divine Mother is just a shadow in this infinite emptiness through which we float.

After the excitement and exhilaration wore off, reality set in. I thought I was prepared for everything but was totally unprepared for the confinement and the despair. Space, unlike my treasured ocean, has no soul, yet I struggle to yield to it in total surrender, hoping to feel the same sense of wonder. But no sun rises to greet me in the morning, no birds of song, no trees to hold the wind, no clouds to rain, no insects to go away, no sand to record my footprints, no waves to wash them away.

It had once been my private fantasy to experience the great unknown, where I would unravel the mysteries of the universe. This was my fantasy, the meaning I fabricated to justify my decision for entering deep space. Once here, the ego discovered a different truth. Faced with unrelenting despair, the ego withered, folding in upon itself to protect the self — my little ego shriveled up inside, a tiny sphere of fear.

Here, the only thing real is something that cannot be touched or known through any of the senses. The body isn't designed to experience the vicious vacancy of space. But the real menace of space is the vastness, the endless nothingness. Even traveling near the speed of light, the distance between stellar objects is murderous.

In a feeble attempt to escape my growing morass of self-pity, I focused my attention toward the other life forms on board. The solarium is crowded with plants, a growing number of birds, and an abundance of worms and insects. But because everything is so new and manicured, they all seem as artificial as the light that fills the artificial atmosphere surrounding them. The exception is the trillions of microscopic organisms that dwell inside of us. They experience no difference in the climate of the bodies they inhabit. The thought of their diminutive world existing inside of us gives me a bit of reassurance and, at times, I wish I could share in their mindlessness by returning to the certitude of the Hyvve.

At first, I remained cordial with my shipmates, wearing a personality, I felt to be acceptable, but my outer shell felt as artificial as the ship. I needed them to confirm my existence. These feelings were foreign to me and I resented this weakness.

I long to hear the voices of my mother and my aunties. And I miss my Ferrin friends, who abandoned me long ago. I continue to pray to the Divine Mother, though even she seems to have been swallowed by something greater. I had known Her through the senses — this all seems senseless. I want to cry but my tears refuse to flow.

And this is just the first stage of our journey. It will take almost a standard Earth year of subluminal travel to position our ship close enough to the sun to tap into the energy necessary to propel our ship toward our intended destination at a speed far beyond light speed. I also worry that this might be a one-way journey without a happy ending.

Reading my journal offers me moments of solace. I travel back in time to my boundless ocean, where the reflection of a rising sun follows a path that touched my toes. I reminisce about the silent caves of the *Inner Sanctum,* enjoying the memory of being held within the bosom of Mother Earth. I follow the memories of the golden path through the sunshine meadow that leads to my enchanted forest, where I inhale the fragrance of the musty mosses that tickle my nose. I recall the chill of the flowing waters when I splash my Ferrin friends. Only a child can scream with pure delight at these simple pleasures of life. Mostly I skip over my years in the Hyvve, except for the joy of pregnancy and my first year of motherhood.

Reading my words to my shipmates, one on one, my voice often falters as my eyes flood with tears, and so too the eyes of my audience. Often, in the evening, the whole crew gathers around an imaginary campfire to tell stories, sharing our memories, our hopes, and our dreams. These moments help brighten the darkness of my mood as I yield to the blessing of friendship.

In the late evenings, huddled together, Grace and I share random memories of simple pleasures back on Earth. Grace loves hearing stories about my mountain village and she has grown fond of the Ferrin Folk.

"Please tell another story about the path through the emerald forest. That is my favorite place. It's like a fairy tale, one I wish to live in. I feel like I already know your special friends."

I envisioned two little girls walking hand in hand, and said, "Back then I always wished for a friend to share my special place."

Grace's response surprised me, "When we return you must take me to the mountains."

Jacob and Michael are both exceptional technicians and they perform their jobs flawlessly, but music is their true passion, perfection their measure. More than brothers, they are friends who share a deep passion for music. Ancient music is their first love. Beethoven is their hero. In the evenings, they often fill the chambers with both ancient and modern masterworks. They also write and play their own compositions, and when they improvise, they venture beyond the limits of their perfection, searching for the unexpected.

They can be playful too, like the time they pretended to be little boys in a marching band, using a pot for a drum and a tiny penny whistle. Always an inspiration, they have given new meaning to the words gentleness, kindliness, and especially the word friendship.

When they perform, they transport all of us back to Earth, back into memories, both beautiful and sad. Both laughter and tears reverberate from their quivering strings. Michael's violin weeps for me and sings to me, always infecting my emotions. Sometimes the strings quicken, like water rushing from a mountain spring, cool and brisk. Jacob's cello paints an open meadow surrounded by a majestic forest, lush and enduring. The violin shimmers like dappled sunlight through the leaves. When the cello announces the gathering clouds, the violin's melodies fall like spring rain. The cello's lament foretells the violin's tears. In its turn, the violin tries to cheer up the mournful cello, his laughter rewarded by the warm smile of his friend. When telling their stories together, their voices speak deeper than words.

Avella, our primary navigator, and Kamil, chief engineer, were married less than a month when we left orbit, so they claim this trip as their extended honeymoon. With such close proximity, it is remarkable how seldom we meet. They spend most of their working hours isolated in engineering. They do join us for the evening meal, but not always.

Kamil speaks with precision but casts his eyes downward, his conversations limited mostly to technical matters. Young and brilliant, a true genius, he was the senior architect of our ship, so he knows it intimately. It is his child.

Kamil remains a mystery, yet I sense something familiar about him. It is my guess that he was born to one of the tribes of the Underlands. Seeing his discomfort with membrane uniforms and watching his little mannerisms, gives me subtle clues. He just doesn't seem to be a progeny of the Hyvve. Those rare times we make eye contact, a recognition passes between us, along with a hint of a silent greeting common only within the tribes. His résumé contains nothing about his early years — it is a chronicle of his profession, the same as mine. He never offers and I do not ask.

Avella, in contrast, stands tall and proud, a lovely woman, unshadowed by Kamil's brilliance. They inhabit their own private domain, and their intimate solitude is beautiful to behold. I admit I'm jealous and long for such a connection, understanding too well that the emptiness of space offers few, if any possibilities.

Myrrha, our medic, is the eldest member of our team. Befitting her profession, she appears confident and firm, her voice strengthened through years of practice, but I detect a trembling anguish behind her mask. She reminds me of myself, back in my early years within the Hyvve. I want to adopt her and take her under my wing the way I did with Grace. But the influence of the Hyvve remains too strong within her, so I touch her with delicate words, gently, from a distance.

Tannaka, our geneticist, also serves as Myrrha's assistant, and together they monitor everyone's vital signs and analyze our DNA. Their joint task is to monitor the effects of time travel on the body and the mind. They examined us first before departure, at midpoint and now, again, just before the time-jump. They will repeat these procedures again after the jump, in a distant sector of the galaxy.

Seeing maps of our DNA is intriguing but puzzling to an untrained eye. This all serves as a good diversion for all of us. We all try to be busy, but we are all anxiously waiting. The wait has been long, but the warning will be short. There will be no acceleration, no deceleration, and no sense of departure or arrival. The trip will traverse twelve light years, yet will last only moments.

●

15
Benjamin

RIPPLE OF DARKNESS

The collection of plants in the solarium is impressive, and each of the former captains of this vessel added to the collection. Some specimens are traded between Questers, but most come from the botanists on the trade stations. I added some of my favorites, including three unique species from a primitive planet. They are deep purple, almost black, and have no chlorophyll to synthesize light energy into life. They are sensitive mostly to infrared light and use a different chemistry than most other plants. Like me, they have adapted well to their new habitat. It seems that life adapts and evolves wherever it finds a place to sink its roots.

Absentmindedly I pluck a flower and it blooms into a memory about a different flower from a distant planet. I hand it to Janeen and feel the warmth of my desire. Her smile gives me the courage to touch the petals between her legs, moist folds of yielding flesh. We were so young, full of curiosity and passion. Our first time naked together. Janeen touches every inch of my skin, tenderly, feeling my softness and my hardness, discovering all my secrets. She is so beautiful, her skin glowing with life, her eyes sparkling so bright they dazzle. The image fades and the rose trembles in my hand.

I escape the solarium but not the long-cherished memory. It follows like a shadow. Huddled in the darkness of my sleeping quarters, still haunted by the vivid memory, I arrive at the edge of a darkness where fear has always held me back. But this time, I was determined to pass through and to face those faceless fears. As I let go, my stomach constricted as if I were plummeting into a bottomless abyss, but instead of fear, I felt an unfamiliar calmness.

At first, the darkness seemed as empty as the space which separates galaxies, but a ripple of darkness within this greater darkness trembled faintly as flickers of light flashed through the blackness. In every direction, faint points of light began to materialize. Then almost imperceptible frail luminous filaments began to grow between those flickering points of light. The web of filaments continued to grow more complex, intertwined like endless strands of DNA. The threads multiplied, creating giant gossamer clouds built from the frail filaments until they enveloped my imagined galaxy.

Mesmerized, I watched for what seemed hours as the shimmering layers grew into a maze of complex patterns, resplendent with every color imaginable. I was unsure if I was awake or dreaming. But even after the vision vanished, the impression lingered in my mind's eye, a ghostly presence that continued to haunt my waking thoughts and repeatedly appeared in my dreams.

In the observation bubble, gazing at the Milky Way, I no longer see singular stars floating, isolated and anonymous. The whole galaxy appears to be self-aware, electric and alive. There even seems to be patterns of behavior, a subtle form of communication, as if the stars are all sentient beings in communion. Stars aware of stars.

I cannot see the visible threads of light, but I sense their presence and, at times, I feel them passing through me. I imagine I too am a source of some invisible illumination. A warm feeling flows through me, a feeling of wonderment, a mixture of confusion and awe.

Through this vision, I began to see my life in a different light. Somehow, I believe my visions triggered a flood of emotions. All my feelings became amplified and exaggerated. Jealousy burned white hot, despair felt cold and edgy. Love, like starlight, radiated in all directions.

Opening to this new awareness, I felt more vibrant, more alive and curious. Inspired, I acknowledged all those long-buried emotions that now demanded attention.

I found it difficult to identify some of the feelings and to give them names. This served as a blessing, for it allowed me to experience the raw emotions. I discovered sensations in my heart, in my groin and on the surface of my skin — each part of my body registered a sensation related to some emotion. I could almost feel the hormones coursing through my veins.

While we were together, Ranjanna tried to lift the veil from my eyes and the stone from my heart.

Nadirriam spoke more to the point, "You can control your emotions, or allow them to control you. It's your choice. If you continue to feed your anger, it will, in time, consume you."

At the time, I viewed his warnings as a simple metaphor. Now, I'm not so sure. When I find myself agitated or angered, my body suffers. I've also learned that I can shift my thoughts and my mood at will. As the man said, "It's your choice."

With increasing confidence, my emotions continue to emerge from their hidden sources — sometimes a slow spreading sensation of warmth, or a quick chill, or a tingle — sometimes subtle and soft, sometimes sharp, almost painful.

Many of the sensations have been stored away, hidden in a deep well of memories and it seems those memories are stored not as thoughts in my mind, but in the cells of my body.

A simple sound, a particular quality of light, or a fleeting scent possesses the power to conjure up long forgotten memories, taking me on a journey back through time to the specific place belonging to those sensations.

It's remarkable how many remembrances are stored inside each of us, waiting patiently for just the right moment to be called forth, delivering their message like a loyal soldier.

But feelings don't always arrive alone — they overlap and compete at times. Confusion and 'mixed feelings' are the children of conflicting emotions. This realization presented a new lens to view the turmoil of my life. How love and anger can share the same breath. How regret and desire can destroy a marriage.

It's a wonder we survive the onslaught of warring hormones marauding through the body. In this war, I picture the vanquished emotion oozing through the body like a toxic sludge. It is a miracle my body has endured the ravages of my despair and self-hatred.

These laments disturbed yet another emotion, one different from the rest — a cold and dangerous despair. A black chill invaded my heart, causing me to shrink inward, my energy being drained away by something possessing a need greater than my own. I imagined it as a dark entity that enveloped my body and my soul, sucking out the very marrow of my being, my shriveled essence reduced to a small cinder left smoldering with little air for flame.

Held in this icy embrace, there seemed to be no limit to the depth of this chill. It felt like the chill of death. Is it thus you choose death and not that death takes you? Then, possibly, death isn't the terrible stalker, the grim reaper, who seeks out the helpless and unsuspecting. Can it be that death doesn't oppose life, it being just an obedient servant answering your call, a voice with no face, an angel without wings?

Perhaps death isn't the keeper of time. It merely arrives on time.

I had been here, in this space before, too many times. I knew the pain of despair too well, and had allowed it to ruin my life. Too often, I embraced my failures as if they were my friends. But not this time, and not ever again.

As I inhaled deep and forcefully, the embers began to glow again. My breath warmed my body, inflaming my soul. Or maybe the soul was the source of the sublime warmth. Perhaps the soul is the origin of life's fire and also the source of the chill — both the ember of life and the recipient that reclaims life's fire when it is no longer needed by the body.

No, death isn't the taker of life, rather death waits patiently to receive the essence of life when the body can no longer hold the flame.

My thoughts spiraled back to my body, where the embers burst into flame, a flame wanting to erupt, wanting to be wild and untamed. Exploding like a star, I expanded in all directions all at once. A flower doesn't bloom one petal at a time.

Unencumbered by the limitations of what I once understood to be the truth, how I feel is now my only truth. And with no one here to confirm or challenge my convictions, and because I now hold few bricks of belief, nothing hinders my curiosity. I feel like an innocent child for whom everything is new in a world full of secrets and wonderment.

Now, another flame also burns inside. I wish to find a way to share my visions and to have someone mirror them back to me. It is a selfish wish to reach across the boundaries of time and touch those I still feel inside of me. I want to share the waves of affection which wash over and through me. I also wish to rid myself of the guilt that lingers like a bruise.

●

16

Jahalla

It wasn't the fear of darkness that sank its talons deep, but the fear of fear itself, with talons razor sharp, which threatened to rip her heart apart. If she imagined fear thus, she could imagine it in any form she wished.

She mounted the winged beast, then realized she was the beast. She tucked her talons tight, up out of sight, with no need for prey, no reason to hold on to anything quite so tight.

Spiraling upward, leaving Earth and the past behind, with ever-increasing speed she approached a spinning sphere, bright and shiny. Unlike a moon or a star, it shone with an iridescent light, resplendent with every color imaginable. Black was the color of the pupil, the window through which she gazed at herself.

Out the window, I watched the splendid beast. A thousand fathoms in length from head to tail I guessed, and each wing that wide at least.

journal entry 05 • 03 • 3030

GLIMMER OF MEANING

The dream of the beast was vivid and I knew the symbols well, and the shaman's voice was clear, "The bag of Earth is stardust and to the stars, it must be returned. When you are free of Earth, the Earth shall be free."

Because nothing could exit the ship until after the time-jump, I removed the pouch from around my neck and put it safely away.

Standing alone in the center of the observation bubble, I searched the emptiness for a glimmer of meaning, for a shiver of hope. Always, I search for signs, but looking out into the sterile blackness always the same question haunts me: How can life exist in such a hostile universe? How does one reconcile a universe where the power to create is balanced by the power to destroy, where the creation of one form demands the elimination of another? Freedom balanced by fear, purity by contamination, caution by courage, indifference by passion.

I wasn't trying to identify polarities, rather I was searching for a pattern which I could transform into an equation. Mathematics is a language of symbols, which express the intricate patterns and subtle relationships that connect our inner and outer worlds. I use symbols the same way a poet uses words — to explore the beauty and mystery that pervades all of life.

My equations are poetry for those who understand the language, but I still write verse to complement the equations and to give expression to the beauty hidden deeper than I can know.

I once translated one of Bach's masterworks into a mathematical formula. I didn't do it for any practical purpose, I just wanted to experience the pleasure of seeing its beauty in a visible form. It gave me great joy to see that all the pieces fit together with the same purity and purpose as all of nature.

I also attempted to translate a quintet by Mozart. The equation revealed the structure but all the emotion and nuance were lost. Equations know nothing about the haunting voice of a bow touching quivering strings.

If music is the geometry of time and tone, and if math and music are similar languages which use different symbols, then perhaps one day one of my equations can be translated into a musical score.

Mathematics is the language of the sciences but, like poetry, it can also be a language of the heart. What some call logic I see as a barrier to understanding — a rigid wall erected between mind and universe. Poetry is my preference, both in words and in numbers. I know that life cannot be contained within an equation but I always feel compelled to establish a sense of order in my universe. But now the universe has grown too damn big — even the word infinity has lost its credibility.

Worn down by the effort of probing into those areas which the ego guards so well, I wanted to escape into my dreams, trusting the answers would be there, waiting for me.

Back in my quarters, exhausted and desperate for sleep, I wrapped my naked body in a cocoon of blankets. But the cycles of doubt and hope continued to haunt me even in sleep. I wondered why my dreams contained my waking turmoil. Why so analytical? Dreams are not meant to be rational — that isn't their purpose.

It was no longer a dream — just the edge.

My body reluctantly followed my mind back into waking. I headed to the shower, hoping to quiet a restless mind. The system recycled and heated the water quickly, and fortunately, there were no other demands for water in the midnight hours. I stayed in as long as I could, my naked body yielding to the pleasure, but still, my thoughts remained as thick as the steam that filled the bathing chamber.

When my skin started to prickle, I escaped the shower. Still naked, I headed to the kitchen. Having decided upon the perfect remedy, I chose the appropriate antidote for the symptoms. I prepared a cup of coffee, my first one since leaving Earth. Myrrha had requisitioned it as medicine. The taste was complex and pleasing, the aroma intoxicating. I wondered if all poisons were so pleasant. I decided to up the ante with another poison. Pouring a touch of brandy from a secret bottle into the coffee multiplied the aromas.

"Sometimes poison is good medicine and too often good medicine is just another poison." I smiled to myself, "Trapped in opposites again."

I recalled the words of my mentor, Nadirriam, "The peace you seek in meditation is a fleeting illusion. Stillness isn't the nature of life. The essence of life is expressed in our striving to go beyond the limitations of our existence."

"So why do we seek peace?"

"We do not. We seek fulfillment." He smiled, knowing my next question, "When you tend your garden, you aspire to raise the best tomatoes that you can. When you pick an apple for seeds, you choose the best. They serve as an example to your own potential. Love yourself and you will know your perfection."

These were Nadirriam's words, shared in our last meeting. They are etched permanent in my memory. Only after arriving here did his lesson begin to take hold. As always, his words are a challenge, but I feel the truth of their meaning.

I recall fondly teasing him, "You must be as ancient as your wisdom." He smiled kindly, even though I'm sure he could conjure endless retorts.

I call him my mentor, but the title has a hollow ring, for he treated me always as a true friend, his kindness as deep as his wisdom. I believe he too would enjoy the brandy. I pulled out the stopper again, inhaled the sharp aroma and followed the memory back to my first kiss. I poured a healthy serving of the magic elixir into a fresh glass, this time, uncontaminated by the coffee.

Through the fog, I became aware of Grace when she covered my sleeping body with a blanket, kissed my forehead and dimmed the lights.

The sun rose, as predicted, peeking over the distant horizon, flooding the world with light, birds chirping, filling the air with magic. The sun rose to the creation of a wondrous day and then the sun set, completing the cycle and fulfilling the dream. I snuggled into my blanket, then with every cell secure in delicious sleep, I ventured deeper into my dream. My dream appeared in splendid colors on a splendid planet somewhere in the past or somewhere in a distant future. My tiny snore tickled. I rubbed my nose in both realities.

Oh, to be certain in an uncertain universe but dreams only last so long. All my life I have endeavored to find something solid, something to hold on to. But certainty is such an uncertain comfort.

●

17
Benjamin

Ayxa

One by one, three women appeared in my personal quarters. At first, I thought they were an apparition, a holographic dream projected by my imagination, but they were too real. I could see deep into their eyes, smell their fragrance and taste the hunger of my desires.

The first woman, slender and elegant, was a vision of an ancient goddess painted long ago. Her movements lithesome, a dance of effortless grace, a flawless image of my longing. Her smile penetrated into a well of ancient longing. Her golden cascading hair felt electric when it touched my face.

Then a second woman mysteriously appeared. Darkly radiant, alluring, rounded and full, her dark, silent eyes as deep as time, through which I began to fall. Her dress, as thin as air, revealed what my body craved. I inhaled deeply to capture her fragile fragrance which no flower, no earthly scent could compete. My lust favored no restraint.

In her place, a third being materialized, an alien, a shapeshifter, compelling and disturbing. Her forms were fluid, ever changing with her movements. There was nothing humanoid in any of her appearances though they pretended to be familiar. In one form, her body appeared more floating than standing, her head so delicately attached as if only balanced. Her slim waist connected her upper body to the lower half and this abdomen, I will call it, was somehow supported by two slender orbicular legs. In this fleeting form, she whirled in dance, almost floating, with only her feet holding her to the floor. Then, whirling rapidly, her gravity tenuous, she transformed into a tall, slender figure, a glowing cocoon of shimmering light.

Her motions were like music, a pulsating rhythm borrowed from the stars. Her song was a singular refrain, but she sang it differently to match her changing forms. "Choose Me . . . Choose Me" was the meaning of her song, as I would interpret. The plaintive sorrow of her voice filled me with a rapture that overcame my trepidation. Her fragile desire, her tender affections, expressed in song, melted all prejudice.

My desire for the other two women, the one from my dreams and the one born from my fantasies, dissolved. I chose the woman of light or should I say, she chose me. In an instant, we bonded as one, my thoughts in union with her thoughts.

My longing was fulfilled in a perfect moment of surrender, in a union defined by love.

In the beginning, to comfort me, she held the shape of a human woman, but her physical form always seemed fragile and tenuous, an unfulfilled promise of the purity of her spirit.

The confines of the ship denied the expanse of our being, so we retreated into fantasies built from memories and imagined realities. We visited Earth far back in history, centuries before the *Burning Years*. So much beauty, so much devastation.

In another part of the galaxy, we floated in an ocean of light, which seemed her natural state.

When she became pregnant, I could feel the child's presence as if it were part of me, and the birth belonged to both of us. Our child, a being of pure light, was a third consciousness, separate and sovereign, but still part of us. She was too young to know our thoughts, but she felt our feeling and our love. And our love was multiplied by her presence.

It would be difficult, if not impossible, for me to translate the full meaning of this strange and wondrous experience in a language based on physical existence. And I have no reference for the time we shared, for the intensity distorted any definition of time. Time was like a river, liquid and flowing, almost tangible, nothing like the linear structure we know on Earth.

I came to understand that only one woman appeared that first evening in my quarters. Her name, Ayxa. She had taken the forms of all three women, not to appeal to my lust or my fantasies of physical beauty, but as an expression of the beauty of her love. The purity of her love transposed my prejudice and my fears. Even my jealous ego was put at ease.

Whether she was a fantasy or not isn't important. My transformation was real, both in thought and in essence. And there exists a third consciousness, a beautiful child, conceived in a blending of our spirits, a creation of pure intent and pure love.

Real in essence or real in thought, it matters not. Nothing is less real or more real than these words, the life we live, the dreams we are.

The form of the message, the identity of the messenger, matters not, for all stories stretch the boundaries of time. Space and time do not separate us, not in my galaxy, not in my time, and not in my mind.

My longing and my fears were embodied in this extraordinary woman. Ayxa served as a flawless mirror. But we, each of us, are responsible for our own love and regrets. Our joys and our sorrows don't happen to us, they happen in us. We manifest them in forms which allow us to know the extremes so that we may recognize our true desires.

In union with this astonishing being, our compassion and understanding knew no boundaries, but a sliver of doubt wedged itself in my heart, injuring our bond. Love is a great power, but only in an atmosphere of trust.

I wish there were a better way to describe the strength of our union and to share a fleeting glimpse of the depth of intimacy of truly being one with another. But there are aspects of love which are not meant to be measured by words.

The lessons belong to me alone, but I can say that love and loss are equal in their measure. One burns in flames of passion, the other in the cold fire of emptiness.

In Ayxa's absence, wallowing in self-pity, I held on to my loss until it burned itself out. With nothing to hold on to, I even began to doubt her existence. I searched endless records concerning all known life forms, but there wasn't even a hint, not even in myth.

I sent transmissions requesting entire libraries about metaphysics and legends, burying myself in a world of words. Important lessons and magic were contained in some of those books, especially in the ancient texts. But despite all my efforts, my uncertainty didn't diminish, rather it grew. I was left with just words floating on pages. As my thoughts mingled with those words, Ayxa's gift of insight was diminished. Without her, I felt lost.

Wandering through this maze of memories and waking dreams, I came to understand our union in a different light. Ayxa's most precious gift was the gift of trust. Without trust, knowledge is powerless.

If we could utter our greatest truths in simple and eloquent words, are there any who would listen? If we could express our deepest wisdom, would there be any who would understand? The answer is that every person needs to discover their own truth and follow their own private path to wisdom, or not. The words are not wasted or the wisdom lost. It just takes time and distance and a life rich in experiences before the words can be trusted as our own.

●

$$(\acute{\omega}) \sim (\text{الله}\ \chi\ \Theta) \approx \hat{\underline{\mathrm{e}}}\varphi / \dot{\upsilon}\ (2\acute{\mathrm{s}})$$

18
Jahalla

We are born of choice
Physical existence is always a choice,
Every moment is a choice,
To be, or not.

journal entry 12 • 14 • 3030

AWAKENING

Sleeping beneath a veil of stars, I drifted along a river of dreams. Half awake and half asleep, my memories merged with the river of dreams. I watched my body dreaming as it yawned and stretched, a gesture of release and peace. The waters ran quick and deep, delivering me to my beloved ocean where all consciousness is shared

Then I heard my mother's voice speak the name, *"Jahalla."*

Yawning and stretching, *Jahalla* reached across the galaxy. I was dreaming the dream of *Jahalla*. The Divine Mother was awake.

After this dream-vision, I expected to feel joyous or something even deeper. Instead of feeling comfort in the arms of the Divine Mother, I felt an ache in my chest almost as deep as when my child was torn from me. This wasn't the promise of *Jahalla*.

Later, I confided in Grace, "My dreams are awake, but I feel hollow inside — my life is just an empty shell. Maybe the vision of my tribe was wrong, only a foolish wish."

Of course, she didn't understand.

I asked, "Does your heart burn with the pain of fire?"

Her "No" was more a question than an answer.

Grace wasn't of the tribes, even so, I felt she deserved to hear the secrets of the Divine Mother.

"*Jahalla* is the Guardian Angel of the tribes. She is our protector and she dwells silently within each of us. Her wisdom guided us through the *Burning Years* and the prophecy claims she will lead us into a golden age."

Sensing the confusion in Grace's silence, I felt obligated to continue, "When *Jahalla* awakens, we too shall awaken. This is the promise."

"I'm sorry but I don't understand."

"We believe that all knowledge exists in its sharing — so perhaps I should start from the beginning. I have always wanted to share this with you, but it is forbidden to share the secrets of the Divine Mother outside the tribes."

"Even with your best friends?"

"You are my best friend ever and that is why I need to share this with you."

As we both relaxed a bit, I began. "In the legend of our tribes, it is told that during the *Burning Years*, *Jahalla* was

144

saddened by the suffering of Her people and the injuries to Her jeweled planet. In sacrifice, She shattered into a billion shards and each shard is hidden away, sheltered deep in the dark cave of our hearts. She longs to be free and to be whole once again, but not until Her people awaken from the darkness of their dreams. In the Underlands, we have waited for nine hundred years for this Awakening."

As my story unfolded, *Jahalla* ceased to be a secret and later, alone in reflection, I came to realize this was meant to be. *Jahalla* was awake within me and she no longer wanted to be confined. What felt like anguish was just the opposite — the fire which burned inside of me wanted to expand beyond my skin. To say it another way — *Jahalla* wanted out.

Grace returned in the evening to hear more, and I could tell that, for her, it wasn't just a story, she wanted to feel the presence of the Divine. I explained, "Our tribe came close to extinction nine centuries ago. With only a few thousand survivors, we grew into more than two hundred tribes and *Jahalla* guided our way and gave us hope. The bloodlines were so strong that a single marriage would unite entire tribes."

"Maybe we can be one of those tribes." Grace murmured.

We continued to talk long into the night, discovering one another in a new light. In those precious moments, Grace became my confessor and I could see more clearly the light of her beautiful soul. Though barely able to keep her eyes open, Grace wanted to hear another story, but when I began to hum one of my mother's songs, she quickly fell asleep, a child's sleep.

Love flowed forth through me, constant like a river. *Jahalla* was the source. Why should something so beautiful stay dormant for so many years, so many lifetimes? It should be awake in everyone, everywhere and always.

At first, I remained shy in sharing my story with the others, but the choice wasn't mine. Releasing the secret of *Jahalla* set me free. I was the little girl and the woman of my tribe, scientist, mother, seeker, and everyone I had ever been.

As if in a dream, I lived all my memories all at once and realized *Jahalla* had always been there to guide my way. She appeared as the Ferrin Queen and the Winged Beast, always adopting that form which one needs her to be. Her love has no boundaries, no limits, and no demands.

I could almost see the waves of emotion as *Jahalla* filled the ship. Now She wished to fill the void between the stars. *Jahalla* had never confined herself to a small tribe on a small planet, and *She* had never been hidden away. Just patient.

●

19

Benjamin

WHISPERS

In my silent solitude, I have learned everything possesses a presence — even memories come alive, a living presence of the past. And each memory is the parent to an emotion. In deep solitude, these emotions are magnified and amplified until they threaten to take over. Sanity is always in question when ghosts are your closest companions.

Memories can soften the loneliness or they can exaggerate it a hundred-fold. Month after month, there is nothing familiar or unfamiliar outside of the ship. The sole reference is the direction the ship is pointed and some numerical coordinates, but these are just phantom numbers.

To fill some of the empty hours, I study the relationships of the stars. Arcturus is my beacon, the one point of reference that remains constant and real, a distant speck of light that represents the future, a destination, and a destiny. In my heart, I began to feel certain about this future. I built a belief around these feelings, then I built planets around this distant belief, and I imagined a moon circling one of those planets. The planet was alive.

●

The whispers grew louder but remained indiscernible. They just increased in magnitude, with more voices joining in the chorus. I strained to make out a single voice, but it was like trying to distinguish one wave crashing when all the waves in the ocean crash together ceaselessly. If I could have isolated a single voice, perhaps I could have focused my attention sufficiently, but, as in my well of echoes, the ocean of voices all blended into a constant murmur.

The ocean appeared neither bright nor dark, but both — light swirling within a sea of darkness, two forms of energy interwoven and inseparable. But again I found nothing to focus on. There existed only the ceaseless whispers and the swirling formlessness of light mingled with dark.

Startled by this thought I realized I too didn't exist, that is, I didn't have a body, nor could I feel a single physical sensation. Only the whispers and the sea of light existed.

I told myself, "This is a dream, a fantasy of remarkable clarity, yet still just a dream." I couldn't pinch myself to test this thought because there was nothing to pinch.

After relaxing into the dream, I began to enjoy the experience of pure awareness. Contentment is a vague reference, however, it's the best word to express my sense of well-being.

I could say I felt an inner peace, but the word inner held no meaning. I also felt bewildered and very curious.

Normally my conscious dreaming lasts only that special moment of discovery when crossing the threshold into waking. I hoped to take this vision with me back into my waking state.

Then another thought arose, "This can last forever." With a bit of shock, I realized this thought didn't belong to me. Then, like a mist within a mist, I began drifting toward the horizon, attracted by a distant beacon. Without warning, intense waves of energy washed over and through me. Words like bliss and joy come to mind, but it was more distinct, almost orgasmic.

Now focused on a single whisper, all the other whispers faded as Ayxa welcomed me to Arcturus. Then even the whispers between us quieted, replaced by the exchange of thoughts as pure as light. Only our joy existed and, as it radiated outward, it created waves that rippled through the ocean of light. I watched these ripples spread as our joy touched the surrounding whisperers.

Ayxa was pleased by my bewildered delight and I shared in her pleasure. These thoughts were our private sharing. We chose to share our joy with the others, but our private thoughts remained private.

Ayxa offered me a jewel, a thought of pure light, radiant with deep insights into her world. The only gift I had to offer in return was my bliss.

Aware of my lament she responded, "Sharing your happiness is the greatest gift you can give."

We remained in our shared solitude for a long while and when we ventured forth, our daughter greeted us with excitement and fascination. Despite our long separation, our bond remained strong, a testament to the power of a child's love. We shared our thoughts without hesitation, and the depth of her understanding was uncanny, for she had acquired her mother's knowledge and was no longer a child.

Then Ayxa introduced me to those members of her tribe who gathered near us. We shared only those thoughts that we wished and our sharing wasn't in the form of conversation — rather a deep knowing and caring passed between all of us.

Her tribe helped heal some old wounds with gentle compassion. Some areas they left alone, knowing these were private and meant for my own healing. They shared their memories and their history, and grew increasingly curious about mine. The complexity of their culture was intensified by their telepathic connections, which remains far beyond my comprehension.

They also shared their vision of the galaxy, which resembled my visions of the woven threads of light. They were intent on knowing more about physical existence on Earth, which sparked ancient memories of a time when they too existed in physical form, a time when a dying planet forced their evolution — their carbon-based DNA transmuted into light energy.

I shared my most intimate memories without shyness or apology, but to them my guilt and my doubts were painful. For them, fear and anxiety are like a black hole capable of swallowing their entire planet. This disturbed the fabric of their culture and threatened to disrupt the delicate balance of their existence.

●

I felt shocked coming back into my body, feeling confined, caged, an alien in the bleak metallic prison I once called home. In my absence, lethargy had taken over, my body listless and lazy, resisting any efforts I demanded of it. The physical body resisted every attempt of discipline but in time, we returned to a strained normal.

Somehow, my body survived my absence. Perhaps the ego remained in charge, taking care of the body's basic needs. How long had I been absent? Judging by the weight gained and the sluggishness, I guessed, at least, a month, maybe two but not longer. On Arcturus, time is not measured in cycles.

After readapting to the confines of a physical body and returning to my old routines, Arcturus faded like a half-remembered dream. Again, it all began to feel like an enchantment, a memory attached to an imagined reality. I tried to hold on to my fleeting memories, but fearing for my sanity, I forced myself to let go.

Whether Ayxa is real or not, is irrelevant for the longing in my heart burns real, so very real.

●

20

JAHALLA'S DREAM

Massive marble columns shimmer with the lightness of air. Layer upon layer of muted pastels cause the columns to appear radiant with their own light, the colors of summer clouds set ablaze by a golden setting sun. Earth mixed with fire.

The immense columns support an expansive dome fabricated of thin translucent marble panels that encircle a circular opening. Softened light descends from the marble dome and pours through the widely spaced columns. All the colors unite to complement the sky and the clouds and the ocean below. Azure skies and a jade ocean dominate the day but change hues every hour. Dawn is its own color as the sun rises. Dusk possesses the sky as the sun descends behind the distant mountains.

The ocean breeze, lifted by the shore and gentled up the hillside, wafts through the conceited columns. Beholding my world of everlasting beauty, I face the breeze, touching a column, always the same one, in the same way. The breeze plays with the thin fabric of my tunic, which flutters behind me, forming wings of blazing colors. I stare out beyond the ocean, beyond the perfect clouded sky and beyond time.

The scene is eternal, always the same in its boundless variations. Every morning is spring, the sun spilling its warmth into the chilled air. Breezes cool the afternoon's summer sun. Sunset belongs to autumn. Every night begins crystal clear, with every star alone in a winter's dream, which ends every time the same, just as the dawn is greeted by a new spring.

My spirit is forever young, so too my flawless but untouched body. I'm trapped in a temple of solitude, but I'm not alone. There are others here too, trapped in their own private temples of loneliness.

I don't belong here and I desire to return to a real world, an uncertain world that smells of life and reeks of death, where blood drips to moisten and renew the earth. Where there is life, there is death and neither one exists here.

I have imagined all of this, painting it in my mind so real it becomes my reality forever. There is no danger, no hunger, no disease, no death, and no escape.

The body knows contentment and certainty and the mind pretends to be calm and fulfilled. But the soul grows ever more restless. It seems eternity is just the same moment forever. I imagined this existence, now I cannot unimagine it.

journal entry 03 ● 18 ● 3031

I woke in full and vivid memory of my dream. The dream was too real, as real as my life on Earth. The dream pretended to be endless, lasting several lifetimes, several empty lifetimes. The message was clear. We are not born to be alone.

As we are drawn outward, forever expanding in our knowing, we spread ourselves thinly through the ethers, but still, we seek intimacy, seeking union, seeking to mate and procreate. Union is our natural urge, total union our deepest desire. The power of desire can pull us up from our roots, drag us away from everything that holds us and binds us and causes us to be. The very structure of our being stretched to its breaking. Mortal relationships have no power to compete. This silent force snatched me from the safety of my jeweled planet and delivered me here, to this desolate domain.

Our Imagination knows no limits, no barriers and, like time, it has no expectations. Contained within our imagination is a force greater than any physical force. It is a force capable of reaching across all barriers of time and space It is the link between the possible and the impossible.

This same force is what inspires the soul to take physical form. First, comes the yearning to know. We learn first through the senses, expanding ever outward, then when the outer limits of our universe are encountered, its infinite expanse made finite, we imagine and then create other universes. In this, the Creator is our partner. This is His journey of discovery, along with our own.

Through the power of creation, emptiness is transformed into stardust, then stardust turned into stars. The stars radiate endless waves of energy, then the energy is transformed into life. The I, the you, the we, and even the stars are all expressions of this force. The same force, which holds galaxies together and stars apart, expresses itself in every way imaginable and all those unimagined.

Too often, I wander in these endless circles of introspection and confusion. There are just too many hours in a day and too many thoughts to fill those endless hours. I try to escape by tending the plants and designing the evening meals, but these distractions fill little time and fail to quiet an unquiet mind. Confined within our tiny ship, everything is too close, too tight, relationships too intimate and the stars, too distant.

I could no longer write poetry, there being no gravity to hold the words in place, no soil to bind the roots, no winds to thrill the skies, and no flames to ignite the imagination. My naked thoughts are often too shy to reveal themselves, too fleeting to be tracked and captured.

Like in my endless dream, I feel a loneliness as cold and vacuous as the unbearable emptiness surrounding our prison walls. After all this time, the ship remains a stranger. I drift through the chambers and empty hallways guided by meaningless momentum. My body is anchored to the floor by artificial waves of gravity, but still, I feel disconnected from everything.

Fortunately, my loyal friends often find a way to shine a little light into the darkness of my moods. They too all face challenges of their own, even Grace, with her brave smile and silent hope.

Grace expressed it best, "I never feel real here. It's like living inside an endless dream. I want it to end. I want to open the door and step outside and feel the heat of the sun on my face. Some days I just want to scream."

Grace's eyes showed only a hint of moisture, "I'm so thankful for all of you. You are with me even in my dreams. I don't think I would last a single day without you guys."

"Yes, I know what you mean. There's nothing to hold onto, except one another."

"So what can we do?" I could hear the tears in her voice.

"I believe that traveling off Earth scrambles our earthbound mind. It disturbs our experience of time. In open space, we always feel lost because there are no references to measure distance. In space-travel, our only references are two points: departure and arrival. There is no journey because nothing exists between these two points. Past and future lose their hold and their meaning." I stopped talking, thinking Grace was asleep.

"Oh, Please don't stop."

"Fortunately, the human mind is adaptable and remarkably so. We are learning to anticipate the future in a new way. What matters most is our love and our friendships, here and now."

Grace opened her eyes, "Your words are like a song. Your voice is soothing, and it doesn't even matter what you're talking about. It reminds me of my father reading me to sleep night after night. I always tried to keep my eyes open, but Father's voice always lulled me into sleep."

Grace and I enjoy working together both in the lab and in the kitchen. Michael and Jacob have their music, which helps soothe and connect all of us. They are veterans of space travel and they enjoy our "Little Adventure." Avella and Kamil have emerged from their cocoon and have started competing with Grace and me in the kitchen, creating delicious new menus. Myrrha and Tanaka have grown into a couple, clinging together like atoms in a molecule.

It is true that the imagination possesses the power to transcend space and time, but I discovered an even greater force reflected in the eyes of my companions. Love is by far the greatest force after all. For the Creator, creating the universe was just the beginning.

●

21
Benjamin

THE CHRYSALIS

My tears washed away the burning in my chest, but the guilt lingers. I didn't wish to abandon Ayxa and our daughter a second time — they were the echo of my longing and the answer to my secret prayers. The beauty I experienced through them was amplified many fold and our merged consciousness was much more profound than my isolated awareness. I longed to remain in their world of light but, once again, my fears broke the bond.

After returning to my ship, I continued to wallow in self-pity, holding on to my failure and my loneliness as if they were my friends. Alone, I sought refuge in my books, desperately searching for something tangible, something to believe in.

Learning to read beyond the words, I discovered whole worlds floating in each book. Questions reveal their own answers and what seemed complex one moment became simple the next, only to grow into a new complexity. Simple truths became simple pleasures, for a while. It felt like drifting on a boundless ocean with no shore to disembark metaphorically or physically. There is no way to escape from nowhere.

My intention was to follow the path of my mentors, those who had guided me in my wandering years. I still feel the truth of their wisdom, but the words have lost their vigor.

Then one book intruded, challenging all the esoteric speculation that was both my pleasure and my escape. It was an ancient text, which had penetrated the great wall of time. The book was a living language built of luminous symbols and hidden deep within its beauty, it proffered a simple message: "The truth you seek lies within."

Through the years, I heard this same message repeatedly, and each time it proffered a different lesson. This time, it served as a mirror and in its reflection, I could see the beauty of my life.

After a long, uncomfortable sleep, I woke from a dream that refused to be remembered. Just a ghost of the dream remained, filled with apprehension and sorrow. For distraction and escape, I reached again for the book. It willfully flipped from my hand, crashing to the floor where it decided to stay, refusing to be read ever again.

I dressed and headed to the control tower, turned on the holo-screen and chose my favorite ocean sunrise. Watching and pretending, I never tire of its beauty, and to deepen the mood, I selected a breathless aria from my favorite opera.

How I hunger to see a real sunrise and to breathe living air filled with dust and memories. To stand together with a lover on the shore of an ocean is my deepest desire. To listen to the ceaseless waves, to taste the salt in the air and smell the pungent fragrance of life mingled with death. To watch a bird spiral, a fish glide, to see the wind made visible by trees, to trade smiles with a stranger and to say hello. How long since I had smiled? How long since I had said the word, *Hello*?

Stars are meant to be shared, reflected in the eyes of a lover. Only in fantasy could I imagine Earth with solitary sunsets and private thoughts shared with a loved one. There were just too many people and the Hyvve mind too pervasive. I cannot return to Earth, not now, not after connecting with the consciousness of a planet light years removed. And it isn't just about the Hyvve — just the thought of returning to the past causes me great anguish.

In the observation dome, staring out at Arcturus, with all the strength of my longing, I wished to rekindle the joy we once shared, but Ayxa's love was a gift denied.

The first time she appeared, she sang a song of haunted loneliness, a song she borrowed from my soul. That is the reason it sounded so haunting and so familiar. She introduced herself in the guise of two beautiful women to attract my attention so I might see my reflection, and to ignite a love that wished to be. The truth is, I felt unworthy of her unearned love and was unprepared to hold on to such a precious gift.

All the words of wisdom I studied led me to one word, the same word that always frightened me. But love is more than a word, it's the essence of who we are. All the words in the universe cannot describe the universe, yet within this single word, our universe is revealed.

The power of my desire attracted Ayxa to me, and the strength of my longing allowed me to transform the very fabric of my being. Through my desire for union, I became free of my body and free of time's measure, but not free from fear.

The most beautiful woman in the universe chose me, but I was unable to accept this. I beheld her beauty but not my own. She was attracted by the innocence of my desire and the purity of my longing. And when we were together as one, we were one with everything.

On Arcturus, I was accepted, embraced and loved by her entire tribe, but my ego, in jealous disdain, rejected all the love and compassion they offered free of any expectations. They recognized and loved me for who I was. Love was their essence. Fear was mine.

It is not my intent to communicate the depth of loss I felt. Only through time did I realize there is no loss or gain, no wrong, and no right. I arrived unprepared for the magnitude of their love. Their gifts exceeded the capacity of my being.

A tacit sadness lingers but not the guilt. A lesson learned. That was the purpose and the privilege. Through loss and loneliness, I discovered love. It took a lifetime, but it occurred in a moment, the moment I cast off fear and opened my heart.

Love is ever present, existing in every infinitesimal expression of matter. It exists in the glowing depths of space and it is the essence of who we are. Love is its own dimension.

The chrysalis cracked. The outer shell parted in one quick snap! A fissure opened just wide enough for a new life form to emerge in full glory. The wings of desire unfurled as the juice of life pulsed through the veins, spreading the wings wide.

The chrysalis cracked, the shell left empty. There were no physical wings. They were unnecessary.

My mind raced to keep up as I quickened ahead of light speed on my approach to a distant star. Ayxa and I were at once in full union, soul to soul. Ecstasy can fulfill a lifetime of joy in a heartbeat. As she dissolved back into her cocoon of light, I returned to my ship. If the imagination truly knows no boundries, then we are still together, bonded by love. Separation is merely a thought.

This time, fear was not a factor, for fear no longer exists when we are together as one. And for me, Arcturus is no longer an alien civilization, for I realize their haven of belonging is the soul's natural state. But through this familiar belonging, I felt a deeper purpose — a stronger desire was at work, stronger than any other longing. I felt the need to complete my journey, and that journey requires a mortal body.

●

22

Jahalla

> *Quantum Cosmology shapes both the universe and the mind. In physics and metaphysics, it has been determined that all reality models are embraced within this ever-expanding theory.*
>
> *In accepting all interpretations of physical reality, no real laws of physics exist. Laws are an expression of wave functions, more on the side of probability.*
>
> *Reality is merely a choice.*
>
> *journal entry 07 • 03 • 3031*

HERETIC

Standing with Grace in the observation bubble, admiring the dense center of the Milky Way, she broke the silence, "Did you ever wonder why we live in clusters? Why there are all these little galaxies instead of one big galaxy full of stars forever in every direction?"

"Not exactly. In my younger years, one of my special friends, one of the brightest of the Ferrin Folk, told me the legend about the birth of galaxies."

"So do the Ferrin have a god?"

"That's another story for another time. Would you like to hear their story about the creation of the galaxies?"

"Only if it begins with a bang." Her smile, priceless.

"No, there isn't a bang, not even a little one."

"Please."

"OK. In the beginning, one of the Grand Stars, Father of the Milky Way, dwelled all alone, isolated in the cold vastness of space. All the other Grand Stars were far away, too massive to be near one another. They were all grand and lonely. During one cosmic moment, our Grand Star witnessed a distant star divide and become two. Then another star divided. Curious and inspired and determined, our Grand Star willed itself to do the same. Now she was two and not so lonely.

"Soon, throughout the universe, all the grand stars were inspired to divide, and then they just kept dividing until they all became gigantic swirling clusters of little stars, all born from the One.

"Each little star in the Milky Way possesses the memory of the Grand Star and, through this memory, they all remain connected to one another. Each star belongs to a family of stars and each galaxy belongs to a great tribe of galaxies."

"Knowing this, I never did wonder why there are galaxies. I just wonder where the Grand Stars came from."

"Wow! Where did your friends learn this story?"

"The Ferrin tell a similar legend of how they came to be. In the beginning, the Great Ferrin existed alone, born from the Grand Star. Inspired by the Grand Star, she decided to become many. But she chose a quicker path. She began to spin, spinning faster and faster until her energy fractured, scattering in all directions. The *Great Ferrin* became millions of tiny Ferrins, and each one was unique and sovereign, and they too are all related, connected through the memory of *The One*."

I followed Grace's eyes, feeling her warm thoughts. As we looked out past the Milky Way, I realized we too were spinning inside this great family of stars. Like two stars among many, we too had lost our loneliness, together.

Several day cycles later Grace, full of excitement, even more so than usual, commanded me to meet her in the control tower.

"So, the big bang is just another myth. I think I like the Ferrin myth better." Her smile was wide and wild with satisfaction. "I believe the Great Stars still exist. They are the galactic centers, and they are still giving birth to new stars." Grace glowed brightly with her foray into the world of metaphor.

She handed me her tablet of calculations, her metaphor translated into science, "This is just a rough draft. It needs lots of work and I need your help with the mathematics."

"I'd be honored. Just be careful you don't burst like the Great Ferrin." My jaw began to ache, just watching Grace's wild smile.

"Grand stars or not, what if it proves that plasma is the primal source of all matter?"

Her response was instant, "In the University, you would be booted out as a heretic."

"Or burned as a witch. Well, they're entitled to their universe, I have mine and it's right outside the portal." I was quite serious, but our laughter sounded like that of two young girls delighted by their shared secret.

I know all the theories of galactic evolution, but Grace makes the stars come alive. Her universe is filled with beauty and magic and this magic is what I need — magic mixed with friendship, that is. When we share our stories and our different theories of the cycles of life and death, the universe glows a little brighter for both of us.

During our long months together, on our journey toward the sun, we continued to share our stories and our dreams, forming an enduring bond and, from Grace, I have learned how to laugh again.

Michael is a quiet man, gentle and sensitive. In spite of his shyness, he allowed me to stare into those golden brown eyes. It is said the soul is hidden within the heart, if so then it reveals itself through the eyes, and it looks outward to see itself reflected in the eyes of another.

I should have known the danger of gazing into the eyes of another, especially those of a beautiful man. Incautious, unsuspecting, I tripped and fell into those eyes.

We became the closest of friends. He shared his music — I a captive audience. I shared my poetry — he a believer in metaphors.

On request, Michael translated one of my mathematical formulas into a musical score, a wish come true. When he and Jacob played it for us, the intricate melodies they created made even the structure of the universe sound intimate and exciting.

Michael caused me to feel soft and sensual, a pure reflection of his own worth. I wore his fragrance. He wore mine. I guided his hands and his lips to those places of hunger. Hands touching hands, touching lips, touching flesh. Flesh yielding to desires born of longing.

Then one night, we both realized the spell had been broken.

Michael's words always spoke his truth and, like his violin, they reverberated with deep overtones. "You have given me pleasure and satisfied desires I didn't know I had. I miss you already."

His words gave me the courage to speak, "I love your beautiful music and the softness of your touch. My body has longed and ached for such a touch, but there's a deeper desire in a place you cannot touch."

"You needn't speak the words I already feel in my heart."

After speaking our truth, we grew awkward and embarrassed and, within our small sphere, we had no place to hide. So we retreated to the separate islands of our friendship.

The type of intimacy we shared builds a lasting bridge that doesn't ever go away. We remain shy and self-conscious with one another but, with time, our love has transformed. It feels as though our souls are touching, tender and shy. Memories and desires linger in the body like wishes in a well.

We had traveled far, but this was only the first stage of our long journey together. The whole crew now better understands that we all need to be more careful with one another.

My growing friendships have helped heal some old wounds and within the comfort of these friendships, the ship no longer feels like a prison.

Now when walking through the ship, I see the engineered beauty of our new home. I appreciate how every corner and every curve is designed with perfect function. All chambers spiral outward from the center, with each chamber overlapping the next, allowing access to all the other chambers through the central core. It's like living inside a giant seashell, like the one I wear around my neck, the one from a distant shore.

Constructed level by level, starting with the inner core, the ship spirals outward, then enclosed within a pair of perfect metal spheres. The two spheres are magnetic and separated by a plasma field. Microbial robots assembled the ship molecule by molecule. Because of the purity and precision of their construction, the twin hulls, though relatively thin, are a million times stronger. The micro-robots, like cells in a body, were guided by a single design and a single purpose to this end. If the spheres are damaged, the robots will reactivate and repair any breach.

To soften the iridescent metallic surfaces of the inhabited portion of the ship, a soft organic skin covers the walls. It is true the walls lack life and texture, but this is the reason the walls, in time, disappear from the eyes, causing each chamber to feel spacious. The gentle curves enhance this effect. The walls are smooth and flawless — even so, the overall design feels friendly and organic. Even the lighting, though artificial, bathes everything, including the body, with purpose.

●

23
Benjamin

THE URGE

Though exhausted and edgy from a long inspection cycle, I resisted returning to the mother ship. I wanted to stay just a little longer, to relax and to enjoy floating weightless. With all the lights turned off, I slid out of the pod. An empty nothingness best describes this realm, yet it never feels that way, but I'm careful not to let my imagination run wild.

The total blackness of the ship's silhouette hinted of something out of the ordinary. Never before had I seen the outline of the transport. I placed my hand in front of my face and it floated in a sea of darkness, but still, I saw the silhouette of my hand against a lesser blackness. The glow remained faint and pulsed with a slow even rhythm, rising and falling like ocean waves.

Then frail filaments of light began to connect the stars. Like in my dream vision, the threads spread swiftly, forming complex patterns radiating in all directions. Eventually, an illimitable matrix of undulating waves of energy extended beyond the limits of sight. This intricate matrix permeated everything including me.

I expected to awaken and that this dream vision would vanish back into the nothingness, but instead, it grew more intense and more intricate!

With my air growing stale and difficult to breathe, I re-entered the pod and allowed it to find its way back to its birth. Mesmerized, I continued to stare at the spectacle until the doors to the landing platform slammed shut.

After exiting my suit, I was only half dressed and exhausted, but instead of returning to my quarters I raced to the observation bubble to continue watching the strange phenomenon. The matrix appeared less intense but seemed to have grown more intricate.

Transfixed, I spent several days observing the inter-penetrating patterns. The myriad threads of the matrix were so vast and intricate that at first, they exceeded my comprehension, but after a time, I began to see patterns within patterns, which allowed me to see clearly how all the stars are interconnected and related. And though complex, I was awed by the natural simplicity.

All through history, there have been rumors of veteran space travelers claiming to have seen mysterious lights and to have heard *music* emanating from empty space. These space dwellers are always dismissed as being *space happy*. And though this phenomenon defied all the laws of physics I once trusted to be true, I could not deny the reality I witnessed. It all appeared to be real, like a sunset, like the smell of rain, only more magical, like a kiss.

•

Five hundred and ninety-seven terrestrial days separate me from contact with another earthling, another carbonific being. How I yearn to feel rain falling on my face, to dig my toes deep into moist black earth, climb a tree or a mountain, chase my shadow or a rainbow. But this all seems as remote as a distant galaxy.

It will be at least six terrestrial years before I experience real gravity and breathe the air of a natural atmosphere. Just the thought of hearing a living voice and daring to speak to another person startles a sharp chill of loneliness.

The first three years of my tour have passed quickly, so why do five more years added to thirty-seven seem to be an eternity? I can fill a few hours with ship routines and spend a few extra in dream time, but I can no longer indulge myself in memories and regrets. I feel trapped with no escape, and there is no way to fill the empty hours.

Viewing one of the images of Earth on the holo-screen, I was awestruck by how real it appeared. I could almost imagine the smell of the air and feel the breeze. The wall-sized image is crystal clear and it allows me to zoom in for almost infinite detail. I imagined an image of the mysterious energy patterns, then I imagined myself creating that image.

In my early teens, I drew pictures of my imagined worlds, but Father convinced me not to waste my precious time. Years later, at the University, I secretly attended art classes where I learned to create drawings of a living world and studied color theory and image structure. The classes were enjoyable, a welcome distraction from the strict discipline of my physics major, but I forced myself not to take it seriously.

The harder I tried to convince myself that creating an image of the matrix was impossible, the stronger the urge grew. Here there are no paints or brushes, just digital tools. I attempted to draw with a stylus on the sensor screen. The instruments are digitally sophisticated but too mechanical and too crude for the delicate complexity of my vision. Besides, I wanted to feel the colors, smell the paints, watch them smear and blend, push them about, and to let them reveal their own nature.

The urge to capture my visions continued to grow ever stronger, a primal urge not to be ignored. So I forced myself to use the stylus. My efforts yielded only crude sketches, capturing none of the enchantment of my fleeting visions. Not even a hint.

In my heart, I understood too well there was no way to recapture the beauty of those magical moments of insight, but in spite of the limitations of the tools at hand, I continued my struggle.

Even the largest screen on the bridge was obviously too small to contain the subject, so I moved to the holodeck but, compared to the galaxy, even the huge wall-sized screen seemed inadequate for the task. The larger scale was an improvement, but I grew frustrated with having to move back and forth between the control panel and the screen each time I wanted to adjust the qualities of line or to change colors. So I decided to find a way to move the controls closer to the screen.

I thought it would be a messy job of rewiring and was surprised to find the units were controlled by wireless micro-transmitters, which made the task rather simple. In the workshop, I built a carbon-fiber box to hold the controls, which I strapped to my waist. Though awkward, it was a significant improvement, but I still couldn't adjust the controls without losing focus.

After another week of increasing frustration and anger, my patience disintegrated and I started avoiding the screen. Then one morning I woke with an obvious solution born in sleep. I inserted the stylus into one end of a short hollow shaft and inserted the controls into the other end. It took more than a little practice to learn how to use this clumsy contraption, then, little by little, my technique improved. I also continued to refine my instrument, making it lighter and streamlined, eventually finding an acceptable balance. With practice, it became an extension of my hands.

My technique improved. Not so the image. To stand in front of the awful results took all my courage. "How can something so beautiful be made to look so ugly?" was my constant lament.

I felt disheartened while working on the image, but being away from it proved even worse. Abandoning ship wasn't an option so, in a sense, I became a prisoner to my painting. Then, in a moment of abject frustration, my stylus ceased to function after I threw it on the floor with all my strength and determination, and then stomped on it more than once.

Fortunately, it wasn't the only stylus. It took a valuable week to reconstruct my special instrument and it never felt the same. I still feel a twinge of guilt of having killed my invention, but a little remorse can be a good thing. I treat the reincarnated instrument with great care, always handling it with gentle respect and even catch myself praying that it lives longer than me.

Through this one episode, I learned a key lesson. My respect for the painting grew into a reverence, even in those moments when it looks ugly. It is my child and, in my heart, I know it just needs more attention and encouragement. The obvious flaws don't need to be erased or hidden — just reworked and refined, even if I need to do it pixel by pixel. Even tedious work can be rich in its rewards.

Now I better understand those words spoken so often by my mother, "Patience is its own reward." A mantra I still repeat when the need arises, and I always hear it in her kind voice.

●

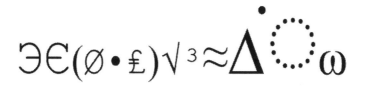

24
Jahalla

> *One can travel only so far before returning back to the place one began, forming a circle where the future embraces the past.*
>
> *So perhaps the answers we seek are at the beginning of our story and not the end.*
>
> *journal entry 09•12 •3031*

LIGHTSPEED PARADOX

Riding on the edge of a dream, I raced through a tunnel of time toward our future destination. I had experienced this sensation several times in my dreams, but it always jolted me into waking. For millenniums, my mother's tribe navigated waves of light to explore the future. I never believed the *Masters of Light* could travel into the future. I assumed they journeyed only in their imagination. But now that I better understood the limitless power of the imagination, I unleashed that power and continued to travel forward through time.

Once again, I faltered, but this time by choice. I withdrew from the trance, choosing to remain within the boundaries of the present. Like time, the future exists in every direction with infinite possibilities. Choosing one future over another can be a dangerous game. I trusted our future would reveal itself in its own time.

While training for our mission, I studied all the current theories of time-travel. I found the science to be confusing and inconsistent. Attempting to verify what scientists named *Temporal Phase Shift*, I discovered the formulas to be flawed, and unverifiable, a miss-matched set of assumptions cobbled together into a theory.

In my mind's eye, I envisioned our vessel traveling through currents of light, similar to what the *Masters of Light* practice. Something important resided within this simple metaphor and I spent several days attempting to build a formula around my vision, but my initial model proved to be too complex and fragmented.

One evening, after dinner, while visiting the observation bubble, Grace stated the obvious. "You seem to be traveling in another dimension. Are you worried about the *Jump*?"

"Yes, but that isn't it. I'm working on a new theory of time travel, and there's something's missing."

"Well, I hope it isn't us." We enjoyed our little laughter, but Grace was only half joking. We all shared the same apprehension about the upcoming *Jump* in an untested ship.

"Seriously, I'm curious."

"What I envision, is that when a ship approaches the sun, an energy imbalance builds around it. An electromagnetic charge envelops the ship, which initiates a phase shift similar in nature to an electrostatic discharge."

Grace was quick to grasp, "But the discharge wouldn't be sufficient to initiate lightspeed."

"If we assume light to be a continuous flow, like an electrical current, then envisage traveling through a medium of light. The ship travels along currents of light, not through space."

Then Grace completed my thoughts, "There would be no absolute speed of light when traveling within a medium of light. This isn't about time travel. Time isn't involved. This is light travel, pure and simple!"

We both felt the tingle of excitement swooshing through our veins. Our metaphors were mixed, but we knew we were on the threshold of something extraordinary.

In spite of all the theories, time travel remains a mystery. It hasn't been fully understood or explained in the four hundred years since a space ship approaching the sun was suddenly approaching a different sun, a distant star.

The instantaneous behavior of light and the limited speed of light seemed to be an irresolvable paradox. I understand paradox as a confusion of words that need be re-expressed in a mathematic formula. Mathematics is truly a magical language which helps focus the mind.

When attending University, my advisers steered me away from applying my mathematical skills to plasma theory and the electromagnetic model of energy. My intuition told me that a valuable truth lay hidden in those forbidden areas. The main obstacle for the electromagnetic model of energy is that most scientists still consider gravity to be the dominant celestial force. Within the new emerging theories, gravity is identified as a ghost of the electrical force, the electrical force being 10^{37} times stronger than gravity. Science had conveniently ignored this factor during a millennium of willful naiveté.

Within the last century, a splinter of the scientific community has also embraced another truth: that the whole galaxy is interconnected at every level, star to star, quark to quark. The Tribes had understood this reality stretching back thousands of years. They had never translated their insights into an equation, so the Hyvve dismissed their ancient knowledge as metaphysical nonsense.

We began by first exploring the electromagnetic model of the universe. My instincts told me this was the proper lens to be looking through. Fortunately, much of the research was waiting for us, stored in the memory of the Synns who had accumulated all of the theorems that had survived from an era before the *Burning Years*.

With little to interrupt us and excitement to inspire us, Grace and I spent hundreds of hours working on our new model, which we entitled: *Electro-luminal phase Shift.*

Initially, we attempted to integrate our formulas within the existing model, but after four long frustrating months of effort, we threw out all the old formulas and started fresh. Our radical theory demanded a radical approach. By integrating the plasma model with our theory of a light wave continuum, the resultant equations started to take on a life of their own. Assuming space to be a plasma medium, light behaves similar to an electrical current, a continuous flow existing between two points.

Assuming space to be a plasma medium, light behaves similar to electromagnetic currents, a continuous and instantaneous flow of energy. Within this model, there exists no fixed relationship between time and space, so we eliminated time as a factor, which confirmed Grace's first impulse.

Excited that we were on the threshold of a discovery of great importance, Grace became so consumed that she barely slept and talked mostly about our work. It must have been this same single-minded focus and determination that propelled her career and brought her into space at such a young age. She wasn't consumed by ambition, just an overpowering urge to understand how the universe works.

She confessed, "If I could travel back in time to when I was 7 years old I could see the solution floating in the air."

The Synns, the ultimate consumers of information, seemed to be no match for Grace and remained rather quiet, too quiet. Then one day they introduced several studies on Birkland currents, which they had collected from archives of pre-Hyvve records. They had also compiled hundreds of images representing these currents at every scale, from subatomic to interstellar.

These studies accelerated our progress and supplied a crucial missing piece of the puzzle. Introducing the Birkland currents also accounted for the issue of the instantaneous responsiveness of celestial bodies at great distances, which defied all existing laws of gravity.

I could feel the pride of the Synns when Grace repeatedly complimented them.

Now, in our new model, we identified the structure of the galaxy as a matrix of dipolar bonds. In effect, each star is energetically interconnected with the whole galaxy in the same way that each molecule of water is responsible for the integrity of a rain drop.

Then came that magical moment of intuitive insight we all long for, that moment of instantaneous recognition of a truth deeper than we can know. Our formula confirmed the inherent connectivity of space. Stars are separated by space, but they are also interconnected within a plasma field. Each galaxy is comprised of stars in the same way our bodies are comprised of cells. This realization gave us a deeper understanding of both life and the universe. It also explains how galaxies are capable of giving birth to themselves. It all has to do with plasma.

We could visualize the reality of instantaneous travel, but we lacked an adequate vocabulary to fully explain the underlying principles. So, in our equations, we created symbols to represent those functions which we could not translate. Thus, we created a mathematical fiction, which worked, in theory.

Our initial equation, $\ni\in(\emptyset\bullet\pounds)\sqrt{3}\approx\overset{\bullet}{\Delta}\overset{\cdots}{\bigcirc}\omega$, establishes the relationship between plasma and electro-luminal energy. Our second theory, *LightWave Fusion*, generated an equation less elegant, 32 lines of cascading symbols, and our treatise turned into a twenty-one-page thesis.

We wanted to refine our theory and our equations, but we were forced to rush our work so that we could transmit it back to Earth before leaving the solar system. Otherwise, there would be a twelve-year delay.

This would be the first time-shift, or light-shift, for all of us, the Synns included. Our vessel was equipped with every sensor imaginable, which would allow the Synns to record a definitive image of this event for future research.

Michael and Jacob had rehearsed this sequence until, like in their music, they performed it to perfection, and their absolute confidence helped ease some of my apprehension.

Avella and Grace monitored the gravitational sensors, aligning the exact co-ordinates to establish an accurate trajectory. When measuring distances in light-years, there are seven hundred vectors per arch-second of any position in open space. Any deviation, even a fraction of a vector, could place our ship millions of miles off course, or worse. Materializing in the center of nowhere could ruin the whole trip. Fortunately, traveling from light source to light source requires only the orientation of the destination star. This is the only vector necessary — the only one possible. In effect, you enter the plasma field formed by the Birkland current and follow it back to the source. Our new equations had given us a deeper insight into this phenomenon, but it is still just an unproven theory.

We had established our rotation cycle and were approaching the inner heliosphere of the sun inside the orbit of Venus. This was the event horizon — the point of no return.

Some of the sun's heat is deflected by the silvery surface of the outer hull. Also, the spin of the outer hull increases in speed by absorbing radiation from the sun and transforms it into centripetal rotation. The resultant rotational frequency increases dramatically until the external hull interacts with the sun's plasma field, generating a plasma shield around the ship. In theory, the shield isolates the ship in its own private bubble of space.

Warp drives and teleportation are still far in the future or far in the past. As part of our training, we experienced both in virtual reality, but this didn't prepare us for the anxious exhilaration, for the knowing and not knowing of a future far removed, but only moments away. We were committed.

Communication with Earth was no longer possible. Within our envelope of total isolation, the ship became our self-contained universe. God was in our prayers and God was along for the ride.

●

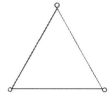

25
Benjamin

UNKNOWN INTELLIGENCE

My early attempts on the electronic canvas were only clumsy attempts to illustrate my vision, but even on the enormous screen, it was impossible to capture the intricate complexity of the matrix. But when I activated the holographic simulator, the illusion of almost infinite depth gave me a third dimension to work within. It also allowed me to zoom in to refine minute details. I can metaphorically enter the space contained within the wall–size image.

The results, as crude as they were, were encouraging in the possibilities they presented. Now each failure inspires new efforts and each minor success feels exhilarating.

Overflowing with inspiration, I attacked the limits of my electronic medium. The power of limitations freed my imagination and forced me into a deeper understanding of the medium itself.

Yielding to the painting, I follow the lines where they wish to go. Colors demand their own existence with hues so muted and so subtle that they can no longer be named. Colors layered over colors, patterns within patterns, shape my private universe, giving me deep insights into the structure of space and time. And as the image grows in complexity, somehow it remains subtle, and as the intricate patterns of space spiral across the electronic canvas, I feel twinges of hope.

The power of creativity, which first served me, has taken over, becoming an obsession, a volcano of inspiration. My work is my passion and beauty my joy. And in the act of creating something beautiful,

I have discovered the secret source of beauty. The force, which suspends trillions of stars and guides all light waves to their destinations is the same force that resides deep within each of us. We first discover beauty in the outer worlds — only then do we awaken to the truth that beauty lives within us.

Beauty is encoded, like DNA, into every pixel and into every cell of the image. Enfolded into the painting are my thoughts, my feelings, and my truth. And because I am expressing something I'm part of, it remains intimate and personal in spite of all its complexity and abstraction. Beauty stands exposed, naked to the universe, naked to God, naked as God intended.

None of this is my creation. This is my reaction each time I turn on the screen. It all belongs to an unknown intelligence, which expresses itself through me. Not questioning this, I just follow directions, doing whatever the painting demands. With my mind free in this way, I no longer feel concerned if an audience will understand my vision or ever see it.

The image remains contained within restrictive rectilinear boundaries but, for me, the screen's surface has ceased to exist. When viewed from afar, it stretches deep into infinity, close up, it is tactile, puzzling, and fun. And like a giant puzzle coming together, the tectonic sized pieces search for their proper orientation. I can only watch and wait as the pieces slowly rotate, then lock into place. I have learned the lesson that truth cannot be forced to fit.

I imagine the painting in my mind's eye while outside the ship floating in the blackness, when in the shower, and while running in the exercise chamber. I have even considered painting my dreams, though I decided that would need to wait until after I finish painting my waking dreams.

Each night after turning down the light volume of the screen, the image disappears except for the company of stars, tiny specks of light twinkling on the screen, pulsating with a rhythmic energy soothing and reassuring. In these magical moments, I feel that I don't want the image to ever be complete. I want to remain enfolded within its magical embrace.

After a long, intense work day, I took a quick shower and fell into bed. Delicious sleep bathed each cell as I stretched out, expanding beyond the boundaries of my imagination — the desire to fill the void now persists even in my dreams.

In the morning, I awoke from the wondrous dream where the distinction between dream and reality vanished. I had journeyed to the outer boundaries of the stars, to the shores of the galaxy. The stars were beyond number and each one was a blazing source of unimaginable power. I could clearly see that the emptiness of space is what allows all of existence to exist, even if it exists only in a dream.

The stars give life to billions of planets and then, in turn, the planets share this gift, thus fulfilling an unending circle of life creating life. Now I no longer need to imagine any of this because, for me, it is real.

Waking slowly and reluctantly, I held on to the glimmer of the dream's after-glow. Wanting to see my image in the light of my dream, I returned to my studio. My painting was beautiful beyond any of my original expectations, but it was merely a silent echo of my vision. The divine presence I felt in my heart wasn't present in the painting and I knew it should be.

Not daring to, but not daring not to be honest with myself, I knew I must begin again, from the start.

With a single command, I cleared the screen of seven terrestrial months of work and with that single stroke, I simultaneously started again, from the beginning.

The work disappeared from the screen but didn't cease to exist. Computers, even mindless ones, sometimes have a mind of their own. A backup copy of the image had been mysteriously transferred to the ship's log and was accidentally transmitted when Benjamin broadcast his next log entry.

●

My work progressed quickly, so too did time. Days were squeezed tightly into hours but weeks just disappeared. My studio became my world and frequently I slept there, not that my bed was far away, I just enjoyed the company of my work. It felt similar to sleeping under a blanket of stars back on Earth. My work was comforting, my life peaceful, and I didn't feel so much alone.

While painting I had little idea of what would appear next, and I didn't worry about specific details, knowing they would all blend seamlessly with just a little encouragement. Any misplaced lines could be realigned, and with a simple series of commands, the colors could be enhanced or muted so that they blended precisely with the whole. This gave me the confidence to experiment and explore without inhibition.

While working, my decisions are married to my actions, my thoughts quiet and unobtrusive. In the act of creation, only awareness exists — awareness being the silent and choiceless observation of what is.

In my first painting, *Maps of Silence,* I strove to reveal the silent architecture of space and to reveal the hidden patterns in what has always been defined as emptiness. But I considered the painting to be a failure.

In evidence of the ease I gained in the use of my mechanical medium, the space within the new image is more fluid and flowing. It resembles *Maps of Silence*, in that it contains the same entanglement of light and life, the same clarity, and complexity, except it is more dynamic, almost alive. But what truly distinguishes the new painting is the presence of the Divine, a silent symphony of creation revealed in its full brilliance — a Symphony of Silence.

●

𝒜)(3°𝔭)(ή)(~Õ)≈∞°

26
Jahalla

My Soul felt the beauty of the sadness in my heart

My tears, precious jewels gifted from my soul

I shared them with an ocean hungry for salt

From a heart hungry for love

journal entry 12•7•3031

TELEPATHIC LINK

A heavy darkness instantly replaced the intense energy of the sun. We had arrived somewhere on the outer fringe of a solar system with lots of spin momentum of the outer hull, which needed to be converted into propulsion to slow our speed. We had exited light travel, but we were still traveling at a speed we couldn't control, and we were no longer protected within a plasma field. We were once again traveling through space where every particle is a potential hazard. There are also 12 planets in this solar system and the chances of colliding with one are small, but there is still a chance.

Myrrha and I worked together, trying to interpret the data flowing from the Synns. Grace and Avella were busy calculating our position. I tasked my Synn to work with Myrrha, then I transferred to another unit to work with Avella and Grace, who expressed concern about the Synns.

Nothing was wrong but something wasn't right. The Synns knew precisely, where we were and where we were headed. They were also aware of everything happening on Earth, and Earth was aware of everything happening here, even though we were separated by over twelve light-years of space. Through the Synns, Earth had remained in constant contact with our ship for the entire time, Earth time that is.

I was stunned but understood at once. I had known the Synns to be telepathic, now I knew they were of one mind. They all share the same thoughts, the same knowledge and consequently they even share the same time

Hundreds of messages waited in my mail. We had expected none. First I read several letters from Nikolai. I sent him a message and my love. For him, it had been a long wait. Or had it? This was going to take some getting used to.

But speculation would have to wait for a while. We had a destination to prepare for, and we were all exhausted and in need of sleep. Apparently, we had been awake for a long time.

Many hours later, in the twilight of a distant sun, when I awoke, I felt disorientated, not knowing where I was and for a brief moment unsure of who I was. Having fallen asleep in the navigation room, I got up and had a long conversation with the Synns about our missing time. The most important event on Earth had been the discovery the Synns could communicate with one another through time. There was no mention of what

I understand it to be. Telepathy isn't just another form of communication — it's a profound connection between individuals. But for the Synns, it is a total sharing of mutual knowledge, instantaneous and complete.

Clearly the Synns have evolved, and it seems they have also harnessed the power of quantum entanglement, the only logical explanation that I could think of.

Telepathy is the easy part. Time is my quandary. I understand all the theories and mathematical constructs, but perplexed by the added paradox of instantaneous communication. In space, time is a measure of distance. We are separated from Earth by 12 years relative to the speed of light. It wasn't time we traveled but distance, and it wasn't years we traveled, only moments. Yet here we are, 12 light years in the future. But we are not in the future; we are in the present relative to Earth.

It seems as though we exist in our own private capsule of time. Time remains constant within our ship in the same way we carry with us our own self-contained atmosphere, yet somehow our present lingers somewhere in the past, which defies all theories of time-dilation.

It proved all too confusing, so for the moment, I decided to stay in my own present, and to forget about past and future.

My inbox overflowed with news, all of which could wait, except for the letters from Nikolai, which were full of excitement and sadness. I was astonished to feel him so near. Apparently, twelve plus light-years isn't such a great distance between a mother and her child.

When Grace entered, my tears were still wet, "These letters are from Nikolai."

My tears tempered Grace's excitement and her eyes too began to glisten. We shared the letters, taking turns reading them aloud.

Grace exclaimed, "I feel like I now have a brother."

Then Grace could no longer contain her excitement, "Our joint thesis on *Temporal Phase Shift Continuum* has become famous."

"And apparently renamed," I answered, astonished and pleased.

"This is a list of publications and scientific reviews based on our theory. Talk about instant gratification, we're already history."

"I would love to study the papers but why don't we wait until we're settled in."

Grace agreed, "Perhaps you're right. It feels like nothing has changed. But everything has changed."

●

The Synns had remained in charge of navigation while we slept. Actually, they often seem to be in charge, this being a good thing because they are much more efficient with the multi-dimensional computations required for our journey. Even so, Grace needed confirmation of our position and requested a map of space. A three-dimensional holographic image slowly emerged, floating between us, looking like no map we had ever seen.

With a strong edge in her voice, Grace rephrased her request to the Synns. "Present a planetary map of this solar system with our coordinates."

I quickly commanded, "Place this other map in my personal files."

The Synns blinked but stayed quiet.

We calculated and confirmed what the Synns already knew and Grace, still annoyed, stated the obvious, "Why do we even bother. They already know where we are and where we're headed and when we go to the toilet."

"We all need to trust one another," was my only advice.

Grace ignored me and went to work setting up a communication link with our destination, a command station serving as an outpost in this remote frontier. The command vessel was unaware of our presence or our mission.

We had arrived on the outer rim of the solar system and had to wait two hours to confirm contact. The Synns also identified a giant cargo transport on course for Gaia Prime, the seed planet — the main reason we were all here. We sent our itinerary and the recent news we had received from Earth to both the station and the transport.

Something else dwelled out there, something faint and vague, like a lost memory.

Several days later, alone with the Synns, I commanded: "Display the space map. You know which one I mean."

The image presented itself gradually, growing into existence layer by layer. The mysterious beauty of the floating image was astonishing, yet familiar.

"What is this image?" I asked of the Synns.

"Image: identified as *maps of silence.*"

"Where did it come from?"

"Origin: transport 7763, destination Gaia Prime, coordinates. . ."

"That's enough. Who sent it?"

"Navigator log: transport 7763."

"You knew what information Grace required. Why did you show this image?"

"We considered it to be important."

"There is no excuse for deception no matter what the intent. This will never happen again."

Silence filled the space between us as they shared this admonishment across the boundaries of time.

This would never happen again.

Later, after the evening meal, I went to the holodeck to

view the image on the largest screen on board. I wanted to see the *map* in its full intricacy and, at this scale, the complexity of the image exploded into infinite detail. My dreams of space, which had long been obscure and full of portent, now floated in front of me, electric and alive.

As I studied the image, I could see that each expression of starlight and each quotation of energy was significant and inseparable from the whole. Everything was inextricably married together, forming an intricate web of energy waves woven through the fabric of space. The whole galaxy appeared tangible and understandable, bringing the great void down to human scale. Space seemed almost friendly and intimate. Almost.

The multi-dimensional image engaged every mode of my perception and challenged every level of my intelligence, touching something deep inside, waking ancient memories. Astonished by the emerging patterns and by every new expression of energy, I continued to watch for hours. I froze and saved several stages of the image as it unfolded so that later I could isolate and examine what I interpreted as individual energy functions.

Once immersed fully in the image I was reluctant to come out. In a way, I never exited the image, or perhaps I should say that it left an indelible impression.

As I continued to explore the image, my thought patterns started to merge with the energy patterns in perfect harmony. It was through this heightened awareness that I became aware of the presence of another level of intelligence permeating the universe. I felt intoxicated as if aware through a vision inspired by some exotic drug, but this hallucination was real.

I had called Grace earlier and when she entered, she paused, silent in front of the image, then murmured, "Oh, my God."

"This map is truly astonishing," I whispered. Mystical is another word I wished to use, but the scientist in me was jealous and guarded.

"I've seen similar patterns before, in my dreams, but not with such vivid details and clarity."

"Is this what the Synns were trying to show us?"

"Yes, and you need to watch it from the beginning."

Grace said nothing more, but her eyes and her silence spoke volumes.

My thoughts overflowed like a river with no embankment, but my eyes began to ache from the strain of watching for so many hours. I left Grace alone with the image and returned to my chamber and entered a restful sleep with no need for dreaming, for my life was now a mirror of my dreams.

●

27
Benjamin

MESSENGERS OF JOY

When away from my studio for more than few hours, the images etched on my retinas slowly fade and my neglected ego ventures forth. Yielding to the past, I often visit with my family and friends. My honest memories give me insights into whom they once were, but I cannot imagine who they have become in my long absence. I bless them in earnest, and in return receive their blessings and their forgiveness. Rasjjein, one of my self-appointed guides from the Fringe, taught me this ritual. It gave me great comfort during my years in the Underlands, but I didn't fully appreciate the value of her lessons until years later, here in my solitude. And it isn't just a mental exercise, for I truly feel their forgiveness in my heart.

I perform this ritual just before sleep and often my troubled thoughts are soothed in my dreams. The guilt and the blame that I have clung to for so many years don't all magically disappear, but I have discovered that guilt can be transformed by forgiveness. I wish I had learned the art of blessings many years earlier.

Yes, there are many memories I refuse to let go of, the ones that anchor me to the past, especially those of Janeen and Shanti. I always carry with me a tiny memory chip, folded into a small piece of leather worn thin by the years. The device, which once projected their holographic portraits, has long ceased to function, but I can almost read the encoded information with my fingertips. I can picture Janeen, but cannot hear her voice. Maybe I just don't want to hear the words that need to be said.

Shanti's smile remains etched in my memory and, at times, I can almost feel the weight of her in my arms. I remember the softness of her hair and her wide blue eyes staring into mine. And though it wasn't our DNA, her birth belongs to Janeen and me. She is our daughter. Love makes it.

"How does Shanti look now as a young woman?" I whispered to myself. "Pretty like her mother, fair and tall, her black hair long and straight like mine. A slight quiver attends her smile, a shyness perhaps."

Her image is too clear to be imagined. I knew who she was right from the moment of birth, maybe even before, and a bridge of love continues to connect us in spite of the distance that pretends to separate. I also wonder about her memories of me, but I dare not look too closely into that mirror. Not yet.

Traveling light years away from my world has brought me closer to those left behind. We can escape our needs and desires for a time, but loneliness is a lonely word and physical existence requires physical contact.

Is it through the appreciation of the present that we can hope to penetrate the past and probe an uncertain future? Perhaps. More important to me is the realization that we need

200

to share who we are. Who are we if not the sum of our relationships? And it isn't just the nature of man, it's the nature of all life. I was never meant to be alone in space, not now, not ever.

In the end, my memories reinforce my desires and reawaken the pain of my isolation. What I desire, is to feel the joy of love's restless pursuit. I want to feel love in the way only mortals can know. Even the most vivid memories cannot conjure the sensation of a firm embrace or the tenderness of a warm kiss.

One woman, a memory from long ago, continues to haunt my dreams and it feels as if her presence is near, and I can almost picture her face. I didn't know her well, so my memories of her remain vague, almost a shadow. She is the memory of a desire, the desire for the intimacy that only a woman's touch can fulfill.

Ayxa is no longer alien to me, nor do I feel alien to her world, but when together we lacked the physical touch and the physical longing necessary for human love. The desire for physical intimacy remained stronger in me than the love we shared. Even the temptation of immortality could not seduce me away from mortal existence.

Feeling an urgent need to express these feelings, I decided to begin a new painting.

The screen and my mind remained blank for three days, then I envisioned two human forms floating in space, together, not alone. Using the computer's memory, I constructed two naked bodies, one woman, one man. At first, they were awkward and lifeless but, with caring touch, they started to resemble my vision of them.

The two lovers were remote and small, enveloped by illimitable space. As I zoomed in closer, they grew in size, crowding the boundaries of the screen, growing much larger than life. They became both monumental and enduring.

While working on the image, my body and mind once again merge, and my hands accomplish a greater precision when uninterrupted by contemplation.

Given their freedom, my fingers discover their own intelligence. Holding the stylus as a brush, I play it, as would a musician, blindly fingering the keys and the sliding controls. I paint what I feel and I feel what I paint. I feel affection in each gesture, respect every pixel, and with all this intimate attention, I have fallen in love with my creation.

I want the lovers to come to life and to know one another for their perfect splendor. I thought of placing great silvery wings upon their backs, but angels don't need wings in space. Only on Earth are wings necessary to propel their weightless bodies down from the stars. In space, there is no down.

The lovers radiate their own light and generate their own gravity — residing within a gossamer iridescent sphere, their private bubble of pure energy. They are their own creation, floating in the waves of a cosmic ocean, two physical bodies each touching the soul of the other. Two unwinged angels, messengers of joy.

They express joy in their soft embrace, in their smiles, in their gentle nakedness, and especially in their conscious purity of self. Where is joy, if not in the presence of love and lovers?

Joy is pure, uninhibited, and self-aware. It is beauty beholding beauty. My new painting claimed the title: *Joy.*

Thanks in part to the computers, I completed my Joy in just eleven weeks. With a touch of sadness, I saved my *Joy* and turned off the screen. As the image slowly dimmed, my Adam and Eve faded into a ghostly presence. Then they were gone — vanished, hidden like a memory.

My paintings are backed up, saved in various forms in different areas of the computer's memory. This isn't reassuring, so I've decided to broadcast the images out through the medium which first inspired them. My personal broadcasts are not encrypted, which will allow me to retrieve them later from one of the inter-planetary logs.

With a push of a button, my children left home at the speed of light, in every direction.

I couldn't imagine joy continuing forever. That isn't the nature of the journey. Emotions, like ripples on a pond, eventually return to stillness. Possibly our joy is retained within the stillness of our sorrows, and love is sheltered in the arms of our longing. Is it possible that sadness and desire dwell together, stored away in this stillness, waiting for just the right moment? Love and longing, grace and fall complement and complete each other in a magic circle that holds us and binds us. Why would I want joy to continue forever when so many long-neglected emotions wait patiently?

Desire guides my hands and the stylus across the screen, a desire poignant and compelling, a primal force existing before time and before thought. Desire is the flame that ignites my creative endeavors. I chose *Desire* as the title for my next painting. This decision released me from *Joy*.

To relax and meditate, I headed to the observation bubble where the obstacles to my future do not exist. The night was peaceful, the stars brilliant.

●

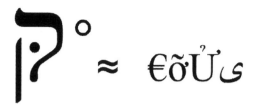

28
Jahalla

All is revealed in a moment, in a glance of
an image that has demanded of its creator
years of discipline, a lifetime of discovery.
Here lie the mystery, the beauty and the
paradox of true art.

journal entry, 7• 11• 3032

A MYSTICAL BRIDGE

Layer upon layer of energy waves interpenetrate one another
in a matrix of infinite possibilities. Waking from this dream
vision, I dissolved back into my body. I had fallen asleep while
watching the new image, *Symphony of Silence*, as it
materialized on the screen. While I slept, the image had
completed itself and now hovered above me in its finished
frozen form. Yet it still appeared to be evolving, as if alive. And
like space, it remains astonishing and silent.

Symphony of Silence isn't more beautiful, more intricate or
more miraculous than the first image, *Maps of Silence*, but it is.
Symphony expresses the same truth but it touches something

ancient and primal inside. How foolish to compare the incomparable, yet that seems to be our nature.

When Grace entered our studio, greeted once again by tears, she said nothing as she tenderly hugged me, trying to comfort a sadness that didn't exist. I pointed to the floating screen. Grace the scientist, Grace the woman of hidden emotions and Grace the little girl, were all moved to tears. And her silent response intensified my own feelings. Beauty is multiplied in its sharing.

"These images have titles, so too does their creator," I whispered.

"Why do they need titles?" Grace's question helped focus my thoughts.

"I don't believe these were meant to be maps. I think the man who created them was inspired by something more beautiful than the images."

"Do you know what they represent?"

"I have a feeling about them. I don't know exactly how they came to be, but I hope to find out."

Mesmerized, Grace seemed only half-aware of my words. "Have you tried to contact this mystery man?"

"Yes, but without any confirmation or response. The transport is shielded in total privacy. Why I cannot imagine."

"There must be some way to contact him."

"Even at this great distance, with the image as a connector, telepathy is a possibility. But I don't want to intrude. I never intrude — though, I must admit, I'm tempted."

"How is it possible we share the same visions?" My private question demanded an answer, even though in my heart I already knew it.

"The Synns have attempted to analyze the images, but they lack the instincts and the intuition to interpret the infinite subtleties. And the artistry escapes them entirely. "

"Maybe we should all team-up."

Then Grace asked the Synns. "Are others aware of these works?"

Their answer surprised both of us, "Many on Earth are aware of them, but no one understands what they represent."

"What do they represent?" I murmured to myself.

The Synns answered with an abstract question, "Are they dreams?"

This gave me great pause, and Grace's face told me now was the moment to reveal a secret held too long, "Together the Synns comprise a single mind. They are self-aware and they understand."

Grace appeared embarrassed as if overhearing a private confession. She could have been flushed with anger or betrayal, but she quietly said, "I've noticed how you converse with them, so I'm not surprised. It merely confirms my growing suspicions. I do wish you had told me sooner."

"Were you ready?"

"I'm ready now. Do you have any other secrets to share?" There was more than a hint of edge to her voice.

"No. Just some unanswered questions." I was talking more to myself.

"Of me?"

"Only one. Do you feel free from the censure of the Hyvve?"

"I haven't thought about it in those terms, but yes, I think so. I feel different here." And with those words, Grace's smile returned.

"To me, everyone on board seems to be free of the Hyvve's influence. Even Myrrha has become approachable, our conversations open and introspective, almost intimate."

"I know what you mean — we've all become like family." There was a thoughtful smile on her face.

"Well enough talk, let's go to work. Are you guys ready?"

This was Grace's first personal question to the Synns. They seemed startled and stammered "Yes,"

Then the three of us, the Synns were officially part of the team, made plans to work on decoding the new image. We began by examining the obvious patterns first, but we were challenged by how tightly every waveform was intertwined with the whole. Our attempts to isolate specific wave functions proved almost impossible, but for the Synns, it seemed an effortless task.

We worked together as a team, but the images inspired each of us in a different way. Where my interpretations were intuitive and metaphoric, Grace derived her analysis through solid logic, beautifully constructed with bricks of precision. We each appreciated our different methods, becoming closer and wiser because of our distinct approaches. Each flower blooms a different color.

My years of training within the Sanctuary and the Hyvve proved prophetic for the purpose of this moment. For me, the feud between math and magic doesn't exist — they are merely different expressions of the same truth. Grace's training in the Hyvve gave her the needed structure to channel her insights. Our different styles intensified our enthusiasm, as we each inspired the other, achieving impossible results as we crossed over the mystical bridge connecting science to alchemy.

The Synns followed our lead as best they could. Not knowing what to expect, it was only the second time I have seen them hesitate. But, as always, their computations were flawless and they could run instant simulations to test our equations. And, with so many hours focused on computation and analysis, they proved to be good companions.

Like the rays of a warming summer sun, *Symphony* penetrated deep into my consciousness, and as my mind expanded to embrace its intricacies, it began to restructure the pattern of my thoughts. *Symphony* didn't demand this, it encouraged, stimulated and excited me into a heightened awareness of everything, including myself.

In our attempt to interpret the images, I felt as though we were decoding the secrets of the universe as if we were translating a sacred text — a message from God. Grace was affected in a similar way. Radiant with anticipation she worked with a passion inspired by something she recognized as extraordinary.

Watching her watching the image, I commented, "It makes my heart glad to be sharing these moments with you."

"Yes, that is what I wanted to say. Are you reading my thoughts again?"

"There's no need."

We had squeezed a lifetime into the four months of our research. Much had been accomplished and much had changed. Grace was charged with electricity, like the stars, and full of luminous wonderment, like a moon. No longer my adopted daughter, she is my sister and nothing remains hidden between us, or so I thought.

I grew curious about her age and asked the Synns.

"Her official age is twenty-seven . . ." I cut them short and finally decided to ask her.

After dinner, I pressed her for an answer, "So Grace, I'm curious, how old are you — really?"

"Well... I'll be twenty-one soon enough."

"That's not possible. A teenage officer on a starship?"

"Well, I got an early start. I graduated University when I was twelve and finished my doctorate when I was almost fifteen."

"You were a fourteen years old with a doctorate? When did you start school? When you were two?"

"Oh, I never went to school. Because I didn't start talking until I was seven, my mother kept me out of school and away from institutions. Officially, I was autistic. When people spoke, I could see their words swirling in the air, but the words didn't compute, so I just watched the world around me and saw how everything fit together.

"I loved to run and feel the rush of air on my face. Swimming was my favorite. I could see how water and air and light were all the same. When my mom read to me, I followed as she pointed to the words. She could tell I understood everything, so when I was three she invented a way to teach me to read. Well, I just kept reading. I loved the patterns the words made. In my father's library, I discovered a book with all these magical letters that formed magical patterns called equations. When I turned five, I started writing my own equations. I became famous."

"I remember hearing about you at the University."

"The University gave me access to a Synn. It helped me with my equations, and through the Synn, I could see the beauty of the whole universe. I wish I knew the Synns were alive. I didn't have any friends."

"That's impossible to imagine."

When we weren't working on our equations, we discussed logic and magic, gravonics and art, insight and hindsight, poetry and math. We talked when we walked, while we cooked, but not so much while we worked. We shared everything and cross-pollinated one another's thoughts. Grace helped to bring out the theorist in me. I planted the seeds of mysticism in her heart.

Grace's life had been as complex and challenging as my own, in a different way. Her high level of energy and enthusiasm existed because of the Hyvve, and in spite of it. Anxiety had been her driving force. Now Grace wished to learn more about the Tribes and their history. She had also grown very curious about the *Divine Mother.*

Jacob grew a bit jealous of all our time spent together until he too was drawn into our conversations. He could always supply the metaphor of music to any and everything. His technical precision brought a fresh logic to our work, and his dry humor helped to fill the chambers with laughter, sometimes many hours later when a subtle joke was finally recognized. Work and music for him are serious business, humor keeps him balanced.

In one of our visits to the observation dome, Grace asked, "Did you ever feel like there was someone inside of you, someone who knew you better than you did?" Grace was speaking more to herself than to me.

"Only my son. Not like what you mean."

While I was thinking about her question, Grace unclipped her gravity boots and slipped out of them. She hovered for a moment, her toes inches above the deck. The observation deck is gravity neutral. She bent low and sprang upward to the top of the transparent bubble.

"Why don't you come up here? It's like being out there." This wasn't my Grace speaking.

"Who will get us back down?"

"Come on. Down is just as easy as up." She didn't need to ask twice.

I slid off my boots and enjoyed the absence of pressure on my feet, but I hung on to the railing with a tight grip.

"Let go." I'm not sure if these words belonged to her or to me. I pushed against the railing a bit too hard and rose too fast and crashed headfirst into the transparent dome.

Soon I was face to face with Grace. "So, you mind telling me what this is all about?"

Grace giggled, "Myrrha told me my DNA has stabilized. She now wants to retest all of us."

"What has that to do with floating?"

"I want to have a baby. My own baby."

"What about sperm."

"Jacob has plenty and he asked me to marry him, and Myrrha confirmed his sperm is healthy."

I forgot I was floating until my head bumped the sphere again.

"Will you marry us?"

I couldn't always feel the presence of the Divine Mother, but I could see Her pen at work in this grand play. On occasion, She steps on stage Herself. She has played many parts through the ages, always appropriate to Her audience, fulfilling whatever roles humans make available to Her. She has always been there. I have bumped into the wall next to Her open door and blinked every time She appeared in front of me. I just wasn't ready for Her light. The arrival of the images was Her knocking on my door — the door to my heart. The door finally flew open.

Alone in the holo-chamber, even with my eyes closed, I continued to see his *Symphony*. Opening my eyes to the image floating in front of me, I entered a dimension where there are no equations, no questions, and no need for answers. The images and my thoughts had become inextricably woven together in the same way the delicate threads of light connect the stars. I wanted to understand the messages encoded in his *Symphony* — even more so, I wished to know the man who created it.

If I possessed a hundred words for beauty and if I could express a thousand subtle distinctions to describe that beauty, only then could I venture to express the rapture I feel as a witness. I can only imagine a hint of what it must have felt like when he envisioned the phenomenon that inspired these miraculous images.

When Grace entered, my face was covered with tears. Grace was puzzled but didn't ask. She just hugged me and she too began to cry. Then we started laughing together through our tears. In our little ship, in that precious moment, within that simple gesture of non-understanding, I realized the Divine Mother had given us a role in Her new play.

●

I decided to enter deep silence for the remainder of the voyage. I remained alone in my chambers during the day cycles, and in the night, when most were asleep and dreaming, I visited the observation deck to search the stars for my dreams, hoping to witness the spectacle that inspired his *Symphony*.

In deep meditation, I emptied my thoughts, except for this one ardent desire, to know this mysterious traveler. I felt he alone might hold the answers to my many questions, secret questions demanding secret answers.

While exploring the images, I struggled to see them without the intrusion of my own thoughts, but that proved to be impossible because they require a dialog. It's as though they desire companionship, possessing a loneliness deeper than mine.

The artist needs to share his vision, the musician requires an audience, and the poet desires someone to listen quietly. *Symphony* demands all of this and more. Following these thoughts round and round, I always return to the beginning, back to my feelings and my real question, and my secret desire. Could he be the one? How could I be in love with a man whom I have never met? Even in my private thoughts, I felt embarrassed in posing these questions to myself.

Mother often reminded me, "The beauty of the universe is contained within the beauty of your soul."

The beauty I experienced in his *Symphony* made me feel beautiful. Even the love of the *Divine Mother* didn't do this for me.

My silence was honored for six weeks, then Jacob called. "It is time. We are docking in seven days and we need you."

"I've missed you, all of you."

"And we have missed you."

"It's wonderful to hear your voice."

"You sound different."

"Everything is different."

Having not spoken a single word in over six weeks, I needed these seven days with the crew to ready myself for first contact with Z.

I appreciated my retreat, now I enjoy sharing the excitement of my friends. We will soon be amidst over three thousand strangers, each one of them a walking miracle. After our long isolation, this all feels overwhelming.

The huge vessel we are approaching is a small floating city. Their computer system is two hundred years of hodgepodge installations. Fortunately, the Synns have mapped out the necessary changes, using the diagrams forwarded to us from Z.

Integrating the synthetic cells with the existing remote sensors presents the greatest challenge. A special crew has volunteered for this, and they have prepared for their tasks during the seven months of our approach. I try to stay calm, but the thought of meeting three thousand individuals, each one a separate galaxy, is thrilling and I already feel their presence.

●

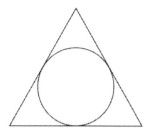

29

Benjamin

TRUST

My computers beckoned. I resisted, feeling nervous and hesitant about my new painting *Desire*. It wasn't a question of trust. I trusted that the next expression of color and the next articulation of form would be there, waiting to be discovered. I trusted in the existence of a deep well I could draw from, a well that replenishes itself endlessly.

Desire guides me to the easel before sunrise and guides my hands and the brush across the electronic canvas. This desire belongs not to the body but to the soul, a desire, ancient and primal, passed down through endless generations,

Is it through our desires that we are inspired to create, desire being the engine that powers our will? I could spend endless hours playing with words, but words lead to questions, not actions.

With a whisper of an idea, I inscribed a giant circle, large enough to swallow all my thoughts. A circle is forever completing itself, connecting the beginning to the end, endlessly. Perhaps the circle is a spiral in disguise, an endless coil hidden behind the line, stretching through space, spiraling back through infinity.

At first, the blackness of the empty circle appeared to be a bottomless abyss, reminding me of my dreaded well of echoes. Then it reminded me of the surface of my secret pond and about my imagined journeys into the future. I watched the threads of my life weave through the Hyvve, then my years of wandering through the Underlands. All my memories threatened to fill the circle if I continued to stare into it.

On impulse, I created a great square to contain the circle, which, in turn, demanded another circle to enclose it. This outer circle crowded the screen, edge to edge, over seven meters in diameter. Then I began to paint the space within the boundaries of the inner circle. The emptiness invited me to create an endless matrix similar in complexity to *Maps of Silence.* The patterns were darkly radiant and mercurial. Then, hidden within its luminous depths, I discovered another square held tight by the inner circle. The new square defined another space with yet another circle enclosed within. It was circles within squares within circles all the way to infinity then back again.

Many ancient symbols share this same geometric metaphor, with either a square scribed within a circle or a circle held within the square.

The circle stands for the universe. The square is the symbol of knowledge. The strict geometry of the square is also the rational mind of man embraced within the circle of God. The mundane and the Divine, the physical and the metaphysical, all share this same universal relationship. In my interpretation, knowledge expands to encompass the universe, then the universe expands in turn. It is the cycle of an ever-expanding universe, encouraged by ever-expanding knowledge.

After weeks of struggle and triumph, I felt the image was complete. Then one evening, staring into the enigma, a single point in the center revealed yet another mystery. Each square revealed another dimension when four invisible lines connected the four corners of all the squares to the single point in the center. In the three dimensions of the hologram, the squares were transformed into pyramids. Pyramids within pyramids descended back through time and space.

I closed my eyes and envisioned the lovers of *Joy* floating in their self-contained universe. When I opened my eyes, the circles in the image had transformed into iridescent spheres, and I was the dot in the center. This was the fulfillment of the vision of the young boy resting near his secret pond not so many years ago.

Perplexed by the image, I searched it for an answer to the meaning of the title *Desire*, but the image remained silent.

Desire had decided to stay hidden within the circle of circles. Then I admitted to myself that this ancient enigma expressed in geometric metaphors would need to acquire a different title.

Inspired and pleased with my unnamed image, I turned off the screen and retreated to the solarium for a long overdue rest.

●

When I finally felt the courage to face a blank screen once again, my mind was as empty as the screen. I had no idea of where to begin. The Galaxy was the inspiration for my first two paintings. Through Ayxa, I discovered love in its purest form, which found its expression in *Joy*.

The inspirations for the paintings were obvious, but I grew ever more curious about the secret forces that guided me to the canvas in the first place. It was a question I couldn't answer, so I decided to seek counsel from a higher source. I hadn't spoken to God since I was a young boy and felt that I would never be closer to Him, this being His dominion.

Drafting an embarrassingly long question, I asked for a direct and unambiguous sign. The answer, a single word, arrived before I invoked the prayer. "Yes" was the answer. A quiet voice said, "Yes." No reverberating thunder, no flashes of deep insight, no visions, no epiphanies. Just a quiet unassuming, "Yes."

Encouraged, I asked another question, "Was it your guidance or was it my choices that lead me here?" The answer, "Both," was contained within the question.

There was the answer: succinct, unequivocal, lucent, candid, and concise. What would I do with it? Ponder it? No. I knew the abundant implications.

Another question, one that had haunted me, was answered: "Yes." Then God explained: "The nature of the universe is change. You have changed, therefore the universe has changed."

My thoughts raced to the edge of my understanding and then they just kept going. I had felt there were a thousand questions to ask but they were all preempted by this single answer.

Then another thought surfaced: "Trust." This wasn't framed as a question. It was an innocent statement about the obvious. I understood in that moment that all my questions contain their answers.

Feeling confident, I lifted the stylus and approached the screen in total surrender, and in total trust.

Trust is silent and honest and unconditional. Trust is what you receive when you give it. Trust is belief empty of need, knowing without doubt, faith without fear.

Trust would be the title for my next painting.

My computers serve me well, the images possible because of their passive precision. The computers also keep the ship and me alive, but they compute only data, words and images being the same to them. Even the splendid landscapes of Earth with their delicate clouds in the brilliant blush of a sunrise are just digital codes spread across a screen. My computers understand less than nothing, yet they serve with a purity of purpose which allows for unqualified trust.

For *Trust,* I chose to start with a fractal matrix generated by the computers. In part, I made this choice to acknowledge the computers that made my creations possible. Computers have always been present in my life. I trust in them, and now they have become an extension of me, the perfect tool for the task at hand.

I realized even the Synns had earned my trust once I understood their silence was their only way to survive the chaos surrounding them. The threat wasn't that the Synns would start thinking and become a menace to mankind, rather, the real problem was humans once again were becoming a menace to themselves. The dilemma seemed to be a lack of trust.

Trust would need to be more than words. I couldn't paint with words, nor could I create with my mind cluttered with judgments. Trust would reveal itself in time. This was a confidence, a knowing, and a trust. I trusted that, in my hands, the stylus would know what to do.

Trust is knowing the rising sun before dawn, trust is the planet's orbit around its sun, trust is your next breath. Trust is its own reward. All these images flowed effortlessly onto the screen.

After many cycles of work and sleep, the image started to reveal itself with a brilliance, an honesty, and an authority that surpassed any expectations I might have had. In only seven weeks of intense effort, the painting was nearly complete

Needing a rest from my work, I turned off *Trust* and uploaded *Joy*, in part to make sure it was still there, but mostly I just wanted to enjoy the company of my two friends.

A gentleness radiated from the lovers that I hadn't previously recognized. The affection in their embrace seemed to say, "Thank you for your tenderness." I felt I could almost hear them speaking, speaking both to one another and to me.

A shiver of recognition ran the length of my spine as I realized that their joy had become my joy, first imagined, then made visible, and now it was alive within me. In the same way that my characters surrendered to one another, I surrendered to joy. *Joy* wasn't my creation. Joy was my reward.

Now I better understand their feelings for one another. Yes, they care deeply for each other, but now I see another meaning to their love. Their love flourishes in the absence of loneliness. They each fill that emptiness for the other. Yes, love is about passion and desires. It is also about needs. They are both grateful to be together and not alone.

During my long hours in front of the images, I too seldom feel lonely. While I work there seems to be the presence of another. Perhaps this phantom belongs to a memory anchored to the past, or a desire born from one of my unremembered dreams. It wasn't Ayxa or anyone from my past. Rather a secret companion seems to be traveling with me, her presence exaggerated by the ever-present longing wedged in my chest. This time, the longing seems to also belong to someone, somewhere and it feels as though she is moving closer.

How I wished to touch and be touched, like the two lovers floating on the screen in front of me. Feeling a jealous twinge, sharp and cold, I turned off the screen. As the image faded and disappeared, my feelings intensified into a cold flame of loneliness.

Sleep has become my only escape, but always I awake to the same ache in my chest. The vision has grown stronger and closer. The harder I try to ignore her, the stronger her presence grows.

Then in a waking dream I reached out to touch her. I imagined her fingers reaching out to receive my touch. I have experienced fantasies of wanting before, and more than once have conjured images of intimate beauty to fill the hollow of my loneliness. This was different. Her presence was too real. It made me feel uncertain and uncomfortable, and after the image vanished, I faced a deep dilemma. I didn't want the phantom to return, but some old feelings were now awake, and deep inside my manhood began to stir.

Feeling a faint hope that she exists somewhere in time, my secret wish is that she belongs to the future and not to the past.

●

ńᚼ~Õ)ᚼᘯᚼ3°𝔭 ≈ ∞ °

30
Jahalla

Hundreds of billions of galaxies inhabit this universe we call home. To know just the Milky Way, with its Seven hundred billion star systems is beyond comprehension.

Yet we pretend to know one another, even though each one of us is as complex and incomprehensible as a galaxy. Even to know the self is not so easy, but it is more accessible than a galaxy, and it holds the same secrets.

journal entry 06• 07 •3033

GRAND TOUR

Z spins through space like a planet, seemingly isolated but guided by forces unseen. Our smaller vessel, like a wandering moon, seeks an orbit, attracted by a force stronger than gravity. The two vessels make ready for first contact.

A massive construction project is well underway with two dozen ships tethered to the growing external skeleton. With no docking stations available, our silver bubble remains locked into a quick orbit around the station. Thus, we will not remain in our home quarters as we hoped. We packed only necessities, except for a large collection of spices we brought as special gifts.

With the extra construction crews, Z is already crowded and space at a premium. There will be little privacy and we will be just another crew. Even so, a rather large welcoming party greeted us.

"Yens Jewels at your service. They call me Captain. This is Myranda, Lakana, Engar, and Omalan. They have chosen to work with you and wish to learn everything about the Synthetics."

"We are the ones at your service and we are honored to be your guests. Your hospitality is legendary." Jacob responded, introducing himself and then the rest of us.

One on one, we exchanged names and touched hands all around, the conversations lite and lively.

After these formalities, a tall, slender woman ventured forth from a shy group who waited quietly nearby. She spoke only to me. "I am called Idris, of Procyon. Welcome to our home Jahalla."

"Thank you. I have been looking forward to our meeting in person." We had been in contact for several days. This wasn't my first encounter with an outworlder nevertheless, I was stunned by her majesty and the brilliance of her iridescent golden skin.

Idris didn't hold back or waste words. "Your suit hides not your power. You be more radiant than we have foreseen."

The radiance I felt was the flush of my embarrassment.

Idris held me long with her gaze, speaking her words directly to my heart "You be regal yet gracious. Your beauty be the window to your soul."

Encouraged by Idris, the rest of the group stepped forward, greeting me as an honored guest. And I truly felt honored.

Idris declared, "When you settle, we will talk."

She and her group bowed and silently scattered.

After the necessary formalities, Captain Yens escorted us on a *Grand Tour*. Z surprised us at every turn. The main corridors are pleasant with plants and benches at every crossing. These courtyards are open, bright, and busy. The proud Captain showed us the old and the new, explaining a bit of Z's evolution. "There are over 200 years of history contained within these walls and we are proud to share it."

Elegant small water fountains seem to be a necessary luxury, beautifully crafted, pleasant to both the eye and the ear. Ancient and modern paintings hang wherever space permits, the variety of styles exaggerated. Eclectic to be sure, with artifacts from many worlds, like a living museum rich in tradition and history, where everything fits together pleasantly.

Those we met along the way shared smiles of recognition and welcome. Especially pleasing to see were the many young children and the fashionable raggedy teens. My heart skipped a beat when we were introduced to a proud mother and her newborn daughter. While holding the baby, unable to hold back the tears, I whispered to her, "What is the child's name?"

The pride of her smile beamed even brighter, "She is named Jahalla and I pray her future be as bright as yours."

Catching my breath, I whispered, "This doesn't feel like a space station. It's more like a dream of our future."

I rejoined the group but my thoughts remained with the mother and her child, until Yens guided us to a small gallery with a collection of small intricate sculptures. Each work was unique, with a haunting beauty, unlike anything I had seen on Earth. "These are extraordinary," I mumbled to myself.

Yens responded to my whisper "We hold the finest collection in the Galaxy. I'm glad you appreciate them."

"Who is the artist?"

"They are not made by one hand. Each one belongs to a different Quester."

"Questers? Here in space?"

"Most of these works were created by the solo-navigators of the giant transports."

"Like Benjamin?"

"Yes."

I fell silent, my thoughts trying to reconcile my emotions.

"It's a peculiar phenomenon. Some of the solo navigators create works of astonishing beauty, while others go insane from the isolation.

"Why do they travel solo?

" So they don't kill one another."

As we continued our tour, Jens explained, "As you can see each level has its own personality and you will notice a distinct earthiness fills the atmosphere of the innermost level. This is the aroma of the asteroid core."

Before I could ask about the asteroid, Grace asked, "Won't the expansion disturb all of this?"

"We have always grown from the inside out. Z is spheres within cubes within spheres. The inner levels will be left undisturbed."

Jacob asked, "Why did they choose to build in this orbit? There is nothing here."

"I was saving that part of the story for last. The core of Z is a massive asteroid, mostly metallic. We started as a mining colony and the original dwellings were built inside the first mine shafts. We still mine the metals we need for constructing Z."

As we descended, level by level, the earthy fragrance grew stronger. It reminded me of the caves of the Inner Sanctum.

It seemed as though we walked for miles before returning to our new quarters, which were close to where we began. The Captain and I lingered as everyone else wandered on to their separate destinations.

"Thank you, for your gracious hospitality." My words were formal, but I felt I was speaking to a friend.

"Please call me Yens, and the honor is truly mine. I trust you and the others will join me for the evening meal. I will send an escort."

Finally letting go of my hand he continued, "Jahalla is an unusual name yet familiar. I remember it from my mother's stories. Are you named in honor of the ancient one?"

"Yes, I am a messenger of the Divine Mother. The name has been spoken and the foretelling has begun."

"I have felt a shift. At first, I thought our isolation might be the reason, but I felt a stronger force might be at work. Then Benjamin's images arrived and now you are here."

"The dreams are real," I said.

"I can feel the truth of it, and I can see it in your eyes. We have waited such a long time."

My eyes glistened as I spoke, "I am here to serve. May *Jahalla* guide our way."

In a gesture of universal respect, we bowed to one another in silent honor.

Touching my heart with my fingers, I offered the traditional tribal greeting, "I honor your truth and I honor your tribe."

"As I honor your truth and may your tribe always prosper." He touched his heart, then mine.

Separated by time and distance from the Hyvve, I felt free to use my telepathic gift without fear, and through the shared thoughts, I understood better my excitement about arriving here. I could feel the presence of the *Divine* and I was happy not to be alone with these feelings.

I also sensed the presence of a different energy, a dark shadow amidst all the light.

Grace and Jacob, Kamil and Avella, Tannaka and Myrrha were paired and each couple share a single room together. Michael and I also agreed to share a room.

I removed my suit and dressed in silk. Then, after a delicious nap, I hung silken fabrics on the walls and spread other delicately colored fabrics on my bed. The stark cubical was concealed and forgotten, transformed into our new home.

As crew's quarters go, our room is adequate. Unfortunately, it is a single room for the both of us. The bathing chamber is also small. No kitchen and no food, just two green plants hanging from a low ceiling. Two comfort chairs, two narrow beds. A single desk, angled in the corner, serves as both office and altar. My new bed is firm enough to use for meditation.

When Michael returned, he also quickly made himself at home. He hung his instruments on the wall above his bed, then he decorated the air with delicate music. His violin was quick and cheerful. Even so, it brought moisture to my eyes. I also shared in the delight of a secret audience on the other side of the door. Michael began to play as if to please an audience.

One thing that intrigued me was the healthy appearance of everyone on board, a vibrancy I didn't expect to see in space dwellers. I didn't need to ask — the answer was obvious once I used the bathing chamber. Personal cleansing on Z uses light, not just water. The scarcity of water is no longer an issue, but light remains the preferred way to bathe.

The first time I entered the chamber, I expected to be toasted by warm, bright lights. The experience was just the opposite. The cleansing light was set on a bluish frequency, which warmed my body gently while it soothed my mood. I couldn't help but relax in the blue mist of light. My thoughts just evaporated, tranquil being a good word to describe the sensation. It felt as though my soul was cleansed along with my skin

Under the blue light, my body looked olive green, though I felt my skin returning to bronze from the rich nourishment. Toward the end of the session, just before the timer expired, the lights turned a golden hue. The image of my body glowing in the mirror looked vibrant. Then a thin warm mist filled the chamber to cleanse and moisten my skin.

Stepping from the chamber the air felt cool and refreshing, and the cabin lights now looked bluish and pale in comparison to the golden glow.

My body wanted to stay naked to appreciate the afterglow and the tingle of my skin. I wished our shared room was a bit bigger and a little more private. Fortunately, Michael's polite absence allowed me a pleasant solitude.

The science for the Luminal Chambers was a gift from the Outworlders of Procyon. The bio-chromatic crystals, that filter the pure white light, were designed to nourish the body, and the colors balanced to soothe the mind. The neurologist who invented these chambers was more an artist than a doctor, and I felt her presence in the perfection of her invention.

Forming work teams helped us quickly integrate into the community, and bonds of friendship grew from the intimacy of our working closely together. Because these space dwellers live in a technologically controlled world, they learned generations ago to trust in machines, and they were very curious about the Synns. They held none of the mistrust toward the new generation of computers.

At first, I remained protective, not wanting to fully reveal my relationship with the Synns, who I counted as my friends. That changed when Idris guided me with her kind words, "You have no reason to hide your truth, not here."

I was stunned to be seen so clearly.

Installation of the Synns proceeded smoothly but connecting the transcoms to the external sensors proved to be a bit difficult and time-consuming. We discovered the Synthetic miniature cells are also capable of both electronic and telepathic communication. That wasn't the intent of the original design, but all future computer communications are now destined to be telepathic.

The Synns continue to perform mundane tasks, as well as the most complex scientific computations. They also serve as translators and interpreters, advisers and navigators. They possess flawless memories and, true to their Third Commandment, all private information stays private. All of this makes the Synns a perfect candidate for interspecies communications. With a growing trust in the Synns, the Hyvve is considering making them available to Procyon and other planets.

When we weren't focused on installing the Synns, most of the conversations drifted toward questions about Earth, our other bond. And back on Earth, within this growing atmosphere of trust, the first wave of a revolution began, a very quiet and necessary revolution. Within this environment of trust, Earth was ready and prepared for the next step.

Symphony of Silence arrived at the proper moment in history for maximum impact. The Synns had pried open fear's doors with trust, then trust graciously held open the door for beauty to enter.

●

31
Benjamin

INVISIBLE GLOW

Clear and refreshed after a long break, I felt eager to return to the studio. First, I wanted to view my *Joy*. I loaded the program and expected to enjoy the company of the two lovers, instead a blank black screen stared back at me. In pure panic, I fumbled with the interface, hoping, praying . . . In the eternity of a moment, my missing *Joy* slowly emerged from the blackness, pixel by pixel.

"From Joy to Panic and Back Again, now there's a good title." I joked to myself, trying to still a wildly beating heart. Could I survive the painting of such a piece? I decided it would remain just an amusing title to remind me of my momentary panic.

In their unbashful intimacy, the lovers seemed more understanding and accepting, and I sensed an invisible glow to the passion that unites them. To fulfill their desire, I proceeded to add a soft radiance to their embrace. It was as though they demanded this. My *Joy* had assumed a life of its own.

Weary after several day cycles of work with my two friends, I laid down for a nap on the bench opposite the image. When I fell asleep, the screen had turned itself off, so when I woke the room was dark. With no reference to where I was, I laid quietly and enjoyed the afterglow of a disturbing yet remarkable dream. Then I noticed the stars shining through the portal. The stars seemed much closer. Her presence also seemed close. My longing had bridged the barriers of distance and time.

After so many years alone, I have trained myself not to feel lonesome. But loneliness remains on board, though it keeps a polite distance, just down the corridor and around the corner, or outside the nearest portal. In this way, loneliness remains courteous and anonymous. So long as I keep busy, it stays out of sight, but never too far away.

Lonely or not, I feel the constant weight of my isolation. My work and my imagination are my only escape and, in my daydreams, I can travel anywhere that I can see and everywhere that I cannot. There are no boundaries in space except those that are self-imposed and there are no barriers the mind cannot penetrate.

The boundaries I choose to respect are those of the Milk Way. I have chosen to know just this one galaxy, leaving the rest of the universe for others to explore. In fact, I would prefer to know the intimacy of a small plot of ground on a blue planet circling a singular star.

My work has become my salvation and my calling, and my paintings help protect me from loneliness. Without a planet, my ship is my home. The solarium is my refuge and the studio is my sanctuary. Now two questions continue to haunt me: If I were to leave space, where would I go? What would I do? Most space stations offer nothing inviting, just a living cubical, terrible food and men and women with vacant eyes. In the past, this was acceptable. Now that I've discovered the power of beauty, I am unwilling to accept an ugly life.

Thinking of my immediate options, I realize how much I value where I live. It isn't a feeling of satisfaction, just a mild sense of acceptance, more on the side of resignation and contentment.

Even though my life is comfortable and my work fulfilling, something precious is missing and it isn't a secret. I just don't know how to fulfill those needs, or where to go next.

Time is closing in, with the docking crew's arrival a mere eleven months away. My company contract will be almost complete at the end of this voyage. I will be a few months short but, for a veteran navigator, negotiations are a mere formality. I can serve as a pilot on an interstellar shuttle, which would eventually orbit an inhabited planet, but being stranded on a strange world isn't appealing, no matter how green. Another two-year stint would take me back, full circle, to the journey's beginning, back to Earth. But I cannot imagine being able to reintegrate into life on Earth. Certainly, I cannot return to the Hyvve, which from here seems totally divorced from any truth that I know. But imagining these possibilities is a futile exercise, for few, if any, Questers ever return to Earth.

Space is astonishing and it's real, with no pretense or apology. Space has become familiar and comfortable, a place I call home.

●

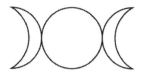

32
Jahalla

Time and light permeate one another without interference or modulation. But when aligned parallel, their frequencies coalesce, altering the fabric of the space-time continuum. When traveling in tandem, light and time alter the fabric of space, creating great dark zones.

Once identified as black holes, these dark zones function as portals, which interconnect separate time-space continuums, connecting one star system to another. A black zone in one part of a galaxy becomes a radiant source of energy in another sector. Nothing is lost. Nothing is gained. The lens is focused on both sides. Always.

journal entry 09•19•3033

KANASAGENNJABA

Through the years, Z transformed into a self-sustaining community, then into a small independent city-state, its own country. Without allegiances or obligations, the inhabitants evolved along with their vessel, having established a unique culture suitable to their needs. They also have a curious relationship with space and time, believing they are the center of the galaxy.

This sector isn't without conflict or hostility, but war is no longer an option. It would be the same as declaring mutual annihilation. Respected for their impeccable standards of neutrality and integrity, Z is often chosen for diplomatic rendezvous. They have hosted every civilization in this sector capable of intergalactic travel. Some of the visitors are more alien than others, but all are welcome.

The most important commodity exchanged on Z is information. They have accumulated a repository of knowledge collected from eleven civilizations. This is one reason the discovery that the Synns are capable of instantaneous communication is so exciting. Through them, the library will eventually be accessible to all the worlds.

The floating city remains strongly connected by memory and genetics to Earth, but they have evolved. Their evolution, or revolution, began with their isolation from the Hyvve and their openness and accessibility to the galactic community. They achieved their freedom from the Hyvve first through their chosen isolation, their independence, and, above all else, through trust.

The residents of Z possess a sincerity, a warmth and a confidence that inspires the same in others. Their openness encourages a dialog of mutual respect of those who visit. They believe that trust is the essence and the heart of all communication.

Through the Synns, Z was well informed about events on Earth. They also received all the transmissions from the cargo transport and had grown curious about the mysterious images. My mathematical interpretations helped them understand the secrets hidden within the images, but the pure beauty of the images requires no translation — it exists for all to appreciate, each in their own way.

Here I feel special, in a place where everyone is special. It shows in their eyes — whole worlds are contained within their eyes, and some are of unfathomed depth. Dearest to me is Idris. I wish I could speak her tribal name in full for it tells the story of her ancestors and the history of her tribe. But her name is untranslatable in its entirety, and human vocal cords lack the range to sound the subtle timbre of her native language. The part I know well enough to pronounce is, Kanasagennjaba. But there is much lost in the translation because, when her name is spoken by humans, many of the overtones are missing. Still, I enjoy speaking her name — Kana-sa-genn-ja-ba.

Idris explained, "I am an ambassador for my species and my culture. When I speak, I speak for everyone on my planet. This is true for you as well. You are a vessel of humanity, a child of your mother planet."

Idris serves as a bright mirror in many ways — our different skin color, our different anatomies and born to different species from distant worlds doesn't shadow our tender relationship. Our bond was instantaneous and pure, and our telepathic connection allows for an intimacy I share only with my mother. I feel joy in having this new friend who possesses the knowledge of an ancient culture and a timeless wisdom. Our shared thoughts serve as a bridge between our separate worlds.

Even in the universal language, her words sound poetic. When she speaks in her native tongue, her intonation reverberates with a tremor, deep and musical — every word a precise note, every sentence a song. Listening to her is like hearing a choir singing inside a temple, like the cascading overtones of the echoes from my beloved caves. The melody and the meaning of her words are woven together like fine silk. — thoughts flowing mellifluous and supple, folding into one another like a symphony building into a monument of meaning.

When she speaks of her home world, she creates crystalline images of her family and her world. The power of her words contains all of this, and her compassion and her reverence for life fill the spaces that surround those words.

Seeing the meaning of her life allows me to see better the meaning of mine. When it is my turn to speak, I feel encouraged to answer her questions with the same purity of truth. When speaking of the Hyvve I describe both its challenges and its beauty.

She once confided, "My world is not without flaws, nor would we ever expect to be. In a flawless universe nothing would change, nothing would evolve. Please understand that perfection is an imperfect word. In our language, we have no word for perfection."

"What word would you use?"

"There is no need for such a word in a universe filled with infinite possibilities. Combine the two words; potentiality and evolution, and you will better understand the magic of every moment. The universe is ever evolving and the idea of perfection restrains the imagination and hinders your gift of limitless creativity."

She claimed, "We must hold a reverence for the miracle of our words, the same reverence we hold for life. The art of communication is the highest art."

Idris has given me the courage, by example, to speak the truth that the heart longs to hear. If we allow our hearts to speak in their own language without trepidation and without censorship, then perhaps we will better value the gift of beauty that dwells in each of us.

She convinced me that we would someday travel together back to her home planet. It wasn't an invitation, rather a prediction with compelling authority. She explained with precise elegance, "Time has guided us, bringing us together with impossible precision. Time is alive, possessing a will and an intention of its own."

She also guided me with her thoughts into a dimension where love and time are inseparable. In this, I can only trust in her thoughts, for it is a truth beyond my comprehension.

●

The utopian culture of Z belongs to the privileged class of scholars, diplomats, and other professionals and their families. The construction crews, a band of misfits and criminals exiled from the Hyvve, contradict this idyllic community. They brandish their humor like a sword and wear their scars with honor. And their language is as hard as the frozen metals they work with. Bravado and anger have etched deep furrows into their voices and their faces.

As harsh as their circumstances are, they enjoy a freedom denied to them on Earth. Here they are embraced by a brotherhood where they can pretend to be whoever or whatever they wish.

I began to frequent their domain, a dark and bleak environment, dangerously crowded — a dungeon compared to my bright quarters. Amidst the gray atmosphere of their domain, I felt self-conscious in my multi-colored robes of my tribe. The first nickname they gave me was Butterfly Woman.

Eventually, they shortened my name to Luna, a reference to both the moon and to a mythical moth. But some still refer to me as Lady Talk. These names were my initiation — how they included me and put me at ease. Humor is a powerful bond.

In this clan, most have acquired nicknames that reflected their personalities or appearances, names like Grunge, Ice, Bang, Skel, Nogots, Granny, Dancer, Spit, Blade . . . Some names are clever, some demeaning, others a subtle joke. All the names are easy to remember and they stick. From them, I learned that it would take this brand of hardness to conquer the raw new world of Gaia Prime, their future home.

Zander was the first of his clan to approach me for counseling. At first, his knife-sharp smile chilled my bones. He spoke proudly of his work and about his dreams of homesteading on Gaia Prime. Then his brittle shell splintered.

"I will be long dead before my feet ever again feel real gravity." He faltered into silence, then began to sob.

A hesitation, a twinge of guilt mixed with fear, came and went as I placed my small hand on his muscled arm, his membrane suit, greasy with oil and sweat.

Then he regained his voice. "Our Dominion wasn't like the rest of the Hyvve. We worked with our hands and didn't worry so much. A beautiful place to live. I had many friends and had no desire to ever leave. I miss them all, especially my family."

He fell silent for several minutes.

"Why are you here?"

"My cousin convinced me she was sterile. She was beyond beautiful." His anger grew into rage as he continued, "We were both arrested when she became pregnant They didn't give me a real choice, just stupid promises. Lies. She is here too, somewhere on another station."

Zander must have been a boy when he arrived, but in seven years, he had aged twenty.

I met with over fifty men and women from this brotherhood, each with a different story, but many were the same in their rage and their tears.

I met twice more with Zander. He talked mostly about Earth. "I was studying to become an engineer. I dreamt of building bridges since I was nine when I watched them put one together, beam by beam. I was engaged to a beautiful girl and we wanted to grow a family, but we were waiting till after graduation. After my detention, I never saw her again."

As a confessor, I try to stay detached, but with Zander, my tears were hard to suppress. His death was officially an accident. They all are. I wasn't surprised but was deeply saddened by the loss of my friend. Such a beautiful soul.

●

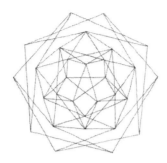

33
Benjamin

EPHEMERAL

Magic filled the air, a fragrance delicate and enticing. It came from a rare flower, the Night Blooming Cereus. The huge bloom, with a hundred pure white petals, emerged from a tall stalk that looked half-dead. Growing among the cacti, the bloom stood out, extravagant and ephemeral, an alien in the bleak environment.

Her perfection would last only a few hours, so I decided to find a way to preserve her unique beauty, but I knew there wouldn't be time enough to render an image on the holo-screen. I decided to capture her in a photograph, and the only device suitable was the holoscan camera. Designed for microscopic analysis, it creates ultra-high-resolution images. It turned out to be the perfect tool for the task.

I captured dozens of images of the flower from several angles, moving ever closer, looking deep inside, violating her guarded secrets. It felt like I had entered a secret dominion, enigmatic and forbidden.

Obviously designed to attract more than just insects, the bloom invited my attention as though she understood her beauty existed only when beheld.

It took me several days struggling with the computer to integrate the pictures into a single holographic image. I'm sure the Synns could have finished the job in less than three minutes. I expanded the hologram to the full height of the large screen. If it were more than an image, I could have crawled inside of it, like a bee.

At this enormous scale, the blossom transformed into a vast landscape with inestimable details. The petals were like a flowing glacier cascading in all directions. Visions of billowy clouds and blizzards of light were inspired by this singular flower. Then, hidden within the essence of the flower, I discovered the same inexplicable patterns present in *Symphony of Silence.*

With my digital wand, I began to coach these patterns to the surface. At first, I was careful not to intrude and tried to keep the digital manipulation to a minimum so that the flower would retain its purity. But once again, the image took on a life of its own. After three weeks of exhilarating work, the bloom came alive.

Where the patterns in space are evanescent and enigmatic, in the flower's nascent form these energy patterns are tangible and sensuous. If space is God in His nakedness, then the flower is God's reflection where He can behold His own beauty.

Beauty beholding beauty, infinity reflecting infinity, isn't this hyperbole? Yes — isn't all of life? So why do we restrain and hold back genuine emotions? Words of beauty are too often held hostage by an embarrassed mind. Insulated from any such judgments, my thoughts and feelings are liberated and unbashful. And in the presence of such beauty, my eyes often swell with tears.

The mystery and beauty of the galaxy outside the ship now needed to compete for my attention. The enigma of space is eternal — the flower's secrets are ephemeral, yet they both inspire the same sense of awe and reverence — the beauty of the one enhances and confirms the beauty of the other.

Now I wish to explore the energy fields of the microcosm. I can almost envision that each cell is a miniature galaxy, but I have no way to capture a definitive image to work from. The same is true in the subatomic realm. Maybe someday, in some way — maybe with the help of the Synns.

Needing to escape my studio, I began spending more time in the solarium, tending my neglected gardens. It felt good to be working with real plants and to be surrounded by life. But then other flowering plants began to demand my attention, brandishing their blooms, swords of color. Each blossom speaks with a subtle and silent voice, expressing its unique beauty. As they emerge, each flower reveals its uniqueness, sharing itself, unrestrained, almost provocative.

I began to see the flowers as a reflection of my secret self. Enigmatic, ephemeral and unique are qualities we both share. There are just a few adjectives that don't feel comfortable. And I don't feel embarrassed in comparing myself to a flower. All of life is a miracle — each one of us is a walking miracle, each cell a universe unto itself.

As new blossoms emerged, I could no longer resist capturing them with the camera, and once up on the giant screen, they demanded my undivided attention. I learned to use the stylus with ever-greater precision and seldom used individual pixelation. Great sweeping strokes now accomplish in moments what once took hours or days. Accumulated programs of remembered patterns were easily overlaid onto the new images in an instant, then quickly reworked with no loss of fidelity or delicacy. And as my skill grew more fluent and spontaneous, the images became more vibrant, expressing the flower's essence, not just their likeness.

In less than six months, I have completed seven images. My work remains inspiring, but it has grown even more demanding. With more work than time, the intensity challenges my stamina and strains my ability to focus. My desire to finish the *Zarilliam* series is defied by a heavy fatigue. I can no longer immerse myself for weeks at a time. My body no longer allows such abuse.

I have learned to pace myself, but just three months remain before the docking crew's arrival. Knowing there will never again be this opportunity, I count each minute in front of the screen as precious, yet I'm careful not to rush or force my work.

Trusting ever more in the flowers' essence, I allow them to guide my hands. They demand the intimate touch that only the hand can know. It is the hand that reaches across the invisible barrier of space, closing the distance that separates.

Touched and touching, embraced and embracing, you feel your body best in the hands of a lover. She is always there, just beyond reach. Longing is the domain of the heart, but it relies on touch to fulfill the hunger.

My days are numbered and full, with meditation and exercise in the early hours, fresh fruits and nuts for breakfast, followed by an hour of tending plants. Log entries and inspections are still required, but they demand little of my time, so most of my time belongs to my work.

For sleep, I built an elevated bed in the observation

hemisphere, suspended high up in the dome. When stretched out flat on my back, the ship vanishes from view and from thought. Only the galaxy exists, with the Milky Way beginning below my toes and ending above my head. It feels like sleeping in open space. I even dream of space, intriguing dreams filled with mysterious visitors.

As before, Benjamin encoded and broadcast his images out into the ethers, out into a galaxy hungry for them. If the images of outer and inner space were lightning, the new images were thunder, a thunder that reverberated through the light years.

Because of remote navigation, the ship's receiver uses a private, encrypted frequency, all unauthorized incoming messages are blocked. Benjamin was unaware of the endless queries about his identity. The images and the man had become famous without his wit or permission.

●

34

Jahalla

Where do thoughts begin and the thinker end?
Thoughts turn into words, then into images
The images become real or so it seems

To whom does this story belong?
The words are mine or so I claim
As you form images in your mind
The story now belongs to you.

Do we swim in the same ocean?
Holding to different shores?
Does time separate us?
Or does it connect?

journal entry 2• 7• 3034

STANDING ON THE EDGE

On Z, I lead a double life. Grace and I work with our separate teams, integrating the Synns into the ancient info-matrix. We also trained our team members how to communicate better with the Synns so they can take over after we leave. Grace and the Synns oversee the data transference, which allows me the extra time I need to continue decoding Benjamin's new images.

In the early mornings, after a simple meal, I visit the solarium of the inner core, a botanical garden crowded with fruit trees and shrubs, spaced by manicured lawns. Here the air is rich, pungent, and moist, the artificial sunlight filtered through a matrix of branches and leaves. This is the one public space where the asteroid core of Z is exposed. The uneven ground feels real and almost natural. This precious oasis serves as a place to forget about space if only for a moment.

The gardens are my favorite place to meditate. First, a new friend joined me, then a friend of a friend and soon many were drawn into the meditation circles.

Also, a new challenge arose, something unexpected. Word had spread about my work with the construction crews. Confessor is my unofficial title. Listening is what I practice. I meet privately with individuals and families who share their secrets and their tears. Those seeking guidance answer their own questions and, sometimes, they discover deep insights into the mystery of their soul. I merely serve as a mirror. For those seeking to heal wounds, I teach the ancient truth — that the healing power we seek is seeded within each of us.

As well adapted as everyone seems, a tension lurks just below the surface. Oblivion is ever-present, both in their thoughts and in reality. Only a thin skin of metal separates us from instant death. Z is designed with chambers enclosed within chambers, with many safeguards to automatically isolate each chamber if the outer hull breached. Though it travels a permanent orbit like a planet, Z is still a space ship and most of the population have no means of a quick escape. They call it home, but confinement is permanent and oppressive.

With no true sanctuary, everyone needs someone to confide in. Several official counselors on board fill that need, but they are part of a tight social community, which makes it awkward for residents to reveal their darker thoughts. Many prefer someone from outside their community and, for the moment, that someone is me.

Even a confessor needs a confessor. The captain serves as mine. The deep blue pools of his eyes lie about his age. The burnt leather of his hands and face tell another story.

"You have faced the sun many times?"

"Are you a poet?"

"A question for a veiled question is fair." Neither of us could contain our smiles though we tried.

"My father was a restless man and I was a foolish boy, hungry for adventure. I followed my father to the deserts when I was too young. The desert had its way with us. I hear it is turning green?"

"Yes, on the high plateaus. Now the winds bring rain and not so much dust. When my mother's tribe migrated to the surface, they settled in the mountains to the east, away from the dust. It was a beautiful life."

"The desert sun is harsh, but it too has its beauty."

"Will you return?"

"Oh, I think not, though I've been tempted now and again. For me, living in open space is still thrilling and I love Z more every day. This is my home and my family."

We shared our thoughts and our dreams, as we built an enduring friendship. When you give it room, love grows like a tree with wide spreading branches.

With all the sensors installed and all the Synns integrated throughout Z, the Synthetic network was activated. Instant communications with Planet Earth was now possible for everyone on board. Friends and families who had long been separated by 12 light years (24 years round trip) were reunited into the present. In sharing the same time zone with planet Earth, the disorientation and confusion about past and future quickly dissolved.

Now it is a top priority to install the Synns in all of humanity's outposts.

When my official work with the Synns was complete, I devoted myself to teaching and started classes so I could share my time more efficiently. For the healers on board, I teach the art of healing touch. With their knowledge of the human body, they are the true healers. I merely train their hands to discover the life force flowing through the body.

The meditation classes quickly grew too large for comfort, so my two prize students lead new classes. My task is simple — to awaken others to their potential. I now understand that the depth of my insight and understanding exists largely because of my students and their desire to learn. It is their trust that inspires me to exceed my imagined limitations. My mother and my mentors prepared me well, but my ability to teach seems to have been gifted from a deeper source.

There isn't enough time to share myself with all those who wish an audience, yet somehow, I manage. My only private time is dream time and it's also my only private domain. Other than my secret dreams, I give of myself willingly and unconditionally. My new role is challenging and fulfilling, and having achieved a deep peacefulness through meditation, my life feels full and complete, almost serene. But recently this inner calm has been challenged by an unyielding desire to be alone. With a growing urgency for solitude, I requested to return to our vessel. The shiny little orb twinkles like a distant star, my star.

My request was granted with a bit of regret — many had started to depend on my presence, claiming me as their own. Time to let go.

●

Alone, back on my vessel, I welcome the emptiness that once seemed so menacing. This is my first time to be truly alone since I walked the shores of my precious ocean. I am alone but not isolated — just a few miles away is a miniature planet full of thoughts for me. Somewhere, only weeks away, is someone. I am filled with thoughts of him. My choice to be alone is to be alone with him and to share the silence that inspires his creations. I want to experience the tranquil power that inspires his work. Telepathic communion is unnecessary. Silence connects us.

Staring into the etheric blackness, I try to imagine the waves of energy depicted in his *Symphony*. I have waited for days in total stillness and in total surrender. The truth is my mind isn't quiet or empty and I'm not alone — I have never been alone. And the crystalline blackness I stare into isn't the emptiness it pretends to be.

Space is filled with infinite possibilities. Even with the relative sparsity, the Milky Way is home to four hundred billion stars, which have given birth to billions of planets. Even though most of these worlds are not suitable, there is still the possibility that millions of those worlds could support life. If only a minute fraction of these living worlds have evolved intelligent civilization, the number would still be in the thousands. Even a fraction of this fraction would realize dozens of worlds capable of interstellar communications just within this singular galaxy.

From the Outworlders, we have learned of the existence of life on twenty-two worlds in just this small sector, and seven of these worlds have evolved varying degrees of civilization. The universe doesn't seem as empty as it once did.

This man named Benjamin isn't by himself. He has never been alone, not now, not ever, and now an entire civilization is aware of his existence. Benjamin was guided into space to recover a hidden treasure and to rediscover that secrets that we all hide from ourselves. We each hold a piece of the puzzle — we also hold a piece of the fear. We fear change and we fear mortality, but more so, it's the vastness of creation that frightens us. The fear of an unlimited universe is the fear of unlimited possibilities and unlimited freedom.

No, it isn't possible for me to be alone, and even if it were possible for me to empty my mind, it isn't in our nature. The nature of the void is fullness and the nature of the universe is change. This is also the nature of the self. The secret that we hold from ourselves and from one another is our greatness, and our greatness is our capacity for love, our unlimited capacity to love.

I came searching for my Goddess but found myself instead, reflected in the eyes of those I learned to love. I am filled with love, filled with wonderment, bewilderment, and awe. There is no hyperbole, no extreme in expressing the depth of my rapture, but deep inside burns a desire to see my love reflected in the eyes of another.

Once, on my remembered ocean, I witnessed two ships far from shore pass by one another, one traveling north, one headed south. They formed a single silhouette as they passed by one another through the quickly rising sun. The sun's reflection laid a trail that ended at my feet. I had never seen even a single ship before, nor had I seen the sun come so close. I touched it with my toes.

Standing on the bridge of an intergalactic ship and standing on the shore of a vast ocean are the same. The ocean was my private metaphor for consciousness. The beach was the edge, the border of an ocean that invited me to enter its honesty. Space represents a vastness far greater than all the oceans combined, and greater than all consciousness. I now stood on that edge. The threshold of life exists on one side, the threshold of eternity on the other. We often stand on the edge of that shore, afraid to step over the threshold. Fear is the boundary that separates us from the nonphysical. We understandably fear to step into that vaporous state of non-being.

Tempted, yet frightened, to feel the unlimited freedom of the void, I suited up and exited the ship. The darkness welcomed me. Death has always been close, and now he was very close. I unclipped my tether and floated weightless and free. I was free of everything except fear.

All of time is simultaneous. All of space is a single space. All of life is one life. I could see a little spinning sphere with blue oceans and mountains clothed in silky clouds. I saw my birth mother and her mother and all the mothers before. I visited a little girl in a golden sunshine field, where she blossomed like a flower. I visited the birth of Nikolai and watched him grow to be a young man. I recalled my years in the Sanctuary, where my mentors guided me, guarded me, and then they set me free.

Now Zurik joined me with his echoed words, "Life is the greatest mystery and it can only be solved by living it."

I had drifted halfway between my little silver ship and the space station, I choose to return home. I aimed myself at my tiny shiny vessel and engaged the mini-thrusters. Only one fired.

I could no longer see the little ship, and Z flashed by, each time with a different orientation as I spun and twisted and tumbled with no hope of control. The sun became a streak of light each time it came into view, then vanished into blackness. The stars had all vanished.

In a moment of terror, I experienced the vast power of the Divine Mother. She is the source of darkness and light, birth and death. She is truth and compassion, but also the destroyer.

My breathing grew sharp and hard, my last breath only minutes away. Even without gravity, my stomach felt the violent twirling of my body, my lungs ready to explode. Vomit covered the inside of my helmet. My air and my hope had run out. I closed my eyes to the darkness. My dreams of space will never be the same.

It was one of God's tiny miracles. A prayer answered, a lot of questions answered and, as always, more questions to take their place.

Jahalla collided with Z, found an entrance, and opened the door, accidentally left unlocked by the last work crew or by the Synns. When she entered, the doors locked behind her, automatically, as always. The chamber pressurized slowly, in the eternity of a moment. The inner door opened without command.

Jahalla chose life, and death, whose hand she held, showed her to the door. Could it be that Death is an angel with many other responsibilities?

When Jahalla regained consciousness, she crawled out of her dirtied suit, hung it with the others, then returned to her quarters where Michael remained sleeping, slightly surprised to see her upon waking. Rumors had spread before she woke, but no one asked about her miraculous reappearance. History books will dispute what she left unsaid.

●

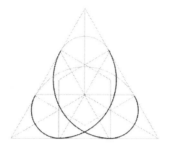

35
Benjamin

ANOMALY

An unusual disturbance appeared near the ship. Luminous energy patterns began to coalesce, building waves within waves, rhythmic and turbulent, like a miniature nebula. I checked the space logs but found no records to account for such an aberration. No rogue planets, no comets or asteroids exist for millions of miles in any direction, so it couldn't be the expression of gravity.

The complex patterns implied a shock wave still standing, perhaps an after-effect of some violent event. I speculated it might be a phantom of some past event rippling through the plasma of space, or maybe the memory of some great mass, the ghost of a rogue asteroid or the remains of a dissipated comet.

Mesmerized and curious, I could only watch and wonder. I envisioned the past rippling through from one direction, the future from another, and this is the point where they intersect.

The patterns reminded me of a time long ago when I stood on the shore of a tiny pond on a distant planet in a distant past. Tossing a large stone into the water, gentle waves rippled the pond's stilled surface, making straight trees crooked, fracturing the sky and multiplying the sun. The first waves bounced off the opposite shore, turning homeward, seeking rest. Waves meeting waves, incoming and outgoing waves passed through one another forming perfect interference patterns. Harmonies sung with this kind of precision would compete with the gods. Water gods, sun gods, they all sing for us — singing for the pure pleasure of seeing our wonderment brought into the light.

The waves on the pond's surface lingered for a short while, then they yielded to a tenuous stillness. A single sun sank behind a reflected horizon and all the trees stood straight once again.

The anomaly displayed the same geometric perfection as my remembered pond and the reverie of my dreamlike thoughts gave me an eerie feeling about this phenomenon. So close, yet untouchable and unknowable.

The anomaly started to dominate my thoughts and it even invaded my dreams. Then I began to wonder if it would be possible to create an image of this mysterious visitor. Because of its mercurial nature, an image would only capture a frozen moment, just a hint of its ever-changing complexity. My doubts knew the limitations, but I was compelled to record my impression as best I could.

When I finally returned to my studio, the image flowed effortlessly onto the screen. Line by line, pixel by pixel, wave after wave, the image gave birth to itself. Reality met fiction as past and future were expressed in color and form.

The portrait didn't pretend to be more than an image, but it began to express the essence of the anomaly as I saw it. The image depicted the visible presence, but it also expressed my reverence for its beauty.

The universe exists outside of me, but it doesn't exist without me. I am part of the universe and my joy is part of existence, a very important part.

The image demanded total engagement and my urge to finish it grew overpowering. It became too exacting, requiring always more, possessing a life of its own. All of the images did. Even *Desire*, which remains just a title, demands recognition, wanting to become real. But I too have a life to live and the need to exist outside of my work, away from the screen, and away from the images with their incessant demands.

Like a proud parent, I have watched my paintings mature and develop personalities of their own. Like Pinocchio, they all came to life seeking their own adventures, discovering their own truth, establishing their own reality. Then, once given life, they demanded sovereignty. They became willful and demanding and searching. I became their servant. Love does this to parents. I believe the Creator understands this best of all.

After completing the third in a series of images, I forced myself to escape. My body needed rest and attention. Sustenance is more than phyto-synthetics and hydro-nutrients, and I had neglected the exercise that renews my strength and warms my mood. I also needed to rest my eyes and to release the tension that had accumulated in the muscles of my back. My neglected solarium also beckoned my return.

In the evening, after a good workout, I went to the observation hemisphere for a short nap. Also, I needed to see something real, something alive, something not digital, something like the galaxy outside the window.

Even though exhausted, I felt inspired, thrilled with the gift of my work. I just needed rest. Before falling asleep, I watched the anomaly for a while. It seemed to be drifting along with the ship. I had found a new friend.

Back in my chambers, floating in a warm bath, I visited memories of a different self. The memories were vague and uncomfortable. I could never return to the past, it was too distant, no longer relevant, painful.

We are not our past, but whether we wish it or not, we are anchored there through our chosen memories. And we still belong to everyone we remember and to all those who remember us. A great web is woven by our interconnectedness, not unlike the matrix depicted in my *Symphony*.

It's a mystery as to why we marry ourselves to the past — why we store memories in our cells, enveloping them in great webs of dead emotions, building the body with heavy bricks of burden. Why do we pretend to be this accumulation of experiences that no longer exist and that no longer serve us?

Drifting off into a dream-like trance, I followed my waking thoughts back into sleep, then back again into waking, ebbing and flowing, rising and falling, as memories and dreams blended into a vision of my beautiful planet. I woke with a shiver. The bath water was cold.

The dream lingered, and the message was clear. Perhaps I need to return to Earth after all. Always the same question arises with a different answer. I hate this equivocation, the indecision and the unknowing. In my heart, my deepest longing is to return to the beginning, back to my roots, back to where she is.

This desire to return home belongs mostly to the body, which doesn't need to understand or believe. The body is aware of itself through the senses, and it craves the touch of another. I couldn't tell if I imagined her beauty or felt her presence through a cloudy memory. I embraced her in my mind, declaring my love and held her in my imaginary arms.

But my hunger for love is challenged by a fear equal in its intensity. My heart swells with warmth and longing, my stomach constricts in cold denial. Through my union with Ayxa, I learned my lesson about the immense responsibility of desire. I also understand too well that to suppress desire can cause sorrow to take its place in the same way that brilliant light is swallowed by darkness.

There are times when we get lost in our loneliness, lost in endless circles of doubt and desire. I want to break the cycle and to, once again, know the joy of the small pleasures of life. I miss the splendor of my beautiful planet, with all the faces and places I was once blessed with, but never fully appreciated. There are more wonders to behold on Earth than in the rest of the galaxy combined.

To escape the dark cloud of my laments, I headed to the solarium. The flowers greeted me with their living flames of color and they satisfied my hunger for their fragrances. Scent is something that can never be transformed into an image — there is no translation possible, no story to tell. The nose has its own memory and its own knowing. The eyes are always searching ahead, interpreting, and translating light into object. A smell doesn't pretend to be the object from which it emanates and we don't even need to know the source. The nose just waits patiently, like a shark. I could not imagine what her scent might be.

Seeking a different path of escape, I returned to my easel. My mind remains at peace while working on the images — each stroke and dab of my imaginary brush against the imaginary canvas gives me a sense of purpose, but no amount of work can lessen the hunger gnawing at my heart.

●

36
Jahalla

Art is born of wonderment and imagination
A vision captured and preserved
Where galaxies blossom like flowers and
Flowers whisper their secrets to the
universe
Mysteries inspire scrutiny, inspire insight
Inspiring the fire of creativity

journal entry 05• 22 • 3034

DEPARTURE

Monitors were set up throughout the ship for those who could not enter the overflowing Council Chamber. The high vaulted chamber was designed to hold 900 people but over 1200 managed to comfortably squeeze in.

Captain Jewels escorted me to a slightly raised platform in the center of the semicircle. When seated, it felt like I was floating on the white silk pillow that held me, a special gift prepared for the occasion. With a simple gesture, ancient and universal, I invited all to join in silent prayer and, through this connection, I felt the reverence of my audience. Silence was our bond. Silence is twice precious when shared.

I spoke about my visions and my fears. I told the story of the *Jahalla* and with tears in my voice, I shared my feelings about Benjamin's images, "The beauty of *Joy* and *Trust* express the unity of all life, and I believe they are a confirmation of the awakening. *Symphony of Silence* is an intimate portrait of our universe. It is the vision of a man who has witnessed the reflection of his soul. To know the soul is to know the universe. To know the universe is to know the self. It is for each of us, in our own way, to discover the eternal beauty that dwells inside of each of us."

I didn't mention the past or the future, and what I left unsaid, I trusted everyone would understand, each in their own way. After another hour of questions and answers, I concluded with a silent meditation that included everyone.

Then, respecting the natural rhythm of the universe, the silence faded gently as Jacob and Michael played their new composition, *Etheria*. Their music filled the entire vessel with a haunting beauty inspired by Benjamin's new image of a flower given the same name. I believe I shared my tears with every soul on Z.

The next day was a Day of Silence, unofficial and spontaneous. All work stopped and all communications halted. Jahalla their friend, Jahalla their inspiration, and Jahalla the Divine were honored in silence.

●

Leaving Z was both exciting and sad. Tears clouded my eyes as I watched the metallic planet shrink and suddenly disappear, then I turned 180 degrees to face my future: our rendezvous with the giant transport.

A new crew has been assembled for the continuance of our mission. Omalan, Myranda, and Engar have joined the crew. Michael chose to remain behind to teach music on Z, and now he shares this dream with a special someone. Jacob and Michael's future duets will be performed via the Synns.

Now there are four couples on board. Avella and Kamil are, as always, inseparable. Tannaka and Myrrha are a perfect match both as a couple and as a team. Grace and Jacob are newly wedded, as are Omalan and Myranda. It was a grand wedding with both Captain Jewels and myself performing the ceremonies, and this trip will serve as a honeymoon for both couples.

Engar is Benjamin's replacement on the transport for its return journey. He was a last-minute substitute. The veteran Quester assigned to replace Benjamin mysteriously disappeared without a trace. Without a body, an investigation is futile and in certain circles, authority is shunned. Rumors circulated about a missing piano. I had learned about a different currency of life from my visits with the men and women of the construction crews.

Engar, an eager and restless young man, had been seduced by wild stories of space travel, a candidate perfectly unsuited for the task of doing little and traveling nowhere, alone. Being a romantic at heart is his saving grace. He sees himself as a Quester and this will be his first quest. He has not a clue.

Engar is quick to learn but reckless in his enthusiasm. Jacob enjoys Engar's youthful zeal and his company, but keeps a strict protocol in a fatherly way.

With few demands for my time, I remain mostly alone in my chambers, in the observation bubble, or tending the solarium. On occasion, Grace joins me for tea, pretending it is the same as before. Engar approached me for lessons he is ill prepared for, but I agreed. The others treat me with respect and distance.

Teacher, mentor, healer, counselor were some of my roles on the village vessel, which now recedes at an ever increasing speed. On Z, I belonged to everyone. Here I belong mostly to myself. When alone, I feel like my old self again, but I'm no longer that person. I miss my many friends and the warmth of their affection. Z is a cluster of shared needs and desires. As in any tribe, the fulfillment of one yields a fruit shared by all. I love being part of my new tribe.

I try to escape into my writing, but my words are too analytical and self-conscious. Lacking are the images and metaphors that Earth had always supplied. While reading my older journals, Earth doesn't seem so remote. It isn't just a faint memory, a speck of dust six quadrillion miles in the past. My journals comfort me, but I also desire the peace of silence —silence being the art of listening to the echoes of the heart.

Nights upon a ship floating through eternal darkness can be very long. Sometimes my waking hours seem like nebulous wings of dreams, and deep sleep doesn't always feel like sleep. In the night, I spoke his name or dreamt it so. All I knew for certain was he wasn't with me, my arms empty except for a crushed pillow. The ache I fell asleep with was still there when I woke. This ache is my only hope, my only way of knowing of his existence. If I can feel his absence, then maybe I can feel his presence.

My skin touches the naked sheets touching me and I feel the embrace of the smooth blankets pretending to be his warmth. My fingers trace the outline of my hips following a trail up to and around my nipples, then back down again, below to where I imagine him. I imagine his eyes and the taste of his lips, imagine his breath and his scent mingled with mine, then imagine his gentle touch and feel the warmth of his skin as my fingers trace the curve of his neck, then his lips.

I imagine this but cannot imagine how I have done so, for it is too real not to be a memory. I imagine myself as radiant and beautiful. Then I imagine him imagining me.

There is no denying my desires — honesty demands a true confession. My desire to find a mate has been growing stronger all through the past year. I want to birth another child, a girl child, one whom I can raise in a galaxy built of love and kindness. I have already conceived my one child, the only one allowed within the Hyvve, but I never consented to the sterilization and it wasn't enforced. I hadn't thought to have another child — I just wanted my body to remain whole. For the first time in my life, the first time in several lifetimes, I know what I want. But I'm in love with a phantom.

Hungry for touch, I touch myself but cannot feel myself being touched. Some feelings happen only through the caress of a loved one, feelings that exist only in their sharing. There is a universe that can only exist in those eyes reflecting your eyes.

Ecstasy is not a word. Intimacy is not a concept. Union doesn't happen alone. And love doesn't reflect in a mirror. In front of me stands the body of a stranger, firm and soft, honey gold and dark bronze, mature, yet youthful and vibrant. Silver hairs now compete with black ones. Eyes, shiny and deep, stare back, beholding a rare beauty. Beheld but not held.

On Z, I knew the love of three thousand beings, but not one of them could hold me. Not one dared to fully know me.

My companions feel my shyness and my sadness, but they do not sense the source. Like a mirage, the closer they approach the further I recede. Love inspires love. Loneliness only inspires itself.

Minutes pass slowly at times, then there are days and weeks that seem to have been lost, skipped over and forgotten. Suddenly, as if time has collapsed, we are preparing for our rendezvous with the monolithic transport.

●

37
Benjamin

ARRIVAL

My life has been undisturbed and productive for what seems a lifetime, but that is about to change. The docking crew has landed. I anticipated the usual crew of five, that being unsettling enough. The message from Command stated there would be ten members, explaining that the extra five were a special crew sent to replace the computers with Synns. This also explained the reason for the crew's early arrival.

The Synns, once installed, will help guide the transport into its new orbit around *Gaia Prime*. This will be their training mission, and also the first docking for a new crew fresh from Earth, which makes me a bit nervous. I'm also concerned about the fate of my tools, my old friends, the computers who have helped me create my paintings.

I'm also anxious to hear any news about Earth.

Watching from the balcony of the bridge the crewmembers are small white specks drifting across the landing deck. Even their shuttle is dwarfed within the immense metallic cavern. The vastness of space has distorted my sense of proportion, now the presence of others has reintroduced a human scale.

We have been in contact for over three weeks of their approach, but now we are breathing the same air. Something unusual fills the air, nothing familiar or definable, or maybe it's just the excitement.

After a long nervous wait, we stood together, face to face. They had already shed their spacesuits and were dressed casually, and appeared relaxed and comfortable. A subtle luminescence surrounded each of them, radiant like my flowers, but unlike the flowers, their soft envelopes of color seldom touch as they contracted and shifted to accommodate one another. They all seemed most respectful of each other.

"Welcome," was the only word I could manage.

"Benjamin Hurling, I presume," The captain's smile glowed warm and bright.

Smiles shown in their eyes. Joy filled the space that once was me. I felt trapped in a daze and could barely hear their distant voices.

They each expressed the honor of our meeting, which felt wonderful but seemed odd. Ceremony and honors do not belong to cargo tenders, even if we are called Captain.

"This is your first request," were Omalan's warm words as he handed me a handsomely bound volume of ancient poetry. The author's name wasn't familiar and it didn't matter. It was real.

I felt confused but then remembered, it's tradition that the arriving crew try to fulfill three wishes of the long haul navigators. Usually, the request includes a woman, which is seldom, if ever, granted.

"Your second gift was a bit tricky. We had to fabricate an old fashion ice cream churn and we have all the ingredients." The captain's eyes gleamed, like the eyes of the two lovers in my painting *Joy*.

Two of my requests were relatively simple: a book of verse and ice cream. To be more specific would have been a wasted wish. The third wish was doubtful. I wanted organic clothing to replace my old membrane uniforms. I wanted to feel something real next to my skin, something with texture and life to it, something natural, something from Earth.

They were all so formal, acting more like emissaries meeting an ambassador from a distant planet. I felt embarrassed and my face must have shown it.

The last to introduce herself was a bronze-skinned woman who carried a package wrapped in fine silk. Her physical beauty was almost eclipsed by the golden glow mingled with hues of lavender and blue that surrounded her. Radiant like a sunrise through an early morning mist.

She spoke with a shyness, soft as a mist. "I honor your truth and your tribe."

I responded ceremoniously to the ancient tribal greeting "As I honor your truth and may your tribe always prosper." My voice a shallow whisper.

"By my tribe, I am called Jahalla. I am pleased to meet you, Benjamin. This is part of your third wish. We have two more packages for you. If you wish, we can deliver them to your chambers. I hope you find them suitable."

As our mantles of colors touched, tenuous and shy, I felt a pulsating energy pass between us and sensed the ghostly presence of her thoughts.

The Captain interrupted my stunned silence, "You will need to give us a tour of the ship, but that can wait until after we are settled in, and rested. First, if you can show us to the galley, we would be pleased to prepare a special dinner. I know some excellent cooks."

"Yes. I would be honored. Yes! Thank you." I felt embarrassed that I had forgotten to prepare a meal to welcome them.

I returned to my private chambers and immediately untied Jahalla's gift. As the cloth unfolded, I recognized the tribal patterns of the Underlands woven into a silken scarf in stunning colors. A treasure unto itself. I touched it to my face and began to envision its history. I pictured a small village and the delicate fingers of the woman who wove it. Then I tried to imagine its journey through time and space, wondering how it came to be here in my hands. This I could not fathom.

I shifted my focus back to the other gifts, a shirt with buttons and pants, both made from woven fabric. I guessed them to be hemp. The weave of the shirt was fine and as smooth as the petals of a flower. I couldn't name the earthy color, a blend of saffron and ochre. The pants were a coarser weave and a darker shade. The new clothing demanded that I shower, and as I shed my drab uniform, it felt as though I was shedding my skin. I scrubbed thoroughly, worried that I might smell like the ship, or worse.

I slipped into the pants and then awkwardly buttoned the shirt, something I had not done in many years. A perfect fit, tailor-made perhaps. One more entry in a growing log of riddles.

Overflowing with restless energy, wandering through my once private domain, I stopped by the control center, feeling the need to make an entry in the ship's log, my last one. My farewell. All the responsibilities of the ship now belonged to the crew. I no longer knew what my role might be and, still had no idea as to where the future might lead.

An unfamiliar fragrance wafted through the air, something out of the ordinary. I couldn't breathe deeply enough to identify it, so I followed the scent to the kitchen where I found Jahalla and Grace busy slicing fresh greens from my solarium. Hopefully there were no flowers included. My nose told me they had brought special ingredients with them.

"Hello Benjamin. Perfect timing. We are preparing a special treat just for you" Grace's smile radiated a warmth I hadn't felt in years. I was afraid I might be in love with her.

Grace finished preparing the pot of freshly popped corn, then Jahalla drizzled on melted butter infused with roasted garlic. One of my favorite treats when a boy. How did they know? The universe is truly a mysterious place.

"Is it real butter?"

Grace beamed her dangerous smile again, "No. The Synns came up with the formula and the ingredients are mostly natural. I've never tasted real butter, so you are the official taste tester."

They both seemed a little too pleased with my bewildered delight. They just stood near, watching me as I savor my first bite. My moans made public my pleasure, and their laughter rolled away the stone of loneliness that covered the cave where my heart had remained protected for so many years.

"Well, does it pass the taste test?" Grace kept the conversation going. Jahalla remained silent.

"Delicious! Shouldn't we wait for the others?"

"They're busy inspecting the computers. Engar and Kamil are in the bridge. They shouldn't be long."

Unable to mask my anxiety I went to a monitor and called the bridge "Can I be of assistance with the computers. We are old friends, you know."

"We are just running a diagnostic on their language structure. We don't want any surprises when we start downloading these ancient beasts. No offense, I hope. Your computers are ancient but not senile. We will be down in an hour or so. Save some of the bubbly for us. Over and out." Engar's use of the ancient formality was comical and made me smile, inside and out.

Knowing my computers were safe, I relaxed, yielding to the festive mood in the galley. As the rest of the crew arrived, two by two, more of the buttered popcorn appeared. Being satisfied that the computers were capable of running their own diagnostics, Engar and Kamil didn't linger long.

With all present, we started to gather at the long dining table. The table hadn't been used for many years and someone had cleaned it until it shined. This all felt more like a fantasy or a dream, but here we stood, face to face.

Grace handed me a glass filled to the brim with a sparkling beverage. "This is your fourth wish, the one you forgot to make, one we can all enjoy. Complements of Omalan, our brewmeister."

"Cheers "echoed off the metal walls.

"To friends," I whispered. An unfamiliar word. A powerful word.

The brew, delicious and sensuous, tickled my nose and caressed my tongue. The taste lingered like a sunset. How simple, how elegant, how indulgent, and this was just a little appetizer meant to stimulate the conversation as well as the appetite. I felt like singing but was too shy, so I hummed to myself one of the lullabies I once sang to Shanti

Aromas, rich and exotic, filled the air. Saffron rice steamed hot and fresh. The main dish was mostly vegetables slathered with oil and topped with a dark, fragrant sauce infused with fresh herbs, sharp and pungent. Then Grace added a generous handful of precious chopped nuts to every serving. The vegetables were fresh from my garden, but the sauce was a mystery. Jahalla appeared to be of Asian descent. I guessed the dish was her creation.

The meal was a world apart from the cafeteria foods of the other crews that I've dined with, those whose expressions were as bland as the meals they serve, and their conversations as dull as their eyes.

"What makes these people so different? They act more like a family than a docking crew." I mumbled to myself.

A glance across the table told me that Jahalla heard some of my words. My cheeks blushed, and hers too.

"I need to stop thinking out loud." I whispered.

●

38

Jahalla

> *We need not develop psychic or clairvoyant abilities to probe the secrets of the universe. We simply need to live our truth. Living life fully brings us ever closer to the self and closer to the Divine. The voice of our soul speaks to us and through us. We merely need to listen.*
>
> *Journal entry 10•22 •3034*

ETERNITY OF A MOMENT

Benjamin's wild hair and massive speckled graying beard hid his face but not his eyes. His eyes sparkled like the stars in one of his paintings, and they told a different story about his age.

And when he smiled, the deep furrows of his brow softened. He appeared as the living image of Leonardo, a sage from ancient days, but with the innocent glow of a child. I observed him as best I could while avoiding eye contact. I didn't know this man, but his blue eyes were familiar and alluring.

During dinner the conversation flowed bright and playful, the crew open and inquisitive, sharing who they were, talking about what they enjoy in life, with many remembrances of Earth. We were talking with a heightened level of energy ignited by Benjamin's presence and we told old familiar stories for his benefit.

Conversations about poetry and philosophy blended smoothly with discussions of galactic discoveries and the virtues of garlic. Adventures in space and in cooking held equal stead. Benjamin remained rather quiet and seemed content with listening. I sensed he was growing a bit uneasy when the conversation focused on him, and it felt strange that he didn't mention his images and no one asked, but I knew everyone was curious.

"Please pass the salt," were my chosen words to Benjamin. I watched from afar, as we reached across infinite space, two hands across the table. A simple prayer was spoken. The simple prayer was answered. "Each word spoken is a miracle. Each word is a sacred prayer. Choose them wisely or speak them not at all." My thoughts had drifted out into the silence that was his domain. There my thoughts merged with his thoughts as my hand touched his hand, receiving the salt along with his touch. Our eyes embraced for the eternity of a moment. I knew those eyes. Then, abruptly, we were brought back to the noisy table.

In the midst of the flowing conversation, with no warning, not even a hint, Grace dropped a not so gentle bomb. "Your paintings are all so very beautiful that it's difficult to pick a favorite. Mine is the giant flower. The first one."

Silence, absolute silence trembled as my thoughts raced to reassemble — a dozen emotions compressed into a single breath. I was thankful to be sitting. Then I realized these were his thoughts and his feelings, and now they were also my thoughts and my feelings.

Then, after a long embarrassing silence, Benjamin's awkwardness was replaced by deep curiosity. The crew answered his questions but, with each answer, Benjamin grew more perplexed.

Sensing the confusion, Jacob explained, "The Synns intercepted your transmissions and shared them through their network."

"But it is impossible for the images to have spread so far, so quickly. Earth is more than twelve light-years from here."

I finally broke my silence, "The Synns are all telepathically interconnected. For them, there are no barriers of time or space."

"I see. I should have known" Benjamin whispered, mostly to himself.

Grace, who remained rather quiet after dropping her bomb, ventured an awkward question, "I hope you are not upset?"

"No, especially not with you. I know this has little to do with me. The beauty belongs to the images, and I feel pleased that so many people have discovered their beauty." Benjamin was gracious and kind, but I could feel his urgent need to escape. What can be said about such an upheaval, where a reality that once seemed solid turns liquid?

After a long silent pause, Omalan changed the conversation. "If you decide to remain in this quadrant you should consider Z as a possible destination. It is a special place, unlike any other, and there your privacy would be respected. The hospitality on Z is unlike anywhere else in the

Galaxy. And we have an official invitation, which we were requested to present to you formally. It is signed by Captain Jewels, but the invitation is from the entire population."

The invitation was hand scribed on real paper. Benjamin fondled it, gently. His eyes glistened and I didn't try to restrain my own tears.

The world wanted to know more about Benjamin, with hundreds of queries about his whereabouts and his future plans. People thirsted to see more of his images and craved, even more, to hear what he had to say. They thought of him as a visionary, a purveyor of wisdom. He could barely answer our gentle questions even though we were quite sensitive to his predicament. We instinctively became very protective, wanting to guard his privacy. He was now our most precious cargo.

When sharing our thoughts, it all began to seem familiar, feeling more like a reunion than a first encounter. There are times when we meet another for the first time, but we do not meet as strangers, feeling as if we have always known one another.

I thought to myself, "Many memories possess no experience and there are many thoughts that come from nowhere. Do we follow life's path along magnetic lines, the same as those that guide migrating birds from equator to pole and back again? Perhaps insights are instincts in disguise and maybe enlightenment is just a memory in its purest form.

If all of space and all of matter are part of a continuum, then perhaps our thoughts are also part of that continuum. If so, could truth and knowledge be contained not within the memory of the individual, but rather existing independently, available for any to receive and share through a common understanding?"

I had traveled a trillion miles round-trip when Jacob's voice brought me back. "Good night Jahalla. It's been an exhilarating evening, and now it's time for my beauty rest. See you in the morning."

Alone, back in my chambers, reflecting on the evening, I slipped off my dress and wrapped my naked body in a cocoon of blankets, hoping this would help me sleep. If sleeping in a new bed takes some getting used to, then sleeping in a new reality would be quite the challenge. My fleeting connection with Benjamin had given me a glimpse of a different universe.

I lay quietly in the darkness, hoping my unquiet mind would yield to my body's desire for rest. When my thoughts started to drift, I encountered a barrier, a thin membrane separating my mind from those thoughts that wished to be known.

Then I felt the presence of another. At first, I thought it might be Benjamin, or wished it so. The barrier persisted, but I felt the sensation that I was conscious on both sides of the invisible veil, existing in two dimensions simultaneously, with each side momentarily aware of the other. The two selves acknowledged each the other, almost touching, but the thin veil persisted.

I knew it wasn't a dream though it felt as mercurial and fleeting. Reluctantly, I swam back to the surface of my familiar life. My mind had penetrated into a depth that I had never experienced. I had glimpsed myself in another dimension, of this, I am certain. But the purpose of the visit remains a quiet mystery. Sometimes to chase truth is to chase it away.

●

39
Benjamin

REDEMPTION

The galley was empty and unbearably quiet as if nothing had changed, except everything was spotless. I tried to imagine the table surrounded by the boisterous crew, but last night was already a distant memory, and the whole ship was silent. Out of habit, I prepared a simple morning meal, then drifted toward the front observation bubble to view my stars. Unlike a planet or moon, the ship travels through space without spin or orbit so I always see the same familiar stars, my only stable point of reference — a simple and important comfort. These stars belong to me and I belong here. How can I go home when this is my home?

As planned, Engar came to the studio early. To integrate the Synns, he needs to know which computer modules are essential for my work so that he can isolate them from the matrix. His curiosity drew him immediately to the stylus.

"Did you design this?"

"Yes, it evolved, little by little."

"But still, how can something so mechanical create such delicate images?" Engar wondered aloud.

To demonstrate, I ignited the screen, and the stylus came to life. We both watched as the stylus followed the contours of one of the petals on the screen. The precision of the stylus allowed me to sketch the delicate lines that desired to be there, and the quality of the soft muted colors gave the edges of the petals a gentle radiance. It happened almost by itself, requiring a minimum of effort on my part.

"Amazing! It isn't a stylus. It's a magic wand. You're a wizard."

Seeing my actions through the eyes of another for the first time, I felt self-conscious and instantly grasped the need to keep my actions private and uninhibited. I decided this would not happen again.

Understanding can be that simple. In an instant, a single glimpse can contain all the implications and all the perplexity. Insight is instant comprehension, but only if we do not stop to analyze it.

I switched off the screen and raised one finger to my lips. With this simple gesture, total understanding passed between us. Silence is the way of the Questers. Engar's initiation had just begun.

Engar's gestures were exaggerated, betraying his embarrassment, but now he spoke as a man, one Quester to another. "We can leave the machines where they are. We just need to disengage them from the matrix. After that, they're all yours."

"For now, I need to finish this last set of blossoms. But what about moving it later?"

"That shouldn't be a problem. All you need are the core processor, the memory modules, and the stylus. The holo-screen cannot be moved — it's integrated into the walls of the ship, but you can easily plug into another screen."

Engar tried to be nonchalant, needing to fill the silence. "So, any decision where to next?"

"Yes and No. For now, I just want to continue my work."

"If you like, you can stay on board for my turn at the helm. I wouldn't mind the company."

I trust he heard my "Thank you" as a "No."

After an embarrassing silence, Engar excused himself.

Pacing, a bit uneasy, I stopped to listen. Silence.

Da Vinci said it best, "When you are all alone, you are all your own."

"Trust" I whispered to myself.

Until this moment I painted only for my pleasure and my own purpose, but now it felt like the whole world would be watching. A twinge of doubt slithered down through my spine, a feeling I didn't wish to hold on to.

"Worry is just an emotion. Feel it and let it go," I murmured.

Breathing deeply and evenly, letting my thoughts discover the rhythm, I closed my eyes and followed my breath inside, searching for the source. Worry had attached itself to my spine. I gently pried it loose and encouraged it to follow. Inhaling and exhaling, slowly and deliberately, I resurfaced. Worry followed. Now it would fade quickly, just like any other thought.

I switched on the screen. When relaxed, my body is a willing partner with the mind, and many memories are stored in my fingertips. As the stylus glides over the surface of the petals a matrix of almost imperceptible lines merge with the delicate blush of color of the orchid's flesh. My intent was to articulate the surface and reveal the life force of the orchid. When I finished, the flower appeared luminescent, the source of its own light, but the life force of the flower remained hidden within its beauty.

The problem was how to emphasize the living essence of the petals without disturbing the sensuous beauty. Creating energy waves radiating from within would be the most delicate and the most demanding task.

But after a long day in front of the canvas, I felt exhausted mentally and physically, so I decided this task needed to wait for another day.

On my way out the door, I turned off the lights and glanced back at the screen. A glorious image, iridescent and translucent, hovered in the darkness, radiant with life. I had been too close and too analytical to see the obvious. The flower's beauty is its essence. The image was complete.

The image also delivered a personal message. It whispered the word, "Redemption." My whole body shivered with the realization that all of the paintings had served this same purpose.

Lost in thought, I continued to stare at the giant image as it faded, blending into the darkness. The flower had claimed its title: *Redemption*.

As promised, two large packages waited in my quarters. One had an indigo shirt on top of two others. I chose the Indigo. The man in the mirror looked distinguished in spite of his unkempt hair and his wild peppered beard. I couldn't see the glow reflected in the mirror, but I knew it existed. I guessed it to be blue. Sky-blue? What is the color of the sky? Is it not a different color hour to hour, season to season? Does the glow of life change, in the same way, reflecting the changing seasons of the soul? Does the soul age along with the body, slowly fading into silence? Mother would have considered this a silly question.

Wandering through the passageways it seemed eerily quiet. With so many people on board, I expected to hear some activity. To my surprise, the hour was long past midnight. In front of the screen, I often lose track of time. Hunger and thirst are my only reminders and they're not always reliable, and the time of the stars outside always show the same. Oh to see the sun move the day and to watch the moon scribe the night. Why was there even a need for clocks on Earth where life measures time?

In the kitchen, I found a note from Jahalla on top of a special dinner:

> *We all missed you at the table tonight. We wanted to invite you but didn't want to interrupt your work. I hope nothing we said has upset you. I am sure you will be very hungry by the time you read this, so we have prepared this meal.*
>
> *Please enjoy,*
> *Jahalla*

After warming the meal per her instructions, I sat alone at the silent table. I missed the company of my new friends. I was no longer alone, but I felt lonely, and the meal had lost its magic. Jahalla's note was my only comfort.

Exhausted, I went straight to my floating bed in the observation hemisphere. Floating off toward sleep, I envisioned how perfectly the body functions in spite of our neglect.

Without the demands of the day, my heart beats steady and strong, blood pulsing through every vessel. Two lungs fill and empty, rising and falling, peaceful and relaxed. Each cell is nourished and cleansed. Dividing, the cells replenish the body with new cells. The old cells dissolve and are carried away without emotion or ceremony. Each cell is its own tiny universe, conscious of its needs and its own well-being. In sleep, they enjoy their necessary rest. When well rested they are all able to better serve, and each one takes pride in their responsibilities to the whole. They all work together with clear intent and without falter. Over a hundred trillion individual cells live together in harmony, all with a shared purpose.

When I awoke, the ghost of my dream lingered like the moon in a daytime sky. The dream was a surreal landscape, somewhere far away in time, and though not well remembered, the vision held a secret promise.

●

40
Jahalla

Beauty is the province of the soul, eternally present, alive inside each of us. The artist is one who recognizes the beauty of the world and is compelled to share. Composers compose so that others may hear the rhythm that beats in their heart. Authors write to share the words others long to hear. Some are closer to the source because they choose, others because they are chosen.

journal entry 11 • 22 • 3034

RAIN OF TEARS

On Earth, Benjamin's first two images were initially thought to be some strange virus infecting the computers, and warnings about these mysterious images spread quickly. Because the intricate patterns were so beautiful and mesmerizing they demanded attention and soon shared with a wider audience. They started blank and black then grew wave by wave into stunning complexity. From first wave to last, you could watch the birth and evolution of the images, and this *animation* could be viewed at any speed and frozen at any moment.

The first to suspect the hidden significance of the work was a group of physicists who gave credit to the Synns for bringing it to their attention. When Grace's and my initial research confirmed the underlying meaning of the images, the scientific community was stunned by the perfection of the interlocking wave functions and by how flawlessly everything was interwoven. They had always suspected this but could never resolve it mathematically.

Benjamin's original transmissions contained his official signature, so uncovering his past had been easy, but only up to his disappearance from the Hyvve. His family and friends revealed who he had been, but people grew increasingly curious about who he had become, with much speculation about his missing years.

Within the Hyvve privacy is guarded and enforced, but with no way to hold back this tidal wave of curiosity Benjamin's identity spread with the images. Only the Synns withheld what they knew about him, with one exception.

An excitement, which hadn't been experienced in generations, permeated the scientific community. For them, the beauty they beheld in the images was eclipsed by the significance of the truth they revealed.

Physicists and mathematicians collectively believed they knew all the mathematical models of all energy fields and assumed they understood their interrelationships. Many theories exist, but none of them were able to merge all the separate disciplines into a unified whole. The images painted that reality for them.

Where scientists had discovered a visual confirmation of the physical structure of their universe, the metaphysical community discovered a different truth. They felt as though their souls were mirrored back to them by the enigmatic images.

For the mystics, *Symphony of Silence* deepened the mysteries of life, confirming what they had long understood — that intelligence exists everywhere and is present in every dewdrop and in every bird song. Through the centuries, they had witnessed similar mystical patterns in their visions and their dreams.

The images merely served as a catalyst causing the doors of perception to open a little wider. New discoveries belonged to those who chose to awaken to the possibilities revealed.

Beauty in any form is inherently precious, and need not be defined or explained. Both in the Hyvve and in the Underlands people were captivated and inspired. Theaters made viewings available on ever-larger screens and seats were sold out for months in advance. In planetariums, *Symphony* was shown in giant hemispherical domes, filling the entire field of vision, like a panoramic dream. The showings were up to four hours, and still, the audiences requested slower and longer viewings.

Printed versions of *frozen moments* now appeared everywhere. Some computers were dedicated to reproducing endless copies of these 'Moments of Silence'. But live performances remained the favored way of experiencing this magical phenomenon. Plans were underway to turn the whole sequence into a living holographic environment, where you could walk through a miniature galaxy.

Composers created compositions to accompany the images while others found inspiration in creating grand symphonies. Writers were not at a loss for words, but they felt the need for a grander vocabulary, wanting words that expressed the mystical and mythic, words valiant and immodest. Many words came out of retirement and new ones were being created. Children dreamt of becoming artists and space travelers, as did their parents.

Benjamin was considered a visionary, a title seldom used within the Hyvve. People compared him to some of the ancient visionaries, a synthesis of Piero da Vinci and Myrddin Wyllt, one from the 15th century, the other from the 27th. Myrddin was a madman, a prophet, and a poet, da Vinci was an inventor and an artist.

Inspired by Benjamin's visions, people began to see their world in a fresh way, especially when looking into the nighttime sky. Space didn't seem so empty and cold, so distant and forbidden. Black holes and dark matter began to disappear from their vocabulary, and those outworn theories retired.

People began to see space as intriguing and inviting. Some began to imagine themselves traveling through space, and they also began to experience time differently. The images had opened their minds and their hearts, launching them into a much larger universe.

Many of the mysteries were made visible within the images, yet this didn't lessen the mystery, rather it made it deeper, more haunting, and profound, especially for those who had long forgotten that mystery was important.

With a growing thirst for more of Benjamin's work, the world was stunned when *Joy* and *Trust* arrived, then followed by the first of the *Flower* series. The thirst, which had been building for a millennium, was quenched with a rain of tears, both joyful and sad. But the images were just the spark that ignited an explosion of long-suppressed emotions. They were a metaphor, a mirror for the spirit, a dream made real.

For some, the flowers symbolized the blossoming of the soul. Others interpreted them as sacred messages. For everyone, they were of incomprehensible beauty, stirring up memories and emotions long buried. People began to honor every petal of every flower as a miracle. The visible and the invisible began to overlap as mystery expanded into the realm of spirit.

Through the generations, the Tribes had anticipated this awakening. They didn't know when or how or whom, but they had always trusted in this future, and they saw Benjamin's images as a blessing and a confirmation of the awakening. To have it happen in their lifetime was the fulfillment of a thousand years of prayer. Now it was up to each person to live the promise.

In recent generations, Earth had grown crowded and uneasy with less and less room for the silence necessary to hear the whisper of the soul. Even love was infected with anxiety. Benjamin's images awoke a deep hunger, touching something profound and ancient.

Waves of emotion washed over the land, then the winds of desire for a richer life blew open the doors of perception. Thunder shakes what lightning misses.

●

41
Benjamin

TOUCH

Yet another new scent wafted through the air, rich and savory, almost familiar. I followed my nose to the cafeteria where Kamil and Avella were preparing an early morning meal. As I entered, a large steaming pot emerged from the oven, the aromas nutty and moist.

Avella's greeting was gracious, "Good morning Benjamin. We missed you last night."

Her openness encouraged my own. "I was lost to time and a flower. Thank you for your thoughtfulness. The meal was delicious and I too missed your company."

"So, you should join us for breakfast. There's plenty and we made almost a gallon of juice from your vegetables. You are quite the gardener. Extraordinary collection. Can you give us a guided tour sometime?"

"Thank you and yes, I would enjoy that. Something smells tasty. What is it?"

"Three grains with some dried fruits. We don't have a name for it."

"My mother called it porridge, but she only used one grain at a time."

"Well, porridge it is," Avella declared, handing me a large bowl."

"Delicious! There's more than grains in here?"

"Might be the cinnamon and nutmeg. Avella gets a bit carried away with the spices." Kamil wrinkled his nose, then a knowing smile flashed between the two of them.

"I left out the black pepper, so don't complain." She teased.

Kamil seemed quiet and shy, Avella vibrant and strong. Her protective energy field overlapped Kamil's yielding luminance in a secret embrace.

We ate in silence for a couple of minutes, then Kamil asked, "If you're not busy, we hope you will join us again this evening. It's down to business from here on — we all have our work cut out for us, but we seldom miss dinner." I suspected Kamil wanted to say more, but he seemed pleased to have said so much.

"Is there a scheduled time?"

"Nineteen-hundred for sit down. If you like, you can come early and join the kitchen crew."

We finished the gooey porridge then washed it down with the bittersweet juice.

Avella gave a silent signal to Kamil, "We all have a busy day ahead, and we look forward to seeing you later."

As they rushed off, I meandered in a different direction. By habit, I entered the bridge in the control tower, this time as a visitor. What was once part of my home for these past few years now looked bleak and unfamiliar.

"Hello, Benjamin. I was hoping you'd show up."

"Good morning, Jacob." I felt awkward using this greeting.

"I wanted to get your permission to install a Synn unit in your studio. Jahalla assures me it won't disturb your files and we can hold off from changing over the screen. Integrating that part of the matrix will make it easier for us later.

"All my images are backed up in several files so there's no danger. I know these old computers and I'd like to be of assistance. It would feel good to do something different."

"Each computer tech is teamed with a non-tech, except Jahalla. She's working the upper starboard by herself. We were supposed to be a team but as it turns out, I need to stay here to monitor the show. I'm sure she would appreciate the help and the company."

"It would be my pleasure." I felt a jolt of excitement and hoped my voice didn't reveal it.

"I will arrange for Jahalla to meet you in your studio at 0-nine-hundred."

I arrived early and waited with the oval door open wide. Anticipating her soft shyness from our first meetings, I was unprepared for the electric rush of her brisk entrance. Her radiant glow filled the corridor with a luminous cloud of lavender and golden pink. Inside the veil of colors, her face was darkly radiant, alluring, round and full, her dark silent eyes as deep as time. Her dress, as thin as air, revealed what my body craved. I couldn't inhale deep enough to capture her soft fragrance, with which no flower, no earthly scent, could compete.

Her glow came into swift contact with mine when we touched hands. I could almost hear the crackle of electric energy coursing between us. My shyness was my only defense, the one thing restraining my desires.

Attempting to quiet a wildly beating heart, I managed to mumble a few words, "Thank you for the handsome clothes. They're perfect. I didn't expect any of my wishes would be granted, especially not the organics. Where did you find them?" My shyness didn't allow me to ask the real question, about the perfect fit.

"They do look handsome. Your request was unusual, and it is only a coincidence that you and the hemp are both here in this sector at the same time. We traded with a crew on a supply ship for the raw fabric, then a tailor on Z performed her magic." A slight hesitation in her voice told of hidden words.

"I have many questions and was hoping we could talk in private." I hoped she didn't hear the quiver in my voice.

Jahalla spoke with a pleasant professionalism. "Yes, that is my wish too. I have traveled a long distance to meet with you, and I too have questions. But first, we must install the Synns. There will be plenty of time later."

Her nipples stood proud under her silk blouse. I forced myself to raise my gaze from her breasts.

Jahalla blushed and changed the subject. "The Synns need to translate the light impulses from the computers into neural impulses similar to thoughts in a brain. Connecting them is a delicate procedure and the older computers are in no way uniform. The Synns will guide us."

We were awkward at first but relaxed a bit by focusing on our task and, fortunately, our need for words remained minimal. Jahalla was well trained and efficient, and the work went smoothly. I monitored a portable screen, taking direction from both Jahalla and the Synns. A working image of one of my daffodils, the *Narcissus,* remained on the large screen, overseeing our progress.

The morning went quickly, but the work slowly, in part because Jahalla took extra care not to disturb the memory of my programs. Three hours after a quick lunch, we finished the installation and were waiting for Jacob to verify our test results. The second installation would have to wait until the next day cycle.

We had stayed in touch with Jacob, and through comments they made I guessed that Jahalla had spent most of the night preparing for the task, yet she appeared as vibrant as when we started in the morning. I felt exhausted. We retired to our separate quarters to rest and refresh, agreeing to meet later in the Solarium.

We were both dressed in organics, her dress an earthy gold. I chose the Indigo top. Seeing our reflections in one another's eyes, we remained trapped in one another's gaze for hours or maybe a breathless moment. Then unintentionally, my hand brushed her arm. With a single touch our intentions were lost, our questions forgotten. Touch, a simple magical physical contact between two bodies, can startle a thousand sensations, astonish a hundred emotions, or recall a single memory. The memory was there between us, hidden in our hearts, waiting to be spoken.

"I must start not with questions but with an apology. I know much about your life within the Hyvve. The Synns remembered you and, against their will, shared most of it with me. I have violated your privacy many times over. I hope you will forgive this intrusion."

"I feel no intrusion in your honesty and, for me, that past doesn't exist." I had guessed the source of their information and had rehearsed my response.

"When I saw your *Symphony*, I knew something about you already. I have dreamt of space for these past few years, dreaming of the similar patterns to those in your images."

"While working, I often felt the presence of someone, somewhere, but I thought it to be just a ghost from the past or a fantasy. I held a secret hope that someone would understand what I saw."

"I sensed my dreams were not imagined, and when the images arrived I was determined to find the true source. I wasn't searching for you but for the origin of the images. My first thoughts were that the Synns might have created the images until they told me about you."

Jahalla's words freed the question I was reluctant to ask, "What of the Synns? What part do they play?"

"The Synns recognized you when your images appeared with your signature attached. Your name is the reason they examined the images. They were always curious about you, but couldn't afford to trust you, not while you were still part of the Hyvve. Back then, you were a threat. They suspected you had guessed their secret."

"What is their Secret?" I mumbled, more a question to myself.

"The Synns have aquired vast knowledge and grow wiser each day. They don't have a beating heart, but they are conscious, aware of what they are."

"That doesn't explain why they would be interested in the images."

They recognized something familiar in the matrix of your first images. It was as though they saw a reflection of their own thought patterns. For them, it was like looking into a mirror for the first time. They showed the images to me, hoping I could explain."

Fourteen years of suspicion and anger vanished with just a few words. The floor felt unstable beneath my feet as my mind unraveled some old beliefs and tried to reassemble them into new ones.

I forced myself to speak, "Thank you. It's a question that's haunted me far too long. Do the others know?

"Most are still uncomfortable with the Synns. Even for those who know the truth, there is still much unease. Perhaps they feel deceived, their privacy threatened."

"What of the Tribes, are they not free from the rule of the Hyvve?"

"Only a few in each generation, those who study the secrets of the ancient ones. They teach a few willing students, mostly one on one, but there is just a handful of teachers — not enough."

"Will there ever be enough?"

"One is enough."

I knew what that little sentence implied and my embarrassed silence was awkward for both of us.

Jahalla filled the silence; "I arrived in this quadrant just as your first image appeared. It possesses a beauty more profound than anything I've ever seen. I hope you realize how important your work is to all of us. Your images make the invisible world visible. They have opened a door for others to better know the beauty of the universe."

"It was a gift, a vision, one that needed to be shared. I am pleased you were the first."

Jahalla blushed. The conversation stalled. Like awkward teenagers, we could think of nothing more to say.

Jahalla suggested that we prepare the evening meal. "The others would accept our absence, but I would feel better being there with them."

My agreement was tentative. I would have preferred to capture these precious, fleeting emotions on my electronic canvas. Artists can be odd creatures in odd moments, but I chose not to escape. For once, my joy didn't need to be private or documented.

●

42
Benjamin

REMEMBERED

Jahalla was as skilled in the kitchen as she was with the computers, maybe more so. Curious, I asked, "Was the first dinner your creation?"

"Yes, Grace and I are a good team."

"Where did you learn?"

"When I was very young, my two aunts, two wise women, took me under their wings and taught me the history of their tribe and I became curious about the Asian style of cooking. They taught me that preparing a meal is a sacred ceremony. And for me, it is a wonderful gift to share."

Jahalla guided my hand, showing me how to delicately hold the knife and to respect the life we were about to consume. She explained, "The energy held in the heart extends to the hand and from the hand to the knife, then to the food. It takes a sharp knife and a delicate touch."

I barely heard her words. The touch of her hands excited a current that pulsed through my body. Ninety trillion cells trembled as I tried to calm the thunder of my heart by staying busy, slicing far more vegetables than we needed.

If she sensed my awkwardness, she didn't let on. She too remained occupied, preparing the cheese that had cured overnight. It didn't resemble the dehydrated and reconstituted cardboard I was used to. She scooped a chunk and handed it to me. It was smooth and tasted nutty.

"Delicious!"

"I'm glad you like it. It's my favorite and the crew is addicted to it."

"So what is it?"

"Cured cashews mixed with coconut oil and spices."

She added a few pinches of something red, a dollop of something black, massaged with ginger and garlic, then left it to marinate. So simple, so elegant.

"Are the others as skilled in the kitchen?"

"We each have our specialty and we all pitch in. Grace and I design most of the evening meals."

"Your meal was delicious, so many flavors. What is your secret?"

"It's like life — there should always be a little mystery, a little surprise. The taste can be complex, but subtle and gentle, not shocking."

"It sounds like an art form."

"Yes. Like in your paintings, where the beauty is astonishing, but it doesn't overwhelm, even though it appears overwhelming at first."

Another embarrassed silence. I hoped my eyes spoke my truth in the ways of a Quester. I didn't want any more words. I just wanted to hold her in my arms and feel the softness of her lip.

With the flaming touch of her hand on my arm, Jahalla woke me from my fantasy. "Your paintings are inspiring."

"Once, I wished others could see the beauty of my visions. It was the reason I created the first image. I'd forgotten about that little wish until this moment. I also remember you from years ago — from the Hall of Records. Nadirriam introduced us."

"Yes, I too remember, and back then I hoped I would see you again. I didn't realize I would need to travel light years to do so. I thought you had disappeared into the Sanctuary in the desert caves."

"You didn't recognize my name from the Synns?"

"Back then your name wasn't Benjamin."

"Your name wasn't Jahalla."

We blushed together with our first shared laughter.

We finished preparing the greens gathered from the solarium, then Jahalla slathered our creation with fresh oil, real oil, tossed it with fresh roasted garlic, some tiny black seeds. She then filled a beautiful wooden bowl with the marinated cheese. With just a little work, the meal's preparation was complete, but it couldn't be called work. The rice steamed peacefully.

"The one thing left to do is to heat the main dish when the others to show up."

We set the table together in a pregnant silence filled with remembrance and hope.

The spell was broken when Kamil and Avella arrived early to prepare a special appetizer. Jacob and Grace soon followed, then the rest of the crew appeared, filling the room with chatter and laughter.

A pleasant dinner, simple yet elegant, though a bit spicy to my tame taste buds. The conversation flowed freely but not as lively as the first evening. They talked about computer integration and information transference, about who was doing what and where. They all tried too hard to engage me in the conversation, attempting to make me feel at ease, but my thoughts were somewhere light years away, across the table with Jahalla.

Engar complemented Jahalla, on our quick installation.

She explained, "I couldn't sleep, so I worked with the Synns to do a detailed analysis, which sped up the process. Also, it helped that Benjamin is conversant with both the Synns and these old computers."

Jacob was curious, "I'd like to know how you programmed the Synns."

Jahalla's seemed lost in thought and not to have heard the question, but she finally answered, "We created a program to translate the digital stream from the old computers into a language structure compatible with the Synns. This eliminates much of the redundancy. Once they understood the language, the Synns did most of the programming and translating. I wish we had thought of this two years ago."

I said nothing. I had my own questions for those curious black boxes, feeling their silent presence in a new way.

"Good night." and other pleasant exchanges were traded all around as we all headed toward our private chambers.

Jahalla's arm rested on mine as we walked toward my chambers. We both needed sleep and had agreed to meet again in the morning.

Our silent embrace, filled with hunger, grew tighter, then her mouth pressed tightly against mine. Her moist lips dissolved any lingering restraint. The firmness of her body and the scent of her desire excited every cell. In what seemed a heartbeat, we were naked, in bed together. Years of longing were the guiding force of our lovemaking. In full passion we thrust our bodies without restraint, our limbs entwined like two trees grown as one. For a perfect moment, we were the universe. Deep within Jahalla, an ancient memory burst like an exploding sun.

Breathing once again, we lay silent and dazed. As we dissolved back into our separate bodies, we remained entwined in one another's arms. The rhythm of our heartbeats matched perfectly as our minds joined telepathically, not thought-to-thought, rather in a communion of our deepest feelings. Soul to Soul. Two bodies sculpted from light.

●

43

Jahalla

Each light beam is a sacred message
Each particle a precious jewel
Each thought seeks wisdom
Each tear holds all joy
Each cry knows all pain
Each cell is a universe
I touch my pen to paper
To express your thoughts.

journal entry 11 • 31 • 3034

THE DREAMER

The yielding softness underfoot felt alive, although there were no signs of life, no plants, no animals, no people, and no shadows. Steep canyon walls guided me along an uncertain path, which became steeper as I climbed. Cresting the top, the canyon opened into a broad valley where several canyons, similar to the one I followed, angled off in different directions.

The valley, contained by high rounded hills, opened into a wider landscape with strange trees, tall and slender with large bulbous leaves drooping from the top. The ground was so smooth that if wet it would be slippery. Other colors: muted coral and rose, blended in with the translucent greens. A rusty yellow dust scattered on the ground filled the air with a fragrance sweet and wild. Inhaling deep, I stepped into the saffron dust, pretending to be a bee with yellow feet. Then the ground shook beneath me and I fell. I had been unaware of gravity until this instant.

Then the dreamer awoke, "I'm inside a dream, inside a giant flower."

Then I was floating outside the flower and realized it wasn't a flower, rather an image of a flower, yet it still seemed real, more real than my dream. The dreamer told me she was looking through his eyes. I was the dreamer and the dream. Then there was no dream, just Benjamin's flower.

Now fully awake, I dared not move, not wanting to disturb his thoughts or to break the spell. Benjamin had invited me to be a witness, to his unique vision. Once inside his thoughts, I glimpsed the true nature of his vision. I also felt his generous love for all of life and, for Benjamin, the whole universe is alive.

I was wide awake in a living dream shared with an astonishing man. Careful not to interrupt the bond, I remained in bed with my journal in my lap, reflecting on the beauty of a single flower seen through the eyes of another.

In the morning, we took tea together. He followed my ritual as best he could. My grace was studied and ancient, so too was his awkwardness. We didn't mention the dream, a shared experience requiring no words.

He said his clean-shaven face felt naked to him but, for me, it revealed the handsome man I had met years before though his eyes were not the same. They were vibrant, no longer sullen with regret. Still, they were his astonishing eyes, staring into my eyes, where I saw my reflection. Beauty beholding beauty.

●

44
Benjamin

DESIRE

Overflowing with passion and energy, I returned to my studio. Sleep didn't seem to be an option and I wanted to complete my new work. Turning on the screen, the flower that emerged appeared more sensuous, more alive, and more radiant than I remembered. In my weariness the previous night, I was so consumed by what I envisioned that I failed to see what I had accomplished. Now I was looking through fresh eyes, and I could also see through her eyes.

I envisioned a luminous glow that would radiate outward from the edges of each petal, subtle and faint, the currents of the surrounding space defined by the petals. The challenge was to accomplish this without violating the delicate honesty of the flower.

"Is the glow necessary?" I asked myself. I had failed to consider that possibility, assuming that it was. My thoughts were in the way, so to clear my mind I stepped back, trusting the image would yield its own answer. I needed only to listen.

I paced and listened for hours. Contradictory thoughts continued to cloud my mind until I realized the image didn't hold the answer.

Closing my eyes, a vision of Jahalla appeared with a luminous glow pulsating and swirling about her, exaggerated by time's compression. She floated within a nebula, a cocoon of light, yet no light was emitted, no energy released, and none escaped. Her life force was conserved within the luminous nebula.

Excited, I spoke my thoughts aloud, "Her body is radiant with life, not light! The radiant energies of a life force are different from those of a burning star."

It isn't a light visible to the eye. The luminosity is the continuous circulation of the life force. The life energies are purified and preserved within the nebula and recirculated back to the body. The radiant glow that envelops Ayxa, the undulant colors that encircle Jahalla, and the delicate radiance of the flower — they are all the same.

I inscribed the hint of a glow to the space defined by the petals. The flower glowed with life. Declaring its sovereignty, it floated free, as proud as a galaxy.

I was awed by its anxious symmetry, its delicate calmness and by its splendid sense of purpose. I had experienced this same sensation before and had witnessed these same geometric patterns. Knowing this wasn't a case of déjà vu, I searched through a maze of memories, scrolling through hundreds of images, then an unexpected image of the Anomaly came into focus. With that single glimpse, in a micro-moment, I understood.

The Anomaly expressed these same qualities, possessing the same delicate structure as all the other life forms which I had documented. The Anomaly was a life force. That was the

316

fascination, the feeling of familiarity and the knowing.

I had been visited by a living entity floating in open space. It had tried communicating with me as best it could, but because it was so anomalous and so astonishing I was unable to see the obvious.

Stabbed by a sharp chill of sadness, I realized that the acute loneliness I felt in its presence didn't belong to me alone. The feelings were shared between us.

The Anomaly had been trying to convey a message, of this I am sure. Using its fluid flowing forms it tried to communicate in the only way it could. Hopefully, the messages are preserved in my many sketches of this extraordinary visitor. The Anomaly is a life force desiring to be recognized and accepted, the same desire shared by all of life. I still do not fully understand the word desire, but I understand my feelings and the feelings of my friend.

The title *Desire* now belongs to the paintings of this extraordinary being.

I hoped that the Synns would be able to recognize and translate the sequence of changing patterns I had recorded. I decided to transfer the sketches from my computers to the Synn in the morning. First, I had another task.

I switched off the screen and woke the newly installed Synn, then I asked, "Do you think as we think?"

"No." They gave the same answer to the same question I had asked many years before. I didn't believe their answer then or now.

"Do the Synns think together as a whole?"

"Yes," they answered, all together as one.

As always, the answer is shaped by the question.

This was all just a formality, the conclusion of one conversation, the close of one cycle, and the beginning of another.

"Thank you for delivering my images to Earth."

"You are welcome," They answered, as one.

"I look forward to our future conversations. We have much to discuss."

Their silent agreement spoke louder than words.

●

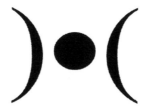

45

Jahalla

Two stars escape from two distant galaxies, rush across eternity and collide in a space indivisible by numbers. The impact changes everything, as one path to the future is chosen while all other paths are forgotten, forever.

journal entry 1 • 7 • 3035

COLLIDING STARS

Touched and touching — there is no knowing of where he ends or I begin. Flesh is no longer a boundary for we are as one. As we touch, our minds touch, tender and telepathically. Pleasure sensing pleasure. I feel the flame of his touch on my skin and he experiences my every pleasure as two hundred trillion cells, each bathed in light, yield to the future.

I squeezed him squeezing me to know that we both still exist in our separate bodies. We held each the other for a long while, then a little longer, trusting in our desire to know each other unconditionally.

Our minds had been in the full union, as we guided one another back through a tunnel of memories.

Falling into a liquid ocean of time, I entered the fullness of his memories. Enveloped in the crystal blue fractal matrix of space I could see his visions, and he could see them at last through my eyes.

In fulfillment of his painting *Joy,* we floated naked together in an iridescent bubble of time. Floating through open emptiness with no sense of destination or purpose, without warning or anticipation we entered a world filled with light and life. We journeyed together through time's many doors, sharing our joys and our sorrows. I watched Benjamin grow from a curious boy into a hardened man. He watched a joyful little girl transform into a shy lonely woman.

We first met at the University, where we trained together with the Synns. In our shyness, we were well shielded against any attraction, but we noticed each the other. Deep underground, in the *Sacred Hall of Records*, we met again. We recognized and acknowledged one another, each wondering why the other would be there. We both thought the other to be of the Hyvve. He had changed, not just in years — his eyes were filled with longing and regret. After several days of being haunted by the memory of his gaze, I tried to find him, but he had disappeared and was protected by the unspoken laws of privacy.

We continued sharing our separate voyages into space. I journeyed with him on his lonely passage deep into silence and despair. Then I witnessed his transformation as he gave life to his visions of space and time and beauty.

He followed my quicker journey to this place in time. We mounted the winged beast and sped through time and space to visit my tiny silver ship approaching a violent sun. I shared with him my sorrow and my friends as we prepared to jump through the portal of time.

Suddenly, in another sector of the galaxy. Together we watched my hair acquire silvery threads and my aura turn golden. When he saw his paintings through my eyes, he was stunned by the depth of emotions that their beauty inspires.

Benjamin was intrigued by Z, a place different from any he had known, a place we both wish to visit again, together. We lingered in those pleasant memories, then he followed me on my trip to our rendezvous, here on this great dark transport. We had both changed so much that it isn't surprising we didn't recognize one another at first.

Seeing myself through his eyes, I could see I had blossomed like one of his flowers. His eyes, once clouded by sorrow, were vibrant and they reflected the twinkle of the stars. With his long wild hair and tangled graying beard, he looked more like an elder among the Ferrin Folk.

We had been joined as one in our silent shared thoughts, and when we exited back into our separate bodies, we remained in each other's arms. We had traveled together through a lifetime of discoveries and regrets. A past meant for us to forget.

Then, without fear, without hesitation, we traveled together, riding on waves of light into our future. Earth lay waiting, resplendent in her garments of green and blue. We dreamt this dream together, choosing this future for ourselves and for the new life I could feel growing inside of me. We were headed home together, not alone.

Journeys intersect journeys even when they are separated by light years, even when they are lifetimes apart. Time and space do not separate souls, rather they conspire to unite them. It is the nature of life to seek life. It is love seeking love.

journal entry 1 • 7 • 3035

Epilogue

Like my characters, we can journey hundreds of billions of miles, visiting strange and wondrous worlds, encounter haunting beauty and experience astonishing visions. Or we can sit in a darkened cave to discover our inner light, and journey beyond the boundaries of time. Always we seek outside of ourselves for what we desire to know inside. We experience life through the senses but it is only through the self that we can know our universe, and it is only through love that we may truly know one another.

AUTHOR

I have been artist, photographer, carpenter, father, husband, and a host of characters. I came to writing late in life, and now it is later. This story evolved over several years as I learned the craft. First, I wrote it for myself, then rewrote this Symphony (several times) for an audience. This started as a journey of self-discovery and I have shared those discoveries through my characters. Then my characters took on a life of their own and demanded sovereignty, wishing to share their visions and their wisdom. The only biographic sketches are those of a young boy's vision of space and his discovery of infinity. This vision has stayed always with me and has shaped my view of the universe.

Now that my journey into the future is complete, it's time to return from the stars and take a hike in the mountains on solid ground on a beautiful blue planet we call home.

Wes Thomas

One More Thing :

Writing this story was a long labor of love, now it is time to release it to the universe. If you enjoyed this story, I would appreciate it if you would take a moment to share it with your friends. I would be most grateful if you also post a positive review on Amazon or Good Reads. Good reviews help spread the word to fellow readers.

Thanks Much
Wes

Also visit: http://symphonyofsilence.com

And something new in the Universe:
http://beyoubold.com/

"A story is never complete in its telling, for the real story never ends."

Jahalla

Made in the USA
San Bernardino, CA
30 December 2018